the
dropper

the
dropper

RON McLARTY

CEMETERY DANCE PUBLICATIONS

Baltimore
❖ 2012 ❖

Cemetery Dance Publications
132-B Industry Lane, Unit #7
Forest Hill, MD 21050
http://www.cemeterydance.com

First Limited Edition Printing

ISBN-13: 978-158767-275-0

Cover Artwork Copyright © 2012 by Les Edwards
Dust Jacket Design Copyright © 2012
by Desert Isle Design, LLC
Interior Design by Kate Freeman Design

To my beloved wife, Kate Skinner McLarty, for saving me

Acknowledgements

Never ending thanks to the incredibly generous Stephen King, without whom a Ron McLarty novel would never have seen the light of day. Great appreciation to Rich Chizmar and Brian Freeman at Cemetery Dance for giving *The Dropper* a home and to Les Edwards for his wonderful cover art. In memory of my grandfather and his brother whose lives provided the inspiration for this novel.

My brother, Bobby Horn, has lived in my dreams for seventy years. He stands bouncing his ball in the shadow of the special school for special people, staring out at a world he cannot understand. He is fifteen and his sweet, beautiful round face perches on that tall skinny body like a new moon. He sways and jerks his hands and shoulders but keeps his eyes on some distant mystery. I stand facing him, night after night, year after year, decade after decade, and while Bobby Horn remains unchanged, I have shriveled into an eighty-seven year old man slowly disappearing from this earth like smoke from a cigarette.

For some years now, when I wake from this dream, I must lie still in my bed until whoever I might be returns and fills me. Each morning I stare at the ceiling wondering if today I will not come back but linger inside the dream to face my brother forever with shame and sorrow. I catch my name and say it for one more day.

"Shoe Horn. Shoe Horn. Me."

I struggle from bed into a chair by the window and look out over the Irish Sea. Yes. I remember now that I have come back. Back to *familiar smells and murky skies. I light a cigarette, my eighty year habit, and gasp between puffs.*

"Shoe Horn," I say to the sea.

Three days ago I closed my shop door and left East Providence, Rhode Island, for England. For Barrow-in-Furness and the life I must call upon and be sure of. This day I will walk through the places and people of that life again and let my old bones do the remembering. I'll begin at St. Mark's Church. Yes. That minister. How can I remember what he said as if it was only yesterday and I was seventeen once more.

"Some say it's Death, Some say it's darkness,
I say it's a game of light."

1

Bobby and me
1922

"But what's it mean, Shoe?" Bobby Horn says.

"Church talk," I say.

"I don't get it."

"I don't get it either."

We walk a bit. Bobby's thinking hard and his fat face shows it. Fat like Mummy's was, but Mummy's was full everywhere and Bobby only carries the fat face with him. The rest of him bony thin, although I see he's fed and know he's clean.

"Some say it's death. Some say it's darkness. I say it's a game of light," he says, wrapping his lips around each word.

"Church of England," I say and shrug.

"But what's it mean?"

His fine hands hang and he shakes them with the question as he does when he needs to understand what he can't. I stop walking and look at his wide green eyes. Bobby Horn needs to know you're thinking with him, needs to see it. I light one now and blow smoke out the corner of my mouth.

"See now lad, he's got to say something doesn't he?"

"Who?"

"Reverend Thomas. You got to say something on Sunday if you're a minister."

"Reverend Thomas is a minister."

"Right."

"But what's it mean?"

"Stop shaking them," I say and point to his fingers. He looks too, thinks hard and does.

"Good lad. Now, what did he say?"

His eyes look somewhere for the words.

"Some…say it's death. Some…say it's darkness. I say…I say… it's a game of light."

Bobby's proud now. He remembered the strange thing.

I turn and start walking toward Ramsden Dock and Mr. Horn's cave.

"I think he meant life is nice when it's light out."

"Is…is…he scared of the dark. I am."

"I know lad."

"I am."

"I know."

"But then I…I…know you're there."

I'm smoking and walking. I'm big for seventeen and I'm known. Bobby's dawdling, watching the gulls a bit, smiling at the old man and woman in the coal cart. I'm still moving.

"C'mon Bobby."

He's run up beside me with two big chunks of coal.

"Look," he says. It might as well be pounds sterling. "They just give it to me."

It might as well be the crown jewels.

" 'For you, ' the old lady says. 'No charge.' For me."

"Well, of course."

"For…me."

"That's 'cause you're a great good guy Bobby Horn."

"You're a great good guy Shoe Horn."

Now I can smell the water and the fish. Now I can hear them that are on the fishing boats. I like the sea smells. I like that you can see what the boatmen do and how it goes. There's no two ways to tie off or repair or even clean a fish. There's one. I like that. I wish plumbing was like that. I wish the bastard had never apprenticed me out. The world passes you and you're still passing wrenches to fools.

"Mr. Horn hit you last night," Bobby says. "Shoe. I said...I said..."

"Mr. Horn?"

"Mr. Horn. I say he hit you again last night."

"A little."

"I heard him."

"Drunk."

"I heard him."

Addy Augarde is in front of her father's candy shop.

"I could hear him."

"It don't hurt Bobby. Don't worry."

"Mr. Horn never hits me."

"You're damn right and if he ever did, father or no..."

"Oh, you...oh you can't hit...fathers."

Now I look over at Addy. She's sat herself on a barrel and I can see her knees. She's pretending not to be watching but she's pretending badly. I heard she'd been to Blackpool with her mother and fancies herself special. She's a bit cakey but I can see her knees and I'm not alone.

"I can see her knees," Bobby whispers louder than he talks.

"What? Her knees?" I laugh.

"Look," and he points.

"Bobby. It's not polite to point."

"But, I can..."

I hear someone shout and turn in time to touch a dirty soccer ball. I stop it and flip it up to my hands. It's soft and soggy. The ball shows itself skinless. Petey Evans runs up to us. Taber with him. That little mick too. They stop when they see it's me.

"Hi Petey," Bobby says with his smile and quiver. "Hi Taber."

They don't really look at him and they don't really look at me. They're looking then, but they're not.

"Whose ball?" I say.

"Mine," Petey says quietly. Not so quiet when they're onto Bobby. Laughing and picking when I'm off lugging the damn plumber tools about. Not so quiet when they set him crying and sometimes bleeding. Bobby's fifteen now and they're about that. Only Bobby Horn is Bobby Horn and I can wonder myself into murder over where the pleasure is at making him cry.

"Who saw me fight under the light at Nuxhall Thursday last?"

The mick raised his hand slow like he had a question. He didn't. I knew he'd been there. Mostly plumber's guild men but some from the street. And the micks. The micks like the fights. They don't take sides.

"The big one," he says shyly. And I know he ain't shy. "You come up from the grab and brought him down."

Bobby dances and shakes and throws silly punches at the air.

"Shoe," he says. "Shoe goes like this and the big...who?"

I answer Bobby but eyeball Petey 'cause I know he's Boss.

"The brother plumber from the hill."

"Shoe goes like this and the big brother plumber from the hill goes like this."

Bobby covers his face and flops on his ass.

"Get up for the love of Christ, Bobby. You're wearing Sunday clothes."

"Oh no," he cries, brushing off the mud. I help.

"Don't cry lad. It's mud. It's only mud."

I'm back speaking to Petey.

"Lawson. That's the guy. Good guy. First time he lost under the lights. He's thirty. He's done. He don't want to hear any more bones cracking. You know Petey, I says to him I was sorry about his cheek, about the kicking of his chest and he says 'That's it. Too much blood.' Bobby had too much blood going last game of yours. What happened Petey? Rough game?"

The little bastard nods. I give him a small one. Fast and light. He goes to his knees and covers his face. Some blood drops off his nose, slides through his fingers. Taber and the mick don't move. Bobby's moving to him. His mouth is open only he can't speak.

"Oh Petey," he says kneeling with him.

"He'll be alright now, Bobby. He needed his head shaken."

"He did?"

"He did."

I toss the ball to Bobby who struggles to catch it but does, squeezing it to his chest. He looks to Petey and the mick and Taber. Back and forth, that fat smiling face going so fast they must be blurs.

"Who…who…who…?"

"Who wants to play?" I help.

"Who wants to play?" My Bobby Horn shouts.

Petey stands up, still not looking. Nowhere to look. My first one under the lights for the guild was that big uncle of his, that Jack. I wasn't yet sixteen. I took him quick and he bought me a beer and Petey knows it.

"I'll play," he says and the others too. They chase the ball down toward the fishmonger. I walk to Addy's barrel.

She has a red flower in her hair. A paper flower with a comb in it and I wonder who she's kidding. It's 1922 and she's still back there dreaming of the actresses on postcards with flowers and combs. Her knees though, are soft and round. I light one and stand next to her.

"That's a pretty red flower," I say.

"Oh, why hello Albert."

Nobody calls me Albert. I smoke and think and wish I had more to say.

"Were you at church, Albert?"

"I was."

"Why, where's that adorable brother of yours? I do not believe I have ever seen you without him."

"I'm without him plenty."

Ronnie Manchester walks by with his mum. He sees me. I know he thinks about Addy. I know he wants to try me too, but his thinking gets in the way. He's twenty four or five and he sometimes goes for the plumbers on Rawlinson Street. He nods and I nod.

"Why, look Albert. It's Ronnie Manchester and his mum."

I don't say anything and light another.

"I will be leaving Barrow-in-Furness shortly," she says. "I hope to be attending classes in Blackpool."

"What sort?"

"Why, acting, of course. I hope to begin attending classes at Mr. Henry Ainley's Academy of Thespian Law and Art. Mr. Henry Ainley has been on the London stage."

I don't know him but I admit it's something alright. London. Acting. Now he's in Blackpool though, and I do know that place. Addy turns on her barrel and crosses her legs. Grey stockings are up to just below her knees and now I see that pink rounding part of the leg where her strength comes from. I'm pretending not to be seeing but I'm seeing and stirring.

"Yes. I hope to be on the London stage shortly."

And I hope to be the bloody Prince of Wales.

"Well, Addy," I say turning so I can pretend not to see her lovely leg better, "I surely wish you luck and I will try to come and watch."

"It will be very costly. That's why it is the London stage. Only the very best perform there and so naturally one would expect it to be costly."

Ronnie Manchester, of all people, showed me pictures on a playing card last year. Above those knees and that creamy top leg is this thing that you might not think would look so nice itself but just does. Look nice, I mean. Other parts too. I seen the pictures.

Addy would have all of it, actress or not. Now I'm greatly stirring and better sit on a barrel of my own.

"I'll sit a bit."

"Please do."

It's warm and the late morning breeze is damp. Down the narrow street I see the wharf and beyond it the water and the Isle of Walney beyond that. The tide runs low and spots of silt dot the space like broken glass. I take off my coat and lay it over my lap and my stirring.

Because of the, tide the bigger boats lie angled and aground in the shallows. I watch some boatmen in mud boots scrubbing the undersides. I'm pretending not to see the higher leg now, her own playing card there somewhere.

The ball rolls into the street from the alley and Bobby follows. He stops it after some tries, sees me and waves.

Bobby kicks the ball back.

"I'll be…I'll be going with Shoe. Thanks Petey. Thanks Taber. Thanks…Thanks…Irish kid."

He comes to the barrels now all smiley and squeezes me and puts his sweet, sweaty face into my chest. Addy Augarde, who may be going to Blackpool, reaches over and rubs his hair.

He looks at me now.

"I…scored a goal."

"You're a great good guy, Bobby Horn."

"You're a great good guy, Shoe Horn."

My stirring has waned enough for me to stand off the barrel.

"We'll be heading on now, Addy."

Addy still shows her leg.

"I'll be right here, Albert."

We walk again, this time Bobby halts ahead, looking back every few steps to know I'm here. The gulls take him and he follows them with his arms stretched out and flapping. I'm laughing but he's dead to it. He flaps them hard but stays to earth. I light another one.

"How come…how come they can fly?"

"They're birds, for the love of Christ."

"But…"

"They got wings. You got arms."

Bobby doesn't like this, thinks about it and lets them down with a shrug. We're over Michaelson Bridge now and Walney Island looks square at us, flat and dull. I hate it so. I hate it that we were ever there and I hate it when sometimes I have to cross the Jubilee Bridge carrying Lowden's plumbing tools. Lugging them pipes and wrenches behind him like he's bloody King George himself. And always the Great Bitch watching from across the shallows.

"What?" Bobby says.

"What what?" I say after a bit.

"You're looking."

I smile at Bobby and myself too.

"That's good lad. I was."

"I know. I saw you."

I start again onto Ramsden Dock Road. Mr. Horn's house is off it behind the foundry. It smells like melting bolts. It does. We smell like that too. Christ. The Channel Lane Hotel is ahead and Bobby runs onto the high porch and to his lookout where he can see over Walney to the Irish Sea. And Piel Island too. I go up to look with him but I've seen them. I've turned the wrench all over the Barrow. I've done the pipes. Bobby points but says nothing. I nod but Christ knows what he's pointing at. I close my eyes because sometimes it's better than what I'm seeing. And thinking. I should never have gone under the lights at Nuxhall Road. I don't like it that Mr. Horn told Lowden I could lay them down. I'm looking different and I've had only nine or ten matches. That Rudy. That filthy Russian. Good Christ but he would not stop. And now, Thursday next. Well, you go 'til you lose.

I open my eyes and he's still pointing. A girl comes onto the porch. I watch her. Mick for sure. Got that catholic look about her. I can tell. I can. And the big black curls. And the skin that's not at all creamy. It's tea cup skin. Black eyes. She goes behind me wearing a blue apron with Channel Lane Hotel on it, carrying some rags. She smells like oil soap. I've seen her before or think I have. She drops some of her rags, bends to get them, but Bobby's quicker.

"Here," he shouts, holding them out.

"Thank you," she says, and I'm right. Pure mick.

"I'm Bobby Horn," he shouts.

"Don't shout it, Bobby," I say.

"I'm Bobby Horn," he shouts a whisper.

She smiles and it's a nice one.

"I'm Molly Reilly."

"I play soccer," he says.

"I work at this hotel."

Addy Augarde's top leg is still in my head and I wonder about Molly Reilly's.

"I'm Shoe Horn."

We look a moment. I do that, I notice. Look at the girls. Look when I should be looking somewhere else. It's a small mouth too, and her lips are round and thick.

"I'm working," she says, getting ready to turn away.

"It's Sunday."

"I'm in service."

"Ahhh. I'm apprenticed out to the trades."

"Ahhh."

She looks about my age but what's that? I might look thirty and not seventeen. I touch my often broken nose. She smiles at me and I wonder if it's true that the Irish girls tend to steal linens. Mr. Horn says they acquire the habit from their mothers. I look at her hands and imagine them reaching for linens not their own. Long hands chapped red and swollen. She sees me looking and hides them in her armful of rags.

"I don't live here," she says out of the blue. "I live over on Shakespeare. Da works for the paper mill. I'm in service."

"You said."

"I don't mind."

"We saw Addy Augarde's knees," Bobby says, like he'd burst if he didn't.

We laugh but Bobby's not finished.

"We saw her knees and…and…and…what Shoe?"

"You scored a goal was it?"

"A goal," he shouts. "I get it and…and…"

Now he's dribbling up and down the long porch with the ball only he's seeing.

"I get it and…Petey comes up but I go like this…and…and I go like this and…"

"Goal!" Molly shouts.

"Yes, yes," Bobby shouts.

Ten minutes later we're at Ramsden Dock Road and Athol Street, looking down the lane to his crooked dark house. Might as well be built of coal. Might as well be chewed into a hill. I light another and check my pocket watch. Past noon and I'm thinking the bastard is still sleeping where he was when I dressed up me and Bobby for St. Mark's. St. Mary the Virgin is closer, just over the bridge. But I don't go there anymore unless I have to. I know the Great Bitch roams there. Bobby starts for the place.

"Bobby."

"I'm just…"

"Wait 'til I smoke this a bit."

"But…"

"You don't go into the house without me."

"I…know."

"Then wait."

He's thinking and watching the glow on my smoke. He's wanting something but not sure what. I'm missing our mum. Who do you tell that to when you lay them down under the light and look it? My sweet mother, stew on the table, salted beef and such and my shirts starched and straight. Christ, but he wasn't the faker then. Up for the work, out to the shop and on Sunday mornings blowing hymns on his coronet. Mr. Horn's horn he'd say. Lunch in the park and kites. But now Mr. Horn is what he has become.

"You don't go in there without me. I'm Shoe Horn."

"I know."

"I know you know 'cause you're a great good guy Bobby Horn."

I flick the damn smoke away and head down to the place and the father.

"And…and…and you're a great good guy Shoe Horn."

2

I lay Phil down and Bobby
picks Blacky up

"Stop. Oh, Shoe stop," he says, stepping out of the circle's dark edges and into the throw of Nuxhall light. Thursday's the night, but I'd gone just two weeks ago and it wasn't right to go unhealed, only tell that to Lowden, the dog. Tell that to Mr. Horn who sets it up and is too drunk to see it. Bobby's crying. The crowd shouting and moving. That prick Gogarty, the Mick Miner, got me a good kick in the privates. I covered and bit his collar. One more good short one in his ribs and that's when Bobby comes crying into the circle.

"Stop…stop…stop…"

Gogarty is doubled and catching breath. I got to hold Bobby Horn.

"Now good Christ, Bobby. It's over when he quits."

"No."

"Bobby…"

"Oh Shoe you're…oh Shoe…blood…and he…he kicked your…things…Shoe…"

"Damn! He's caught the breath! Do you want me to die!"

"No! No! No!"

"Then get back! McAvy! Will you get him back and hold him!"

The McAvy's a tree. He's got him now.

Gogarty comes again. I grab and lean into him.

Gogarty tries to box my ears.

"That's not fair," Bobby screams.

I jab his Adam's apple. I bring my knee to his privates. I do a hard butt on his cheek. I knee him again. He's done but he spits at me.

"He's spitting," screams Bobby. "He's spitting at Shoe and he's... he's a great good guy."

I step off to the side. I'm feeling young now and he's got to be twenty five. What's that feel like? Phil Gogarty's a good one though. It's not the first time he spit on me. I was fourteen and he come by Ramsden Road with his boys looking for it. Mr. Horn had gone at my face and Mummy had put me out of the house with ice. They all got me that time. But he was a good one and never ran or laughed or said he was sorry.

"How do you want it, Phil?"

"Up yours. How's your father?"

"You want it long then huh? You want me to keep it going 'til the skin peels right off your ugly mug."

He doesn't speak for a bit. Watches me circle him. Sees what I feel, the blood filling my arms, my fists, my face. He looks down.

"I'm sorry I asked for your father. Don't make it long."

I go at him now but he's not done. I'm watching his trousers and ankles for a pin or some ointment to blind me but it doesn't come. He comes up with his elbow and I grab it and turn him and it's the back of his ugly head facing me. He ought to sprout a nose for me to push out the right way. He ought to have eyes to see what's coming. I give him three straight hard ones to the fat back of his head. He's falling. He's done.

There's three tonight. Me and Gogarty were second up. The third one started before we could clear. These two wanted to go. Jesus. There's no reason to do it, much less want it. Gogarty's to his feet and rubbing the back of his head. Those other fools clinch and punch and roll between us.

"You punched the back of my head," he says over their grunts and the crowd of guild men.

"There it was and I hit it. It was inviting, you big mick. C'mon Bobby, let's count our fortune."

We walk back toward Ramsden Dock, The McAvy with us. He's quiet and thinking and it makes his walk scary because his huge feet never make a sound when they touch ground. None of us say anything, even Bobby, who runs ahead and waits. My eye's closed, my teeth ache and I didn't bind myself tight enough for Phil Gogarty's kicks.

"I been thinking," The McAvy says, his awful hands stuck in his pockets, his great shaggy head bent to the road. "I been thinking that America would like me."

We walk on, Bobby hears a dog whimpering in an alley and runs there, whimpering himself.

"Bobby! Bobby!"

"Yes…yes…Shoe?"

"Don't touch it."

"But…"

"You don't know it."

"It's crying."

"He's right," says The McAvy.

"Listen," Bobby says holding up two fingers. He pays attention in ways I can't imagine. I listen because he's Bobby Horn.

"There," he says, his mouth open. He does the whimper to me and The McAvy, then to the dog itself. Then goes into the alley.

"Did you hear me, Shoe?" The McAvy says again.

"You're going to America. I heard you."

"I didn't say I was going, Shoe. I said that America would like me."

"And where would you stay? That brother of yours don't want you."

"I didn't say I was going to stay with Donald. I said America would like me."

We light one and Bobby comes out of the dark with a black little thing that might be a dog. He's cradled it and they're both whimpering together. I don't say nothing but Bobby knows better. He runs ahead stopping and twirling like he's dancing. My thing is swollen and not in a mysterious way. Addy Augarde could stand on a sugar barrel and pull that damn dress over her head and I wouldn't stir. Or maybe I would but it would be a painful stirring. Or something.

"I meant I'm not looking for trouble," The McAvy says.

If you look to The McAvy for trouble you'd be a goner. Look at the thing. My good Christ on the cross but if he's not as big as three men. I smile on that but my face doesn't like it.

"Stop making me smile, McAvy. It hurts my damn mug."

"You know what I mean."

"I do lad."

The McAvy shrugs.

"I'm going to my mums."

"Say hello."

"I will. Good night to you, Bobby."

"Good…good night…McAvy."

I watch him start away. He's always got his mind working. They took his job at the boatyard and give it to a one armed soldier last year. He's eighteen and hasn't had anything but running errands for the foreman and sometimes cleaning up the bathing beach at Biggar Bank and that's summer and that's nothing.

"He's a big one," Bobby says. Only he says it to the thing he's holding and holds it out to see The McAvy round the corner, bowed in thought.

"Isn't…isn't he a…a big one, Shoe?"

"Yes, lad."

It starts whimpering again and he pulls it back and whimpers with it. There's stars wanting to come out but Barrow-in-Furness don't like them. Smoke lays just over the roofs from the brewers and millers and ships and that cuddles up to the fog coming in from Walney Channel. It's like walking through Bobby's head. Nothing changes. I'll be plumbing before the sun's up. Hours before the man who is supposed to be teaching me the trade. Lowden has the hands of a lawyer. He hasn't picked a hole clean for years. Not since Mr. Horn give him me. It's plumbing, not a miracle. I learned all he knew in ten days and I'm apprenticed for seven *years* and most of the money goes to Mr. Horn. Says he's my broker. He won't get none of tonight's purse though.

Bobby's far enough ahead.

"I almost can't see you, Bobby, slow down."

"I'm...I'm...going to my lookout."

"Slow down so's I can see you."

He climbs the porch of the Channel Lane Hotel and goes to his spot. It's soupy with the fog and smoke but he still stares out and points for the dog.

"Look," he says.

I sit on the steps. My smokes are damp from the night but I work it up. The McAvy says I smell like tobacco. It's true. It's also true I take them from my mouth and look at them falling into ash and think there's something I should be learning here. Or should already know. There's a mystery in them is what I'm saying. Now the thing is barking and Bobby's joining him.

"Bobby! No barking!"

"We're not...we're..."

"Stop him, and you too. People are sleeping."

"We're talking."

He's looking at me and the thing is too and they're both barking.

"That's yapping, Bobby. That's not talking."

"No...no...yapping is...yapping is..."

Now he's crying. The thing stops and looks at him. I let him go a bit because his crying is quiet and smooth. Bobby's always every way at once. Arms and legs dancing out, speaking and shouting and whispering in a storm. I have combed his hair ten times today and it still rides his head like barley. Truly, only crying orders him a bit. When it bubbles out of him and he's still, I know there's more in there than any of us imagine. I pat the side of my step and after a bit he brings the thing over and sits. We're quiet for a time, him all lined up in his tears, me thinking about everything going on inside him, forgetting myself. It's good getting lost inside Bobby. There's no dark corners. I hold out my smoke to him.

"Oh…oh…Shoe…I…you know I don't!"

"I was offering it to your mate."

Bobby's stopped crying and starts shaking. I point.

"Stop."

"They just…go."

"Just stop."

"I can when I think."

"Then think."

He looks at his shakes and squeezes his face in thought and they stop.

"You're a great good guy, Bobby Horn."

"You're a great good guy, Shoe Horn."

Molly Reilly comes to the bottom of the stairs.

"Molly…what?" Bobby shouts.

"Reilly," she shouts back. She's swaying and I see a smoke in her hand too. She puffs it and grey ash falls onto her long black coat.

"Look," Bobby shouts and stands and holds out the thing that's whimpering again.

"What is it?" Her heavy Irish voice is swaying along with the rest of her.

I don't say anything and I don't need to. I don't want to either. I keep my hands close to my broke up face.

"What?" she says, pointing right at my nose.

"Gogarty," Bobby says seriously. "And…and…he kicked Shoe's things too."

Bobby hands me the dog without looking.

"But Shoe…but Shoe does…this and this…"

And it's displayed for wobbly Molly Reilly. I remember some, but Bobby shows it exactly the way it was. So he *remembers* too, with everything he is. It's all in there. That's the greatness of my Bobby Horn and I feel it and want to say it. I don't though.

"Stop that bloody bouncing around and stop that bloody punching the air."

"I…I was…"

"Molly Reilly doesn't care."

She wobbles but her legs seem sturdy. She won't tip as long as she's looking and she's looking at me.

"I'm sixteen and don't call me a mick."

A red velvet hat with a red velvet bow on the side was pulled low over that coal black hair. She took a short angry puff and let it fall out of her hand.

"Shoe…Shoe's…he's a…he didn't…say mick."

"Shut up, you," she says to Bobby. I'm down the stairs and got my bleeding, broken mug in her potato eating face. She steps back and almost falls. Catches herself. But she's not afraid.

"I'm sixteen. I'll say shut up or piss off or good morning."

Now she's got her hands on her hips and I'm sorry.

"I'm sorry I got so close."

She's watching me. She's swaying again and her eyes are dewy. She doesn't answer me and we're quiet until the thing starts barking and Bobby does too.

"Bobby…"

Now Molly Reilly's barking and goes to Bobby and strokes the thing, all the time barking and smiling. There's nothing to do or say. My thing has begun to throb again and the one clear eye is closing up. I sit back down and they go quiet. She sits too.

"I went to Nina Sevenings evening for girls in service."

I nodded.

"Oh, so you know Miss Sevenings evenings do you?"

I might know but what of it. My business is getting Bobby sleeping and my tools laid out.

"It's every Thursday night. Some girl plays piano and Miss Sevenings reads Sonnets from the Portuguese and punch is served."

Bobby's going all over. His part of the step marches, like the Coldstream guards.

"Shoe goes…Shoe…he goes every Thursday too. He…"

"Not every Thursday, Bobby."

"He got…he got that Phil Gogarty," he explains to Molly Reilly. "And he's a big mick."

She turns her face up at me, one hand still on the dog.

"Mummy made this hat. It's just like that one Phyllis Dare wears on her postcard."

"I know it," I say, and I'm not lying.

"That was last year. She's gone. I don't live here, I live on Shakespeare with Da."

"Where…where did…our mum's gone too," Bobby gets out.

Molly nods.

"She's…she's…right Shoe?…She's with God."

"My mummy's with Da's cousin, Robert. Run off before last Christmas. London we think but don't know."

Now Bobby Horn nods but his eyes are into the soupy night. The dog looks with him. I stand.

"We got to go now."

"I don't live here," she says again. "Only I got to heat the bricks up for the beds."

"My mum did that," Bobby shouts happily and thinks with his two fingers up. "But…but…Mr. Horn…what Shoe?"

"Mr. Horn don't do it, Bobby."

Mr. Horn don't do nothing.

I stop at Jubilee Bridge. A little cool breeze parts the smoke and I can see halfway to Walney Island. I'm ready to talk about that damn black thing that Bobby's holding close to his wide face. I cannot look after him and that thing too. I cannot have it into a house of kicks and slaps. My hands are deep in my pockets and I hear him.

"A…A…A nice day to you too, Miss Corony."

I should have felt it, should have noticed the air grow colder and the breeze that cleared the bridge come sour. I don't move a thing. I am Shoe Horn and I am known but I don't move. Now I hear the stiff brush of skirt against the cobblestones. I hear the wooden heels of its shoes hollowing the night air with each step as if those horrible feet were laughing. When it's by me, I close them tight so I don't see it either coming or going. I feel Bobby now and know he's staring at me and at its back too.

"You…you…never look at her. Is it…is it 'cause she's ugly?"

"We have to talk about the dog, lad."

"She's…old. Do you think old people are ugly, Shoe?"

"No."

"Some…are ugly. That…Bill, who cleans the toilets in the park."

"He's French."

"Do you think he…lives in the toilet?"

"C'mon."

We turn up toward Mr. Horn's house. Before I go to Lowden's, I'll dress Bobby and have him at St. Mark's by 4:30. He'll sleep again there and then play in the yard with the others. I don't call them unfortunates, although the little Cooke girl who is blind and deaf might be. Some others too. Mostly they're just in a world they probably know wasn't built for them. How else can it be? I'll leave until tomorrow to worry about the dog.

"Blacky," Bobby says from behind me, as if he's reading my mind. "I'm…his name is Blacky."

We stop outside the alley to our dark place and I light my last one like I do. Bobby watches the dog in his arms and then I feel him watching me.

"You…you never look at her…I…I know why."

I pull on the smoke and look at him.

"She's the dropper," he says.

I don't say nothing. I'm thinking there are stars somewhere but not in the Barrow.

"Evans and…and Petey and those…say she's the dropper. That's why you won't…look at her."

I'm thinking, somewhere there might be tools that are mine and mine alone, and I would lug them for myself.

"She's…she's the dropper."

I finish the smoke and flick it. I get close to his face. We stare like monkeys. I love him. I love him so.

"That's right, Bobby Horn. She's the dropper."

I'm half down to the house when I hear him.

"But…but…what does she drop?"

3

I plumb for the
Scotsman from Africa

Even though he'll sleep again for Mrs. Bulmers in Victoria Hall at St. Mark's, on the floor in the big blanket I brought with him that first time after Mummy died, I see to it that he's cleaned good and done his privy.

"Young Mr. Horn and Mr. Horn," she always says, her words crispy.

"I've…I've…I've done my privy," Bobby shouts.

The first day and the second and the third, he sobbed a river and would not believe that Shoe would be there for him when the sun started down. He would not believe our mum had gone either. Mr. Horn had pounded me that night. He was bigger then. I was thirteen and could mostly stand and accept it but I remember he knocked me out that night. I promised my mum I would not fight back, promised her with that dirty Dr. Clausen by the side of her bed, making it a blood oath. He knows about Bobby though. He knows not to go for him.

I cleaned my face and licked my tongue over my loose front teeth. I was thirteen and had not begun going for the plumbers but Mr. Horn was stacking me with welts and changing me, even then.

Now Bobby was used to it. Almost four years of mornings before the sun. The cold, wet streets of the Barrow glistened under gas lights.

"Did…did…did…?"

"No Bobby. Mr. Horn wasn't awake."

"He didn't…hit?"

"No lad."

We turn on Rawlinson and I'm shifting the damn plumber's box from one hand to the other every forty steps. Jackie Robeson, Lowden's apprentice before me, always carried in his right hand and his bloody arm went twice the size of his left. It's the whole bloody business in a box and you got to carry it. I hate it. I hate it so. Bobby's back is to me when I hear it.

"Stop," I say and stop myself.

He doesn't turn around. He doesn't stop. I see his cap is too small and it sits up there sad and funny. I had laundered up his shirt and tweed pants but he looked like he just played a rugby match.

"Stop," I say again and he does.

"Turn around Bobby."

He shakes his head.

"Bobby…"

I wait because Bobby wants to make me happy, only he needs to think it's his idea. Sometimes I'm short and then I'm sorry all day. Bobby teaches me to be quiet, to watch and to wait. He's turning, but slowly, as if he's giving me the chance to call it off. He's full with second chances and he makes me think before I open my mouth. The black thing's head peeks out of his shirt.

"You can't be taking that thing to the hall."

He's thinking and it shows on his fat face.

"I'm…I'm…he's not being taken to the hall."

"What's that then peeking out? A bloody Mau-Mau?"

Bobby's eyes go wide.

"It's…It's…a dog."

32

He pulls his coat back a little more so I can see the wee thing and it can see me.

"Look. It's not a...a...Mau-Mau."

"I don't care if it's the Prince of Wales, you can't be taking it inside."

"I'm not."

"Put it down."

"He's Blacky. He's got a name now."

"Lad..."

"He waited...he...last night he waited to go to the privy with me."

Bobby turns and walks again as if the privy business has settled things. Ronnie Manchester comes down the street toward us. He's got his plumber's card. Someone will meet him with his tools. I've heard he's good with pipes. I don't know though. He never looks at Bobby.

"Hello...Ronnie," Bobby shouts.

Ronnie passes him without a nod, even though Bobby's opening his coat to show his secret. He stops at me.

"Got one?"

I give him one and light them. He's no apprentice now but he's always begging the smokes. I watch him close. He blows out smoke and smiles.

"You did Gogarty last night huh?"

"Shoe...Shoe...he..." Bobby gets ready to show.

"Bobby, stop. Ronnie knows how it's done."

"He fainted you know."

"Naw, he got right back up."

"I mean after, at his mum's. He fainted right out. He's still out. She had that dago Doctor, what's his name?"

"Ricci?"

"Had the dirty bugger there an hour and still couldn't get him up. He's in bed now, still fainted."

We smoke together and Bobby watches us. Last year I got the Russian to finally stop with an elbow in the heart but he never fainted. They got some cold water on him and he was back. Ronnie tilts his cap back.

"I'm taking Addy to the moving pictures after work."

He winks at me.

"She's like a plum, she is. All this actress talk and she's about to bust wide open."

"We...we saw her knees!" Bobby shouts.

"I'll tell you about it," he says to me and saunters away.

We walk and don't say nothing. I'm sorting through the headache Gogarty gave me and working at not thinking too hard about Phil or his mum. I know that Doctor Ricci. My mum used to call him Doctor Eyes, Ears, Nose and Throat. So it wasn't my kicks, I guess. Or my elbows. But the bloody steam pipe fitting at the shipyard better be done before that bastard Lowden walks in. My head's full of what's been done and what's to do.

"Wait," I say at the Lower Victoria Hall door.

Bobby's got it half open and he's telling the dog about the place.

"It can't go in, lad."

"Blacky."

I nod.

"Blacky can't go in. Mrs. Bulmers won't let you have a dog."

"I...I don't have it...we're...we're..."

He's looking to explain it to both of us. Me and Blacky. We both look at Bobby, his hands out and pleading as if the words might drop out of this dark, clammy sky. His round mouth is open and nothing's coming.

"I know lad, you and Blacky, you're friends."

"Yes," he says in amazement and pushes that wild head onto my chest again. "Yes. We're friends."

"I know. Right Blacky?"

The thing whimpers.

"See Bobby? Blacky knows you're friends but he knows Mrs. Bulmers won't let it into the hall."

Bobby thinks and looks close at the dog.

"He'll…you'll…be good, won't you?"

"It can't go in."

"But…"

I'll be late for the damn steam pipe and it'll be catching up all day long. And now, for the love of Christ, it's starting to rain.

"Put it over there, by the grass next to the church lane."

"He'll…he'll…oh Shoe!"

Now his free hand is whacking his thigh and he's crying.

"Stop that Bobby."

"I…I can't."

"You can."

"He's…my friend. He'll get wet."

"Bobby…"

He marches crazy when he can't get it and even the tears don't stop him. His face up to the clouds, his bony little fist striking his thigh.

"Bobby…"

When Mummy began to die and Mr. Horn had hidden in the pub and that dirty Dr. Clausen had left me alone with the wet cloth to try and soothe her and she would shove my hand away and even her friend Mrs. Moody couldn't help me, only Bobby knew. Only Bobby rolled onto her bed and put his mad head under her chin. Only Bobby knew, understood what Mummy needed, and he gave it and he gave it and gave it. I say it again. What my brother understands, he understands with his whole wee body. He knows in the bottom of his feet things I can't imagine.

"I'll take the damn thing."

He stops. He's crying still but he's hoping.

"What?"

"I'll take the dog, I'll take Blacky with me and I'll bring it back when I get you."

Bobby dries his eyes on the clean shirt and halts to me.

"To…to…"

"I said I'll take the bloody thing to work. Only I got to go lad."

"Shoe's an…apprentice," Bobby says to the thing. "He works… he's…he's…"

"I'm a plumber. Give it here."

He does.

"Only work hard today, Bobby."

"I…I will."

"Learn what Mrs. Bulmers teaches you."

"I…promise."

"Well, it's a goodbye now, Bobby Horn."

"And…and…it's a goodbye now, Shoe Horn."

He whispers something to the dog and goes in, where he'll get down his blanket and sleep until the sun wakes him. Mrs. Bulmers, who is not married, is always at Lower Hall. She smells like that olive soap Mummy liked and she's as big as the ships that bring it to port. She says Bobby is a flower and the others are flowers. I don't know. Flowers? I came early for him once and those that could were standing in a circle, still as stones, with their hands pointing up to the ceiling and she was telling them a story about Tom the Tulip. She asked them if they could feel their roots. Every blessed one said yes to that. Bobby said, with his eyes closed, he wanted to be red and started to cry.

"Tulips don't cry Bobby Horn," I said.

"Some do. Oh yes they do," Mrs. Bulmers said.

Now I'd like to be a tulip, anything but the plumber's apprentice. I'm soaked and my arm's aching because I can't shift the toolbox and hold the bloody dog too. I stick my head into the boatyard office. And Christ if it's not Charlie Burt who took The McAvy job.

"What's it?" he says, not looking up from the card game he's playing with himself.

"Lowden got something going with the steam pipe fittings."

I'm just wanting to get to the spot and fit the bleeding thing.

"Steam fittings? Nobody said anything to me about steam fittings."

He's looking up as if I've lied. He says it like that too. I'd like to give him a few short bleeders and see if he'd talk to me like that again. But he's got the one arm from the Krauts, although he wears the pinned sleeve like it's everybody's fault. He stands up so I can get a better look. That's right, he wants to say, one arm and it's all your doing.

"How's that friend of yours? How's that big lout McAvy? He'd fall asleep in the office. Did you know that Horn? He'd have the Krauts all over us if it was up to that big lout."

He would not say that to The McAvy. No one in his dreams would look on The McAvy and say such a thing. He knows I know that. He moves some papers around his desk top and picks one up.

"Righto then. Shipbreaking. Yes, here it is. Anchor Line Basin. You know Rogers?"

"I do."

"See him then. That's where he should be, the bloody filthy African. Down there among the hot pipes."

Charlie turns back to his card game. I turn for the Basin.

"And no dogs," he says without looking up.

"What?"

"You can't bring a dog down there."

"Says who?"

"It's a rule."

"I never heard it."

"No dogs allowed. Now you've heard it."

He's still not looking up and he's grinning at his cards. I don't know much but Blacky will be down there. The rain's harder and I'm walking across the yard toward the Basin when I hear him at the door.

"You hear me, Horn? Do you? You can't bring that dog down there."

I turn up the alley between Dock and Basin. Rogers' stream room is the last entrance on the left and I can hear his machines under the heavy door. It's dark except for a furnace flame and I feel my way down the steep stairs. Rogers is looking hard at the furnace gauge. He's bald and shiny and Charlie Burt is right to say he's African, although the accent says he's Scot. Maybe Scots don't know what they are. Or care. It's icy cold despite the furnace but the bugger's not wearing a shirt. His trousers bunched around his stomach by a fat brown belt. He found Mr. Horn one night drowning in a muddy puddle and carried him home. When I took the bastard from him, Mr. Horn called him a filthy nigger.

"Lowden's got me here for a fitting, Mr. Rogers."

Rogers points to the tangle of pipes behind the furnace.

"I dabbed some red paint on the flawed one."

I put down the box and check it. I forget Blacky until he licks my lips.

"Aww Christ."

"What's that?"

"Damn thing licked me."

"Give it."

I hand the thing to Rogers who holds it in his big hand. They look at each other and I want to laugh at the two Africans. I find the red paint and pull on the pipe. The thing is cemented to the wall. Someone must have known an apprentice would be there one day and wanted to make it as difficult as can be.

"Christ."

"What?"

"Cemented."

Rogers shakes his shiny head and speaks to Blacky.

"Steamfitters that can't fit, shipbreakers that can't break, plumbers that can't plumb."

I look now and I'd go on that and Rogers knows it.

"I don't mean you lad," he says in his thick brogue. He's maybe fifty and hard. But you can't accept an insult here. Ever. He smiles at Blacky.

"I don't mean him do I? What's his name?"

"Blacky," I say, feeling for the wet spot. "Is this shut down?"

"It's shut down. Right Blacky? It's shut down good."

I've got it. They leak in a lot of places at once. I get my cutter and saw and light one before I start. Working overhead is tough. It's the blood, I'd guess. It rushes down your arms and fills your chest. Also the buggers put the things on top of one another which makes it hard to grip because the pipes on either side are hot. Christ.

"I'm going over to Hindpool Road and see about boiler castings. I'm taking the dog if you like," Rogers says.

"Name's Blacky."

"You said," and they're off.

Bobby and Scots and Africans rolled into one. The dog is on holiday. Lowden would whisper to just bind the damn pipe and seal it. Then he'd tell them he did the fitting so smooth it looks like the pipe's not new. I want it right to spite the greedy beggar and take the old section with cutter and saw, frame-up the new length and fix it. I got Addy on my mind. I don't know why I don't want Ronnie Manchester to see a moving picture with her and I think about that while working the pipe in place. I would take her to watch a picture and I wouldn't sneer and talk of ripe plums and such. She's not pretty although she's fair and her hair is soft. You can see it's soft. That Irish servant, that Molly Reilly. Her hair is not soft. It's coarse really, and tangled on top, just sitting there as drunk as she was. Addy keeps distance. Her clothes and eyes keep distance. Is that what it is? Or does she say nothing with her eyes and dress? Molly's hands are hard and her eyes are small. I don't believe she is a linen snatcher though. Addy talks like she's knowing what she don't. I light another, then get my hands back up there. My closed eye has opened a bit in the cold and damp of Rogers' cellar. I look up at the pipes but I'm seeing Molly's mouth and the stuff she'd rubbed onto her lips to go to Mrs. Sevenings evening for girls in service and in that dress that didn't have the puff or fullness of Addy's sitting there on the barrel, her knees all creamy. And Molly with that dare on her eyes. Her mouth and then her nice thing probably not all wrapped and bound in puff like Addy's, and smelling like oil soap and not sweet like Addy at her father's shop. But both their things all nice or nicer than the postcards and lying that way all open and such, and me with my thing stirring and us watching one another's things and…oh good Christ!

My thing's done it again. I'm working and it's launching the goo and my damn hands not even near the silly thing. Christ! I go up to the outside and pee on a corner of the red brick building, to clean it out. Rogers is right. Water closets that don't flush. Furnaces that don't heat. Plumbers with oozing things. Jesus, Mary and Joseph.

4

We fly a kite and
I go see Phil

"Raise it up! Come on lad! Raise it!"

He's got the bloody thing dropping like a potato. Blacky's got a squirrel he's interested in and Bobby watches them and not his kite.

"Bobby!"

He looks over on that like he's in a miracle of places all at once.

"Hold it high now," I show him pretending I've got one. "Hold it over your head."

He looks up surprised as if he forgot he's holding the damn string. His mouth goes open and he halts to me, frightened. But now the breeze scoops it and it flies up, its tail making nutty loops.

"There she goes, up to the clouds."

"I…I…got it."

"You got it, Bobby."

"I…I got it good."

"That's a great good guy, Bobby Horn."

"It's…it's up…with the birds. It's…flying. I'm flying."

"You're flying, Bobby."

"I love…you," he yells.

"I know."

"Thanks. Thanks Shoe. The...kite and...and the...park. The park. Mummy took us here. Mummy...Mummy liked it."

"Now Jesus, Bobby, that tree. Raise it..."

"I...I...know. Raise it up."

It's over and around the tree and he's a bird. His free arm flaps with the thing itself. It's great. It's big. It's bigger than everything. Bobby among the clouds. I sit on the grass and lean on my side. He pilots the thing and comes to me, standing there like everything's new all over again. He's thinking hard. I can see his face go all pinched concentrating.

"Mummy...Mummy took us by that...that elm."

That is the pleasure, right there. He takes you, he does.

"Now, how'd you know that was an elm?"

"Mummy...Mummy would...she'd say 'Let's take our lunch under that...elm.' And that's...is that...is that...?"

"Yes lad, that's the elm."

"Then...that's an elm."

Now he's pointing up at the kite and waiting for the words. He's shaking and going like fire. We had to leave church before the sermon at St. Mark's today. It's a bright Sunday morning and Bobby could not sit still for thinking about my promise of the park and kites and bangers.

"You...see it go round and round?"

"Round and round," I say lying flat. The rare sun so good all over.

"Why?"

"Why what?"

"Why round and...and...round?"

"I don't know, Bobby."

"The wind."

"Must be."

Bobby points again at the kite. It's white from a torn sheet and we wrote Bobby's name on it so the gulls would know whose it was. He's pointing but his mind's bouncing.

"That…that…banger was good. Thanks Shoe."

We watch the kite and now watch each other.

"Why…Why do they call them bangers?"

"One name's as good as another."

"I'd…call them sausages."

"Why?"

"Cause…that's…that's what they are."

"Then I think you should call them sausages."

"Oh no…I…I'll call them bangers, everyone else does… And…and Mummy used to bring…she'd…what?"

"Bananas."

He smiles and I see our mum clear in his fat face.

"I…I…love them."

"And cold steak and kidney pie."

Bobby laughs and shouts and sees Mummy's food spread in a line.

"Steak and…and…kidney pie."

"And that big pitcher with the red and blue flower on the side filled with milk."

"Cold. Cold…milk…and and something on the ground."

"The Indian blanket," I shout.

"Indian blanket and the Indian was…was praying."

"That's right, Bobby. Praying on his horse and he had that big feather headdress that dropped all the way to his saddle."

"Yes…yes…"

"When it got a little dark and cool we'd wrap you up in it. Do you remember?"

Now he throws his head back and sends out his joy into this cruel world.

"I remember Mummy's…fat red face. I remember her big big face."

He looks at me and spreads his hands out wide, fingers apart, letting the string go.

"This Big!"

I pop up pointing.

"The kite!"

He looks and points and shakes. The thing rises up to the sun.

"My kite! My kite!"

"Jesus, Mary and Joseph," I say, and we're after it. Blacky forgetting his squirrel, runs with us.

The Barrow lies in the Lake District but any fool sees we're at Morecambe Bay and then the Irish Sea and that ain't lakes. We follow the kite like dopes until it does a goodbye loop and flies over Walney to the sea. Bobby's still chasing and he's halfway toward Jubilee Bridge before I catch him.

"I'll make another, Bobby."

"My...my...Oh Shoe, my kite!"

"I'll make another."

"My...my..."

"Bobby! Stop!"

He settles slow into what he can but his feet are still going and his fingers too. His mouth is open round and the words and thoughts that move so differently inside my brother catch in his throat and come as a moan.

"Bobby. Bobby," I say soft so he has to strain to hear.

"Bobby Horn."

"That's...I'm Bobby Horn."

"You are."

"I'm...I'm Bobby Horn." And he's smiling.

"And you're a great good guy, Bobby Horn."

"And...and...you're a great good guy, Shoe Horn."

He holds my hand and I give him a tickle with the free one. He giggles and gets mad because I tickle too long. He's pulled away and not talking. Bobby loves to make up and forgive. I pretend like nothing's wrong. We walk over to Salthouse Road.

"I'm…you tickle me."

"That's because I love you."

"I'm…I'm mad."

"At me?"

I'm waiting for his part of the game. It's very serious business, being mad and forgiving. It's the most important part of Bobby because he can forgive everyone everything, even if there are those that shouldn't be. Blacky starts to jump around and he picks the bugger up and nuzzles him.

"We're mad…we're…aren't we mad Blacky? Be…because Shoe tickles too long."

He holds the thing up to his ear.

"What's he say?" I ask him.

Bobby makes a silly face and looks at me with some astonishment.

"Why…why…oh Shoe…dogs can't talk."

"No?"

"Oh…Shoe," and he smiles at me despite being mad or saying he is. I've got our Sunday jackets over my arm and have rolled Bobby's pants a bit. We walk though Rawlinson and cross onto Salthouse.

The Gogartys got the top three floors. Sun hits the front so the windows spark. I think I hear someone call behind us when we're standing in front of the place but I turn and see no one there. The curving street is wet and shiny even though there's been no rain. I look up at Phil's window and his mum and sister, Liz, and those two brothers and God knows how many others squeezing into the corners of the place.

"Bobby. I got to go see Phil."

"You…got to go…see Phil."

"That's it, Bobby. You and Blacky stay here, only don't go out of sight of the place."

"I…I…"

"Bobby?"

"I'll…we'll stay and…"

"You and Blacky play."

He's thinking with his mouth open.

"Play…what?"

If everybody had a life inside like Bobby Horn I wouldn't be out here wondering why Phil's mum wouldn't speak to me at the sausage shop. I wouldn't have had to pretend that only getting his kite up to the gulls mattered on this sunny day.

"Why don't you and Blacky march? Why don't you and Blacky change the guard?"

"Change the guard," he says to me and again to the dog that looks, by Christ, like he understands. I walk up the stairs and clack on the brass clacker. I clack again and hear someone on the stairs. Liz opens it and looks out at me with flat, green Gogarty eyes. She's tall and full and would be pretty with her reddish skin and high cheeks, if she would only smile, which she will not.

"Horn," she says and I begin to put on my coat.

"Good afternoon, Liz. I was out to the park with my brother and I thought I'd stop and say hello to Phil and all."

I remind myself she's a pretty one if she'd only smile because her eyes make you long to be anywhere else. I do want to see Phil though, so I put a smile on my own mug. She keeps her eyes on me and shows nothing. But Phil does that too, and his brother Tom. Now I've got the jacket on and buttoned.

"Ronnie Manchester said Phil wasn't feeling well."

"He's right."

I hear Bobby stomping his feet and making sounds like drums and trumpets in the street.

"Well, that's what Ronnie said."

She looks past me to Bobby's marching.

"What's he doing then?"

"He's marching."

She nods and puts them back on me.

"He's in the kitchen."

Phil is at the table, sitting straight but he doesn't look at me. He's looking at the red cloth over the table like he's reading. He's not reading. His mum is sitting in the parlor right behind the sliding doors and somebody else too, except I can only see the trouser legs. Liz stares at Phil a moment then raises her head toward where her mum sits.

"Well, here's Horn then."

Phil looks up on that so slowly you'd think his head was on a string. The mum stands slowly too and steps into the kitchen. A guy follows her in. He's dressed nicely. I don't know him. He might be Phil's age or older. Short. Dark.

"Hello Phil," I say.

Nobody says anything. Like I said, the Gogartys don't give it away. You just never know for sure. You guess at what it is. I'm guessing he's glad I've come.

"Well, see, we were in the park after church with a kite and… see my brother let go the string and it went to sea and so I was thinking I'd stop by and see how Phil is getting on."

Phil's face stays flat and he moves it back to the red cloth. The silence makes the kitchen seem much larger than it is. I can hear my heart pounding. I'm here because Ronnie Manchester told me Phil fainted but he's up, he's sitting and staring. Ronnie Manchester also said he was taking Addy to the moving pictures and said she was like a plum. I see her nice thing in my head and shake it out. I wait and try to look as if it's the most expected thing in the world, this bright and windy Sunday, to be covered in Gogarty quiet. There's nothing to do but leave. Liz follows me down and when I turn to ask something she closes the door and rises back to her people.

"Where's…where's Phil?"

He's still marching. Blacky's on the street now, yipping and yapping.

"He's up there. C'mon."

I light one and see it again, how I turned Phil and that big back of his head was there like an invitation. Bobby stops marching, picks up Blacky and halts up the steps of the Channel Lane Hotel, to his lookout at a corner of the porch. He stops and looks out like he always does, at something and at nothing. He's as still as he ever goes. I'm sure he sees the truth out there even if it's a mystery. I wish it was me looking out, seeing what he does, knowing something for certain and not guessing at everything. Molly Reilly comes out in a leather apron and heavy gloves, bits of coal flakes up her bare arm. I salute with my cigarette and bring it back down. She sits next to me and I can smell the coal.

"I'm piling coal in the basement."

"Hello Molly."

"They have this guy, Rudi, a Russian…"

"I know Rudi."

"He didn't come in yesterday and I worried all last night that he wouldn't come in on Sunday when he loads the bins, and the bastard didn't come in and I have to do it. Which is what I worried all last night. I'd be worrying still if I wasn't having to load the thing. Got a cig?"

We smoke without speaking. I see her arm rise with the smoke and see smooth and pretty skin. Maybe I was wrong about the Irish not being creamy. Liz isn't creamy, it's true. Her skin comes nutty smooth but now I see that Molly's skin is really the color of linens she may or may not steal. Her hair, in wild wide curls is nice too.

"Well, I'm sorry you're stacking coal."

"Then that makes the both of us. What's Bobby watching?"

"I don't know."

"He doesn't tell you?"

"I don't ask."

Now I smell more than the coal flakes. Sitting this close on the porch steps there's something like flowers. Mummy would float petals in a warm bowl of water, different types of petals and different colors too. You could hardly tell what was on you after you soaked your arms and face and patted some water behind your neck, but something surely. Mr. Horn too, smelling like a rose sometimes and calling her missus.

"What?" she says, flicking her smoke to the street.

"What, what."

"You were looking at me."

Bobby sees her on the steps.

"Molly Reilly."

He runs off his lookout holding Blacky out in front. He sits next to her and she puts a gloved hand around his thin shoulder and gives it a hug.

"Bobby Horn!" she shouts.

He sees her apron now, her gloves and smudges.

"What...what...you..."

"I'm loading the coal bin. The dirty Russian didn't come like he was supposed to."

"Russian?"

"Rudi."

"Rudi the...the...Russian. Shoe! Rudi the..."

He puts Blacky on Molly's stiff apron, goes to the bottom of the porch stairs, dancing and punching at the same time.

"He...Shoe is going like...like this and when Rudi falls he grabs...he...oh Shoe..."

"Sand, Bobby."

"He...he grabs sand and comes up and...and...throws the..."

Molly looks at me on that. I shrug.

"He threw sand in my eyes."

"...in...in Shoe's eyes."

"Bobby's kite ran away," I say to change it.

"Now, how can a kite run away?" Molly asks with a nice laugh.

"Well, see, Bobby had the kite up like this, and it was a beautiful one..."

"White!" he shouts.

"White, and Bobby's name was on it. Big so the gulls would know who it belonged to."

"Gulls…can't read," he says to Molly.

"But it got away, didn't it Bobby? That's okay because I can make another one for next Sunday."

"We…fly on Sunday," he says seriously.

"If that dirty Rudi comes in next Sunday maybe I could fly with you."

"Molly!…oh…Shoe…oh…"

"Sure. That'd be great," I say getting up. Then without thinking I say, "You smell nice."

She stands too and looks.

"I mean…I mean you don't smell like you been in the bins."

"I make lilac water."

"That's it then."

"I'm sixteen. I'm a girl," and she goes back across the porch to the cellar door so fast I can't see if she's mad or not.

We stop for sweet tea on the way to Mr. Horn's house. Bobby has some bread and butter. He looks tired. Little black shadows are going under that round face. I wipe some crumbs off his lips.

"You look tired Bobby."

"I'm…not."

"Still, you have to go to bed early tonight."

"I…will."

Later, in front of the alley to Mr. Horn's house, I watch him play football with Petey Evans and Taber and those. I watch them close and when it rolls out of sight and they fly after it, I follow too. They know I do. It's why I tell him to wait with Mrs. Bulmers inside Victoria Hall. It's why I tell him he can't go into Mr. Horn's house without me. Jesus, I think. I'm tired myself. I'm so bloody played out.

I've bought a bit of nice plaice at the fishmonger and I boil it up with some potatoes. Plaice is for Sundays.

"Mummy…Mummy made it…made…"

"Mummy made it crispy, Bobby. Is it good though?"

He nods and chews.

Mr. Horn is God knows where. I hope he comes back soon. I can't sleep until he does. Now that he's sick with the stout, he likes to hit me when I'm sleeping. I cannot stand to be hit as I sleep. And now, with the bloody nose broken again and the wobbly feeling in my left eye, I cannot stand it even more.

After dinner Bobby takes his bath. He's a big boy, he says, and can take it by himself but I leave the door ajar while he pours the soapy water over himself. When he's clean and dried and tucked to his neck in Mummy's quilts and blankets and only his face is out, I take down the Cowboy and Indian book, with the drawings of horses and buffaloes, and pretend to be reading it to myself.

"Oh...oh...Shoe," he giggles.

"What?" I say, my eyes still reading.

"You...you...stop...you can't read that."

"And why not?"

Now he squeals and shakes and laughs.

"Be...because you have to...read it to me!"

I do, and the Cowboys and Indians chase each other until his eyes blink and I sing 'Dublin's fair city' for him like Mummy did and brush his forehead like Mummy did, too. The moment they close and his fingers and feet fade from the dance I know that Bobby has tramped another day to its end.

The small parlor with Mummy's treasures is dark and the oil lamp flutters. I meant to buy oil but then I meant a lot of things. I sit in the dark and smoke and bring Addy into my head without all her fluff. Just all of her, standing in the middle of the room. Ronnie Manchester pointed at the playing cards and said that what that nice thing was, right there, was the cunt. But I'm not sure. The cunt doesn't seem enough of a word for such a nice thing. But even thinking about words makes my own thing stir. I have to think about something else, so I go to the kitchen for the cold potatoes, and sit with my tea, listening and watching at nothing. I see thick fog hanging over the channel like smudge. I don't want to cross the filthy bridge. With all of Shoe Horn, everything I am, I don't want to cross the bridge. I grab at the metal rails, my nails claw into the heavy planks but still my legs move over it. Biggar Sands peeks out across from Ramsden dock but no one is there. The beach, the dock, all of Vickerstown too. Empty of souls. Or filled with half ones. I hear myself calling to Bobby. "Bobby," I say. "Bobby. Stop. Don't go to her island." But he turns to me and says "I must. I'm supposed to be here." And I'm running now and Bobby is running ahead. I hear Mr. Horn. I hear his coronet blow once. Loud. Clear. I turn to it still running and he stands there, tall and straight, and Mummy is standing next to him looking past me to Bobby and waving, waving him on. "Bobby!" I'm screaming, "My Bobby Hor…"

"Here lad. Shoe? Wake up lad."

I push my head from the table. Sweat from my running dream lies on my face in small beads. I rub it off with both hands. The McAvy is standing over me like a hill.

"I've carried your father home. He's in the chair in the parlor."

I'm still halfway on the bridge and I shake my head to run the rest of the dream out of my ears.

"The chair?"

"In the parlor. I was helping at my uncles. I was washing the glasses when he fell."

The McAvy looks older tonight. He might be sixty and not eighteen, in the light from the lamp. He sits at the table and lays his hands out flat like he does. I stare at them. They are hands like a country and they look beautiful and awful at the same time.

"He called me a filthy giant."

He says it to his hands and if hands could have a life of their own, his could.

"He's a drunk, McAvy."

"Well, I am a giant, aren't I, Shoe? I'm walking by Sacred Heart this afternoon and some wee girl with her mum shouts out 'Look, look. What is it?'"

"Papists," I say, as if it explains it. But I know what she meant and sometimes wonder 'What is it' myself.

"Donald wrote a letter to my mum. America's big you know and I'm not looking for trouble. There's no work in the Barrow because everyone's afraid of me. Donald's making baking soda. He works at the Rumford Chemical Works. He sent a picture of a house he might buy and it's a big one, by Christ, where a guy isn't always having to duck at the door."

The McAvy speaks in a kind of whisper. It's like he's holding back the storms inside of him. He puts his hands together as if he's praying and maybe he is. I get up and get my smokes, give one to The McAvy and light them.

"I think America would like me. A job and a house with doors big enough to walk through."

He says this like a warning. I have never seen The McAvy angry but I feel something in my stomach and look away.

"Well, Shoe. I'll be going to my mum's."

"Will you say hello for me, McAvy?"

"I will. And hello to Bobby."

"I'll tell him."

He ducks at the door and I watch him walk to the street at the end of the alley. His head is bent low and he stops and looks both ways, as if deciding where his mum is or where he is supposed to be.

5

I sink in toilets and
speak the word

I'm at Mr. Taylor's place where his wife has let a bloody
spoon down the sink. I'm on my back trying to wedge the thing
out while all the time he's talking about when he was young and
I've heard it all before the time the Mrs. let her cat down the tub,
by good Jesus Christ.

"…that would have been 1881 and the old man looked him
square in the eye, took the measure of the bastard and said 'You
may own the bleeding Shipbuilding Company but I run the bleeding Shipbuilding Company.' And that bastard had to agree. What
was the choice?"

He's sitting on the water closet. Soon his wife will flush a
bloody love seat down the thing.

"Know what I mean?"

I've got the handle of the spoon but it's slippery and unyielding.

"Yes sir."

"But the lockout of '89 is a different story altogether. I was
singled out for grave retribution because, God help me, I was what
you boys would call 'dapper.' I had a certain propriety, a refinement
if I was forced to say it. They hate that. But Jesus, what's wrong

with a man who can string a word or two together? And I'd have my cap angled and my hair set just so and if somebody would ask me 'what's it?', well I could tell them and I don't mean in grunts and promises. But like I say, it was lockout and stay out so I took the train at Market Hall to London where there's people, by Christ, who don't blame a man his enlightenment."

"I think I've got the spoon."

"I come back, of course, otherwise I would not be in the Barrow still. I come back from London, a city, by the by, that looked on myself with much favor. Admiration really. But she was here and my sweet mother, bread in the oven, that creamy fresh butter, she wanted me to marry and, by Christ, how many mothers can a fella have? Disappoint my sweet mother? Them that think that can go to bloody hell in a hand basket. So I joined up with the Wood Pulp Company, which, by the by, produces easily the finest stationary in the entire country and has been cited by world authority, and you, as a young man, can only imagine our deep bafflement over the failure to receive an appointment from the Queen for, as I said, stationary that speaks for itself."

"C'mon. Bloody filthy thing."

"What's that?"

"I'm talking to the spoon, Mr. Taylor."

"Ahh. So 1892, on the very day they finished installing the new paper machines, I took myself, Jumping Jack Taylor, pulper and cutter, out the factory's double doors, back to the market station and then Barsea, where my future Mrs. was in service to the Honorable George Fell, and that gentleman, by the by, was a man of powerful sophistication, which was proved that very spring when he took the floor of the House of Lords and delivered what is considered to this day a..."

"Got you! You filthy bugger!"

"What's that?"

I hold it out and up, so he'll stop talking. My head's still under the sink but I wave the bloody spoon like a sword. He keeps talking but I stop listening. I clean it and pack up my box and I'm at the door.

"I pay Lowden? Is that right?"

"Same as before, Mr. Taylor."

"There it is then."

"Yes sir."

Outside there's a bit of thunder and lightning but it's not raining that cold, clammy October rain, so I'm not complaining. The Taylors are the far side of the park and I'm to meet Lowden at the Channel Lane Hotel at nine. It's seven-thirty. Who in bloody hell works a job at five? And who is awake to talk and talk at five like Mr. Taylor is? But I finished early enough to lug the box across the park and still have a bite at the portages' place next to the fishmonger. He'll have boiled up the coffee and, if you don't mind the grounds sometimes in a swallow, it washes the hard biscuits he makes, right down easy. I'm in the middle of the park, by Bobby's big elm, when another white flash comes together with a bang. The storm's right over me and still no rain. I'm glad he's with Mrs. Bulmers who is not afraid to hold him when the thunder comes. There is nothing that frightens him more. At night, if it wakes him, he screams for Mummy and I have to sleep the night with him like she would do, rubbing his big high head and whispering songs she would sing, and even Mr. Horn, before the first of his "disappointments," before the first punch and first kick, even Mr. Horn would sit on the edge of Bobby's bed, stroking Mummy's fine brown hair while she stroked Bobby. Now he may be more afraid of the storms than Bobby. I hope so. I bloody Christ hope he's afraid and curled in his terrible bed, crying like...aw Jesus Christ on a fucking crutch, I've forgotten the bleeding dog at the Taylor's.

"Here he is. Blacky right?"

"Thank you Mr. Taylor."

"He'd climbed up on the bed and him and the Mrs. were sleeping the sleep of the just."

"Thank you Mr. Taylor."

Now it's past eight and I take my coffee and biscuits standing. The little black beggar stares at me and I must dunk a chunk of biscuit in the coffee for him. He eats and goes right back staring.

When he sees the Hotel, Blacky rushes ahead, up the porch stairs and goes to Bobby's lookout where he sits and looks and maybe sees what Bobby sees. I go into the hotel.

"I'm the plumber," I say to the guy by the keys and letter boxes. He's got a little hair under his nose and a little belly over his belt. He smells like cigarettes, I think, but how would I know? He looks up at me and sniffs.

"The plumber. Of course. Yes. Well, the entire water closet bank on the top floor has ceased to eject waste material. This is the third time it's happened and so naturally Mr. Raymond and Sons who had previously done the Channel Lane's plumbing was replaced by Lowden's Plumbing. Are you Mr. Lowden?"

"No sir. I'm Shoe Horn. I'm his apprentice."

"Apprentice?"

I know what's coming. Jesus, Mary and Joseph. And Lowden's not soiled his shiny little hands for at least the two and a half years he's owned me.

"Yes sir. I'm his assistant. He'll be doing your water closets personally."

"Because an apprentice would not do."

I walk back out to the porch and Blacky. There's a bit of a sprinkle now, but it smells better than that fella. Or better than me.

"Shoe Horn," she says and I turn to the door.

"Molly Reilly."

"I've some tea in the kitchen. Come on. Bring Blacky."

Blacky's heard her and he's jumped onto her arms with his black face looking like nobody loves him but her. I follow them into the kitchen. She sits me at a long table and goes for the tea. A small woman, her grey hair bunched under a net, stands at the big stove with her back to me.

"This is cook. Annie."

Annie waves some cooking thing she's holding but doesn't turn from her duties. Molly pours and sits.

"Want some bread?"

"I had a biscuit at the portages."

"I don't eat bread. Bread makes you fat. Are you plumbing the water closets?"

"I am."

"That's a dirty job."

"It is."

We sip. It's good and black. I notice her cheeks have come red in the damp air. Her hair is pulled back and held there with a ribbon the color of her cheeks. Her mouth doesn't seem so small and her big green eyes have a secret. I remember her hands on her little hips after her evening at Mrs. Sevenings for girls in service. I remember those eyes narrowed and brave.

"Tomorrow I'll be seventeen," she says, those eyes on me, bringing that tea cup with the flowers around it to her lips.

"Tomorrow?"

"Seventeen."

"I'm seventeen now."

"I guess tomorrow I'll find out what it's like."

Blacky dances around cook's feet and I see her dropping bits of sausages and not looking down. I can hear the rain come hard now and I turn to the window, but Molly's mouth and arms call to me. And it's not the rain but the cunt that's in my mind. And it's the cunt that's stirring me. I want to speak but the cunt has got my brain. I'm seventeen and don't know the moon from a cat's asshole. Cook leaves through the swinging doors carrying a tray. Blacky turns and looks at us.

"The cunt," I say.

Dear Christ on the cross, I said it. I hear it bounce off the walls and shake cook's hanging pots. Blacky's ears prick up. Molly's face stays open. She does not so much as blink. Lowden pushes through the doors.

"There you are, Horn."

The nasty fat man's wearing white gloves. He's got his name sewn in black over his starched white shirt. Like a rake, he keeps his bowler tilted on his head. He's no rake. He's as old as Mr. Horn but short and round. His voice is a bark and the head it comes out of is bald and shiny. Lost it all from the scarlet fever when he was a kid. All gone. Eyebrows. Eyelashes. So it's a fat hairless baby I'm slave to.

"Molly, this is Mr. Lowden."

"How do you do?"

He jerks his head to her like a turkey.

"I'd do fine, girl, if I could get my apprentice to do a decent day's work. I've got a line of water closets that that terrible plumber Raymond and his terrible sons have made such a mess of it will take a miracle to bring to order and now I find he's been carrying a filthy beast around with him on his assigned rounds."

He jerks back to me. Blacky bounces over Lowden's little feet.

"Is this the filthy thing? I might kick it then."

I'm careful with Lowden, it's true. The guild card can't be had by a failed apprentice and guys like Lowden, well, work and the heart to do it only counts a little. But I have promised Mummy on her bed only to accept Mr. Horn's blows, and that is hard enough.

"That's Blacky," I say, standing up, young and hard and willing. "That's my brother Bobby's dog. I'm watching him."

I give him the fat man's way out.

"I'm sorry if it's against the rules Mr. Lowden but I keep him out of trouble."

"Well…see you do then."

"Yes sir."

"Come on then, let's look at the bloody water closets."

He walks out the way he came and I follow him. By the door I turn to Molly.

"Thanks for the tea."

She nods and I follow him out. I set up at the first water closet. If I lay out the tools in good order, after a bit it becomes like someone else is doing the filthy job. I begin to lay them while the fat man jabbers loud, hoping the hotel owner will hear.

"What's here, Horn, is cheap materials courtesy of Mr. R.P. Raymond and Sons of Hindpool road. Let's just thank God that the firm of Lowden Plumbers were able to find a bit of time for the job."

He lowers his voice, watching me make my moves as if he's never seen a pipe and wrench before.

"What's it then? A reaming you think?"

"Maybe."

I top the big pipe that should be lined and open and hear the garbage clinging all up and down it. Yes, that Raymond and his sons have used the cheapest pipes, just like Lowden will want me to.

"Now look here Horn, how long do you think this will take?"

"How many are there?"

"Seven on this floor and one below."

"Let me go on this one and we can figure from there."

"Righto. Then I'll be going down to the truck for a bit. And I may have to be running back to the shop."

I don't say anything and he's staring like there's more.

"There's a good one coming this Thursday," he says. "That boatman, that Tom Ward from Piel Island. Know him?"

I know he's never lost. I know he's a big dog and a hard one. His face is marked high on his forehead from his charges. He doesn't talk to anyone. Comes over on the ferry and goes at it.

"He's fighting some joker under the light."

I keep working.

"Nobody'd go it with Tom Ward so the guild had to put money on the table. A good pot. Twelve pounds or so. Ward's ten to one."

I've followed Ward under the light. I watched him keep a guy up only to hurt him more.

"I was speaking with my dear friend Albert Horn several evenings ago over a pint and I mentioned that his son, Shoe, and Tom Ward were the only two going who haven't lost and it was your father who suggested that perhaps the guild could arrange a match for after Ward disposes of this amateur on Thursday."

Now I look at him. The sun comes through the bath window and bounces off his polished head. I wonder what it's like to be him, all the edges rubbed away.

"Well I'm thinking about stopping all that, Mr. Lowden. My eye's loose. My nose's loose."

"We meant later. A few weeks later, when they're not loose."

Jesus Christ but I'm a fool. I worry about my sight. I can never be sure if I'm smelling what I'm smelling and still the guild's twelve pounds fills my head like the cunt did earlier. Now Phil makes his way into my head. I light one to smoke him out. Lowden stands in the door.

"I'm sure your father will discuss it with you. A good man, that. Tom Ward versus Shoe Horn. Can you see it? It will be the nearest to professional since Blackwell fought the nigger in '04. Remember?"

I was a year not born.

"Sure," I say.

He nods like he don't believe me. I want to give him something to stop his talking and I settle for a question.

"Who's he meeting on Thursday?"

"Some lug who's never been in it before. Can you imagine?" he says. "The guild hangs out the pounds and here comes a fool willing to try Tom Ward."

I take my middle wrench and reach for the box.

"Who?" I ask again.

"Fool name of McAvy."

Oh my good Christ Jesus.

6

I am sent to Walney where the Great Bitch keeps her lair

"So the damn fool goes charging up over the hill after these red Indians and one of them, nothing on at all except something around his privates, one of them starts making these crazy sounds and yells, and Custard thinks that the noise is coming from the bloody Indian's horse and Custard says, 'Look at that Crazy Horse.' And that's how he came to be named Crazy Horse."

Bobby's looking at me, his eyes all wide and his mouth open. His fingers grab at nothing. It's Thursday lunch and I've spent all morning at the police station where the swine have tried to put a new radiator in themselves. Now there's water everywhere and the dogs are pointing fingers at one another. The station is around the corner from Victoria Hall so I grab Bobby and sit on the steps letting some sun warm us. I'm eating my baked potato. He's holding his like he's forgotten it's there.

"And...and...what happened?"

"To who."

"Wha...what happened to...Custard?"

"Well, see, he follows the Indians over the hill and before he can say 'bloody hell,' he's in the middle of thousands of them. Eat your potato."

"Did…did…they kill him?"

"Killed him. Scalped him. Cut off his head. America's tough. Eat your potato."

He takes a bite but he's off with Custard and Crazy Horse. Mrs. Bulmers had boiled eggs for them and milk too, but Bobby wanted what I had.

"Mr.…Mr. Horn hit…"

"No worry."

"He…was hitting and…and crying."

"Bobby, Mr. Horn doesn't know."

"Know…know…what?"

"Mr. Horn doesn't know anything."

Last night after I got Bobby calmed and sleeping, with Blacky at his feet, he comes into the house quiet and drunk. He pats a chair at the table and I sit in it. There is nothing to say. He said everything on my twelfth birthday when he took two teeth. He said it on the ribs and chest. He has said it and I have heard it.

"Lowden says you're quitting. Is that true? Have I raised a bloody coward?" he says, puffing his poisonous breath onto me.

I stare at him. Nothing, nothing to say.

"I told him, by Christ, you will not quit. I told him that Tom Ward will feel the Horn fists in three weeks time."

He nods to me as if he's settled it. When I don't speak he stands and comes close.

"Three weeks. Do you hear?"

He cuffs my ear. He slaps the top of my head. He grabs my nose but I stand and he falls to the floor. He starts to cry in his rage and struggles, bent and leathery, to his feet.

"Knock me down will you?"

His punches are like a child's now, milky little fists lashing out behind his tears. I move my head. I save my nose and my eye but

I stand and take what Mummy told me I must until he leans onto the table and then sits weeping into his hands. He's finished. He'll sleep soon and I watch him like this has happened to someone else. After a moment I walk out for a smoke knowing in my young bones what no one in the whole bloody guild knows. Tom Ward, a hard and cruel boatman who comes to fight under the light tomorrow night, should keep himself on Piel Island.

Bobby's finished his potato and Mrs. Bulmers, God bless her, has brought us both milk and cookies. Some of the others chase Blacky and Blacky chases them.

"See...see..." Bobby points.

"Blacky plays good," I say, but I know what he's thinking. "That's because you're outside and he can run and jump, lad, but when you're inside learning, why, Mrs. Bulmers can't have a dog around playing, even if it's nice."

"But...but...look."

Blacky's jumped into the wee Mongoloid girl's lap and she's laughing and kissing.

"Yes," I say and think that that alley dog is better than most people. He don't have to think about it. He just jumps and kisses. Bobby squeals and points and puts his big face under my chin and squeezes for joy. I rub his hair and light one for after lunch, his face still pushing into me.

"I love...you," he shouts.

"I know, lad."

He smiles and is off the steps and with the others, chasing and laughing. If that is not a decent world then go find one. Mrs. Bulmers sits with me and watches too. She lets a sigh go and then another.

"Are you leaving?"

"I've got another ten," I say, my eyes still on them. Bobby's picked up Blacky and is holding the little buggar to the blind girl who never smiles or speaks. He takes her hand and runs her fingers over Blacky's fine hair.

"I mean are you leaving?"

I look over to her on that. She's fat and old but very pretty. It's true. Mrs. Bulmers is such that she looks the way she should. Beautiful maybe. It's her grey eyes and what she knows and has seen.

Has she read my small mind too? Does it hang over my head like words written in chalk?

"No," I say.

She looks at me longer than she might and she nods but for the first time in my life I think there's things I can't see that others can. The bully boy walk and the hard hands are cut bare and the truth lies behind me. I don't know why, but right then and there I want to weep. She turns back to them and I catch myself. I am Shoe Horn, I say to myself. I am known. I hope it's true. I give Blacky a whistle and we're off.

Lowden is at the station when I return. Not working, of course, just talking it up with the blue buggers. I'm on the stairs to where they've ruined the radiators when he sees me.

"And here's the tough little buggar…How old are you now, lad?"

Now I am entertainment, by Christ.

"Seventeen."

"Seventeen, and he's laid them down under the light for…well Jesus. It might be three years now or maybe."

Lowden holds wages and cuts himself in. He's that dog that's always nibbling the end of the bone until all the flavor is gone. Mummy said that. Not about Lowden, about the mayor's wife, I think. But Lowden wears it. I leave him talking the buggers into betting and lay the tools back out. Lowden says to leave them strewn at lunch to save time. How can a man work strewn? And time is cut in half when two are working and two are not, by Christ. I rock the old radiator to the side, having fitted a stem on the new one, where the cheap buggers downstairs snapped it off trying to do the plumber's job themselves because the lazy dogs think that what a man does that leaves him dirty by day's end must take no mind or skill. But even though I hate plumbing, I might not except for Lowden. And Mr. Horn, of course, who takes most of what little I earn and drinks it up. When Mummy went, the bastard took me from school and sold me to Lowden. Jackie Robeson, the apprentice before me, who looked, it's true, like a lout with a plumber's box, surely was not a lout. He taught me to lay out the tools and do it "correct." He would say, "if you do it correct lad, then they will have no choice but to respect the profession." One day, maybe a week after I'd come and some days before he was freed, he looked up from a soapy, greasy section of pipe at the hospital and he holds it and he says, "This is a lead pipe, lad, and the word for lead in Latin is *plumbum* and that's why we're called plumbers." Jesus, but that was something. Roman plumbers for the love of Christ. There's a system, that's all. There's two pipe families. One family for clean water going in and another family for dirty water going out. You'd think such a grand trust would raise a man, but you'd be wrong. Even Lowden who got his father's and grandfather's shop couldn't speak of its history or importance. Jackie told me of Egyptian plumbers. He told me of Roman sewers and pipes of clay. Jesus, all this history and still I feel ashamed. Maybe it's not the pipes. Maybe it's myself.

"That should about do her," Lowden says behind me.

He don't know much but he knows when it's finished.

"It's done," I say with a last turn of the wrench. "Can they drag the filthy thing outside or do we do it?"

I ask it innocent enough but I know what he's thinking. He's thinking "we" and he don't want to wrap those lady fingers around no rusted radiator.

"Well, hell, let them that broke it, move it." He smiles like he thinks he's in on it with me. Some big joke on the blue buggers. Right then, I'd kill him for a penny, by Christ, I swear it. I'm dark and dangerous and if he don't see it, he's a fool. He does.

"Look," he says with one eye on the door. "Look, how's that brother of yours?"

"He's good," I say, and stand and face the hairless beggar.

"Well, good. Good. He's a good lad. Now look, what I'm going to do is let you off early. Say you finish at St. Mary's by four-thirty or five then off you go. That's it. Over and done. And it's just the sink by the choir room. Take you no time."

"St. Mary's is on Walney Island."

"That's it."

Phil and The McAvy are pushed from my head by the Great Bitch itself. Walney is hers. I can smell her through the smoke of my cigarette. I have only seen the thing at night, in fog and street-light. I should be able to do the choir sink quick and be back over Jubilee Bridge well before dark. I look at Lowden and calm myself.

"St. Mary's then?"

"That's it."

I hurry onto the street to the dock and bridge. By her father's candy shop, Addy Augarde carries a big bag of sugar to a barrel. She waves and I have no choice but to walk over. Her hair is curled high. Her wide mouth shows teeth. She puts her hands onto her hips like Molly, but without anger.

"Why, Albert Horn, I haven't seen you in ages."

"Hello Addy."

"Can you visit?"

Her shoes have heels raised and I see that a lot of the puff under her dress is gone. Now the clothes arc and fall and mound a bit over her bottom. Her neck is creamy and it falls and dips in my mind through soft hills. She smoothes her dress and flattens it where the cunt lives. I must sit, quickly.

"A bit," I say sitting on a barrel.

She smiles and for a moment I think her eyes have seen my stirring.

"How was the picture?"

"What picture?"

"The moving picture Ronnie Manchester took you to."

She looks at me seriously and then looks over her father's shop to the Irish Sea beyond. It's very hard when people are talking and then stop talking. It lays too much at the feet of the poor fool who's listening. It was her turn and now it's my turn again. Blacky jumps at my leg and I pick him up.

"And who is this?" she asks like the actress she hopes to be.

"This is Blacky. This is Bobby's dog."

"Why, Blacky, what a handsome thing you are."

Blacky smiles. I swear it. It's a wee man inside that black hairy thing. Addy is petting him but looking at me.

"Are you free for tea on Sunday?"

"I am," I say but there's Bobby and something else I can't remember.

"We can take it in pa's shop. Cakes too. Mrs. Claire Irvington of the west end favors cinnamon cakes. Do you know of her?"

"I think so," I lie.

"She played Mrs. Westerbrook to Mr. Addington's Arthur. I read her notices. They called her alluring."

Ten minutes of talking. If that damn choir sink is difficult… Well, I won't be on that filthy island after dark I can tell you.

"What about the island?" She asks.

Oh good Christ, I'm talking out loud.

"Goodbye, Addy," I say picking up the plumber's box.

"Until Sunday."

In the middle of the bloody bridge my legs begin to feel they aren't my own. I pick up the dog and hold him for my own reasons. St. Mary the Virgin overlooks Walney Bridge. It's not cold like St. Mark's or even St. Luke's over on Poore Road, two churches that frighten you to your knees. But then there's no mystery to St. Mary. Mr. Horn laid bricks and cobblestone on it when he was young and I remember Mother and him and me and the baby would sit in those long pews and listen. But Mother knew it lived on the island and no word from Mr. Horn could change her mind. And so it was

St. Mark's, or St. Luke's, from then on, until the "disappointments" poured a river of stout down his terrible throat.

I enter the small chapel to the side of the main altar. The sexton's office is a room between the two. Sunlight sprays through the stained glass in reds and blues and greens and I am as glad for it as Christ on the cross looking down on me is miserable for his nails and crown of thorns. There are no shadows in this place for the Great Bitch to hide. The sexton opens the door slowly and stands shrunk and old in suit and tie. It's a wonder how such a man can clean this place, can care for the corners.

"Yes?"

"I'm the plumber, sir."

He looks me up and down.

"I could have fixed the choir sink myself. I have the tools. I simply did not have the time."

That's right. Any fool can do what I do if any fool had the time. Clean water in, dirty water out. The old bugger.

"Yes sir. Where?"

He sighs.

"Follow me."

We cross back through the church to the vestry. The rector comes from his room. He's the same one was here when I was young. Round and soft. Lowden with hair.

"Mr. Thomas, have the scratches in the podium been sealed?"

"Not yet, sir."

"Well, my sermon papers catch on them."

"I simply have not had the time."

"Because I'm turning these pages at communion and they… catch."

"Yes sir."

The rector goes back into his room and I follow the sexton who is moving so slowly, he seems to be not moving at all. I look at my pocket watch. By Christ it's after three.

"…this corridor was established to allow quick access from the choir room to the choir stalls. In 1904 the stalls themselves were re-configured to give additional fullness to the voices."

Can a man move slower? Has he stopped? Are we backing into the night? He turns to me at the choir door.

"The thirty-nine steps to the corridor, and so to the vestry, re-flect the thirty nine articles of faith. You'd do well to remember that."

"Yes sir."

He steps aside and I rush in.

"Where?"

He points to a door behind the choir master's piano and I go to it. The floor is wet and the faucet not only drips but the pipes below are clogged or worse. I lay my tools on the wooden floor just outside of the bathroom. I stop the drip quickly then squat watch-ing the pipes. A moment of looking is better than an hour of doing, especially if what you're doing isn't right.

"Those pipes will not repair themselves," he says at the edge of his nose.

I don't say anything. Bobby has taught me that people can ap-pear cruel at times out of an unsure spot in their stomachs. He has also taught me to wait. I run my fingers up and down the pipes to feel for moisture where I may not see any. My loose eye's getting better but it blurs if I watch a spot too long. Thirty nine articles of faith, my ass. Bobby's got that right too. He can see God in a sau-sage. The old man lights one. I can see where his time goes.

"So?" he says with a cough.

"What's below? That's where the clog is."

It's the water closet of the rector and he's not happy to see me. He stares at Blacky as if I'd brought the devil into his place. We close the water closet down and start drilling on the big pipe to give it a ream. By the time I've got it flowing and pack up, the church is empty and filled with shadows. Blacky walks with me to the chapel door and out into the soupy night. Christ, but I'm a great fool. I pick Blacky up as though he might come between me and the Great Bitch who must surely know I've come to her island and stayed too long.

The fastest way out is the road by Biggar Bank but it circles and cuts by its home where it might wait for me like the night Mummy said she waited outside our house, knocking to come in, long fingers curled bloody around her tools. The dropper at Mummy's very door. I go to the front of St. Mary's now where street lamps struggle with fog. I put Blacky down and light one but pick him right back up. My legs are as heavy as the plumber's box. I stay in what light there is. Somewhere shouts and laughter come into the street.

"It's okay Blacky," I say to him and to me too. "It's okay."

I'm at a trot now, the heavy box holding me from a run. I see the arch of Jubilee Bridge in and out of the mist.

"A good evening to you, Mr. Horn."

I stumble and go to my knees with my box falling and spilling out heavy pipes and fittings and wrenches. She crosses just out of the throw of light.

"I startled you," she says evenly.

I'm scrambling for my tools, box them quickly and stand. She has the red wrench, the big one, in her awful hand. Is that coarse black hair over her fingers? Tall, her long black dress swishes without wind and the whoosh it makes is louder than the rush of water under the bridge.

"It's a poor idea to run on these stones," she says with ice. "I know them. They are like eels in the damp."

She holds out the wrench as if it weighs a feather. I reach for it but keep myself away, eyes pinned to the stones.

"That brother of yours is the sweet one, isn't he? He always has a big hello for Mary Corony."

I set the wrench in my long box and pick it up. When I raise my eyes, I am alone. Nothing on the bridge but mist and voices, still laughing from the Vickerstown houses lining the Walney Channel. By Christ I've become my own nightmare.

"And you say hello to him from me," she rasps from behind.

I stagger into a run.

7

The McAvy and Tom Ward
and Bobby too

Though it's cool and the mist is like fine rain, I'm sweating when I turn on Ramsden Dock Road and stop running. My heart has moved to the front of my face and it pounds against what teeth I have. The bridge has disappeared in the smoky air. If I wasn't just now slipping across the bloody thing, I would swear the Great Bitch has taken it with her. Blacky is still in my arms, although I forget scooping him up. His small eyes have seen it too and he is as still as my heart is not. I put him down and we walk toward Victoria Hall.

Bobby is alone with Mrs. Bulmers, who buttons his jacket when she sees me and gives him a kiss on the head. He runs over and puts his face into my chest and together they say,

"Thank you for this beautiful day
And all the ones we love.
Thank you for the day and night
You send from up above."

"A…men," Bobby shouts into my chest.

I look up at her lovely smile.

"I'm sorry I was late Mrs. Bulmers. That Lowden had me…"

"No worry," she says, and means it.

The McAvy is walking slowly by as we come down the steps. He's got a smoke in his mouth. He's dressed as always, in the starched white shirt buttoned to the neck with black trousers and suspenders his mum lays out each day. He raises his hand when he sees us and waits at the bottom of the steps.

"Hello Shoe. Hello Bobby."

"And…and Blacky too," Bobby says, thrusting the dog at him.

The McAvy rubs Blacky's head with two fingers that are like hands. We begin to walk together a bit without speaking, only Bobby and Blacky growling and whimpering at each other fill the street.

"I like foggy nights, Shoe. I don't feel like making myself smaller. Do you think it's because it's harder to see me? I don't know. I fit better in the fog, you think?"

"You fit everywhere McAvy."

We walk a bit further. Bobby puts Blacky down and they both run ahead.

"Now you stay where I can see you and you can see me," I shout. I look at The McAvy. Jesus but he's right. He's straightened himself and he's bigger still. His brother, Donald, used to tell stories on him before he left. He would tell that The McAvy was born with all the hair he has now, rolling and curling like a bear, and he would tell he had paws instead of hands.

"Lowden says you're going under the lights tonight."

He shrugs. His shoulders rise and fall like clouds. My Christ, can he really be this big? I'm walking with a bloody countryside.

"I'm last up. A boatman from Piel Island."

I nod.

"Tom Ward," I say.

"A good one?"

"The best."

I can hear them, in the wind like whispers that grow with every step. Bobby's marching now and, by God, so is Blacky. We both watch them in our slow walk. The McAvy points and smiles. He envies Bobby's game and so do I. More this night than ever.

"Why?" I say.

"I'm eighteen. My mum still sets out my trousers. Donald wrote Mum there's some big guys working at his chemical plant. In America nobody cares, it's true. America's so big, everybody fits."

He looks at me and spreads his hands out.

"I'm saving, Shoe. I'm saving for America. There's twelve pounds up tonight, did you know?"

Now it's a low roar and I can imagine the kicking and punching. We turn and the light pulls us in. Lowden, the dog, is standing with his back to us and Mr. Horn, swaying but still straight up, stands beside him. They jab and shout as though they are in it.

"Lean on him, for the love of God," I hear Mr. Horn's reedy voice above the rest. "C'mon, you dog."

The McAvy walks over to Lowden. He knows he holds the pot. Lowden is startled but Mr. Horn, who can't help himself, shakes his head as if The McAvy is a fool. Only a man who's soaked through with stout would ever be so sure of what he don't know. If The McAvy sees his head going, he doesn't show it. Bobby halts over to me, Blacky in tow.

"You're...you're not...oh..."

"No lad, The McAvy's fighting."

"The...The McAvy?"

He says it like it should be said. There's majesty to The McAvy. Even stooping to speak with Lowden, there's something great about him, and Bobby sees it.

Now the second one has ended and a great hooting comes up. I did not see what happened but not enough blood, I suppose. Not enough breaking and bleeding. I look around the circle of watchers and see men and lads I know would never act to a dog the way they do to those who get under the light and fail to entertain. It's like plumbing all over again. Those that do and those that think they could, but can't.

"Here's Ward," someone shouts and Tom Ward comes out of the crowd into the center of the light. He's shirtless and his suspenders hang to the back of his knees. He's a big one and thick. He's chalked his knuckles to keep them tight but also, I know, to see where each blow falls. His face is battered only about the forehead and, in the light, he dances and throws hands at the air like a professional, moving his head side to side and back and forth. The crowd goes for every feint and punch and lets him know he's theirs with a roar.

Now The McAvy steps out. He has not so much as unbuttoned his neck. The crisp shirt crackles as he swings those arms easily by his side. The crowd goes quiet the way they do at the beach when he goes to straighten the chairs in high summer, dressed as he is now. Bobby is shaking and bursting next to me until he lets it out and holds his name full and loud and long.

"The...McAveeeeeeeeey!"

Mr. Horn looks over on that and points at us.

"You keep that little bugger quiet!"

Lowden looks too, and laughs and then Mr. Horn laughs with him. I'll remember that. I will remember exactly how Lowden looked and laughed.

Tom Ward's hair is cut close so no one can grab it when he's on them. The McAvy's hair waves like Mummy's elm. Is that a smirk on the boatman's face?

"The...McAveeeeeeeeey." Bobby shouts again and he turns and smiles. "I...I...love The McAvy."

"I know, lad."

"He's...he's a big one."

"He's the biggest one."

Now Ward comes out and circles, thinking, wondering. Maybe he already knows. In his dance around The McAvy, he feints and bobs, giving the crowd the idea he's playing and can drive the lug down at will, and they're with their man, roaring with each perfect slap at the air. The McAvy turns with him like a gentle top, spinning slowly or looking it, playing tricks on the eyes. Ward's coming in and out without throwing one punch. It's his taunting, I guess, like what George Carpentier tried last year to Dempsey. I read that Dempsey laughed but McAvy's face stays as pressed as his starched white shirt. Tom Ward will have to do more than taunt. He charges in to put his hard head under The McAvy's chin and to then work the ribs. Before he can throw one, The McAvy grips his shoulders, turns him like a doll and a push, high to his back, sends him out of the light. Ward is up and back but what has happened, has happened in an eye blink and now he sees that the awful hands that hung open and turned him have balled into mauls. McAvy throws some at the air himself, and by Christ if Tom Ward doesn't just stand for a moment, and watch in quiet with the rest of us. The McAvy is eighteen and might have lived forever. He could bring a day down with those fists. This time Ward tries staying away, he throws one, misses and dances out of reach. Now he's hearing it from the crowd. Now the buggers, safe outside the light, are yelling for him to charge The McAvy. Ward stays jabbing, thinking of other ways. But guys like him don't have other ways. For Tom Ward and them that weigh all of themselves on beating other men there's only that swaggering lope and charge to take another man's place.

Across from him The McAvy waits, set in stone. Tom Ward knows the answers but he's back to himself again and charges, head down, holding back the left he hopes can make a miracle. The McAvy clubs him high on his head and Ward flops, not moving, except for a wee flutter of his feet. The McAvy's not sweating and his shirt is still crisp. He doesn't savor any of it and it shows on that huge, flat face. He begins walking to Lowden and where he moves the crowd goes quiet. Bobby rushes in and grabs him in a hug.

"The...the McAveeeeey!"

The McAvy smiles and ruffles his hair. He looks over to me in some apology. For what? When he reaches Lowden, I see Mr. Horn standing importantly next to the dirty so called plumber. The McAvy has his paw out for his money but Mr. Horn's mouth is going at his ear. In points and gestures too. Bobby rushes to me and puts the mug under my chin.

"The...McAveeeeeey!" he shouts, muffled by my chest. Blacky dances at his feet.

Bobby pushes back and does his aping of the fight. He's got Tom Ward down to his nasty smirk and The McAvy too. And something more, that Bobby sees and no one else. Sees inside himself as if his heart had eyes. That The McAvy lives only in the dignity of the moment. Whether it's stacking Biggar Beach chairs or cleaning the dirty bar of his uncle, it is splendor or nothing. The McAvy is a king without a crown and Bobby sees it. We walk over to him. I hear Mr. Horn going on. Lowden cannot open his mouth, in the shadow as he is, of The McAvy.

"You take your bloody money," Mr. Horn slurs, "But don't think they'll be more. My boy, who I've trained myself, is no lout like Ward. He'll bring you down. He'll..."

Mr. Horn is still yapping when the three of us walk out of the light and away from the crowd, Bobby in the middle, The McAvy and myself each holding one of his hands. Blacky follows like the rear guard. We're all looking ahead and I take a smoke and hold the pack out to The McAvy without looking.

"I'll need twenty two pounds," The McAvy says. "Even if I work a ship over, the dirty work I mean, I'll need twenty two pounds to get out of New York and into America. I think I'll need twenty two pounds. I'm pretty sure."

Bobby and Blacky march ahead but the fog is lifted and I can see them without worry.

"What does your mum say?"

"My mum lays out my clothes. I'm eighteen years old. I'll be nineteen next."

I nod and may understand, although, Christ, I do wish Mummy was here to lay out *my* clothes.

"I'll need food and money for things. I'll walk out into America and see where I'll go. Nobody staring. Nobody going quiet. A big country for a big guy. A big guy who knows how to work hard and will. My mum will know it's right. I know my mum."

We go silent again and at Craymore Street he stops and I do too.

"Bobby!" I shout to him and Blacky. "I'll be saying goodnight to The McAvy now. So wait and march right there."

"I…I…will," he shouts back. "And…and…goodnight to the… McAveeeey!"

We laugh and smile at his beautiful voice.

"And…and…and…goodnight to Bobbeeeee Hornnnn!" The McAvy shouts out.

In the distance Bobby hugs himself and dances for the joy of The McAvy.

We shake and my hand disappears to the middle of my forearm. He is eighteen, I tell myself, and he is a world himself. His huge face flashes in a smile and goes serious.

"You're my only friend Shoe."

"Go on now, McAvy."

"It's true. But there's more in America. There's room for such as I am."

He goes up his street and I watch. I can't help myself and call after him.

"There's room for you everywhere."

He turns in the shadow of the streetlight. I will never see him and not be startled. He shakes his head.

"No, Shoe," he says, in that echo of a whisper. "Only America has the room for a monster. Look at my hands for the love of Christ. I hate them so."

He holds the things out and I cannot speak. I watch The McAvy turn up to his mum's.

"The…the…McAveeeeey!" Bobby shouts far down the street, in his march, Blacky in his arms.

I stare until only his shoulders sway in my sight as if he truly is a dream.

It's past ten when I tuck Bobby in and see those black bags hanging under his eyes. Tomorrow I'll see him in bed at eight, I promise myself. Blacky takes his spot at his feet, and I reach for the Cowboy and Indian book that's been done over and over and over. When I look at his fat face he's smiling and sleeping. Tiny snores come out and somewhere inside I know he's with Mummy. I envy him so many things. His long fingers lay splayed and still.

"You're a great, good guy Bobby Horn," I whisper and pat his wild hair down. Blacky looks at me and at him, and damn if there isn't a promise in those black eyes.

I sit in the kitchen with tea waiting for Mr. Horn so I won't get hit in my sleep, but I fall asleep in the chair. I wake to a voice in the house. A hollow and stale one, half talking and half crying. I find him in Bobby's room, dribbling gibberish while Bobby sleeps. He looks up when I enter, tears down his cheeks.

"So it's the great coward I've raised," he says, with a snort.

"Leave the room."

"How dare you speak to me in that way."

He don't stand because he can't. I say it again.

"Leave the room."

"This is my house, you little…bastard. And I'll stay…where I will."

I go to him and stand in all I've got.

"This is your house, but by Christ you will leave this room."

He looks at me with hate. His "disappointments" coming fast. What's on my face I'm not sure, but it's hard and it's black and it's everything sleeping in that bed. He sees it too. I never think of it but tonight, now, I cannot believe I am a part of him. I don't know what I have done to be a part of this. He looks away.

"Then…then raise me up and…and help me to my bed."

When he's on his bed, in clothes smelling of vinegar and beer, I look down at him. I may be crying myself except that I never do and was taught never to.

8

I give the Anchor Basin a good reaming and comfort Molly

Lowden's got me back in Rogers' basement at the Anchor basin. I know where I'm going and don't have to ask that one-armer Charlie Burt. If it's information you need and he has it, he'll make you perform tricks to get it. It's the reason me and Blacky take the entrance by the water and away from Charlie's office. Rogers is the same. Shirtless and steamy, that head of his as shiny and black as wet slate.

"Blacky," he calls when we drop down his steps. "Come give us a shake."

He bends, ignoring me but holding out his hand to Blacky, who puts a paw up and, by good Christ, shakes it.

"That's a good lad," he says in his heavy Scottish roll and picks the thing up.

"Lowden says there's more."

"There's more, right Blacky? There's lots more. This is down now. Over here, see the one behind what you fixed? I've heard when one pipe goes they all go…true?"

I get a grip and feel the corrosion.

"It's the sea."

"Ahhh."

I give it a tap and flakes come off the outside. He's right. One goes and they all go.

"More?"

"We're down to two flowing and the rest pissing," he says laughing. "Right Blacky? The rest pissing?"

I've got my plumber's box and have some fittings with me but I'll need lengths of pipe.

"Lowden ought to show within the hour, maybe. Shut these others down and I'll start cutting. He can measure them on the floor and take his truck for more."

Rogers and Blacky duck through a small door to another part of the basement where the valves are. I run my hands over the pipes feeling for wet beads or where it might seep.

"Here. You. Horn. What the hell do you think you're doing?"

It's Charlie Burt for the love of Christ. He's climbing down the steep stairs barking like Blacky. He's got a full shirt sleeve over the stump and has it pinned right across his chest to his far shoulder, so no one could miss it.

"Remove your hands. How dare you try to avoid proper channels?"

I keep working and feeling for water.

"I am speaking to you, Horn."

"Piss off, Charlie."

"What did you say?"

"I said, 'piss off.'"

"Piss off?"

"That's it."

"You can't speak to me that way. Where's Rogers?"

I pay him no mind and go back to touching, measuring the lengths of cuts inside my head. He's angry and red by now and I don't have to look to know it.

"Rogers? Where are you? Horn is here and here without authorization."

I take my metal saw and begin cutting the fattest one, three inches from the wall. I'll ream both ends but replace the taken piece with new lead. Charlie's shaking when I glance at him. The one hand goes into a fist.

"I should beat you, you lout, for all your disrespect."

I light one slow and go back to cutting.

"You can try if you like, Charlie. But don't think I won't go back at you 'cause you're a one-armer."

Rogers pops through the doorway, Blacky at his feet. "Rogers...you...Horn hasn't got the...what the good Christ? Is that a dog?"

Rogers reaches down and picks him up.

"This is Blacky. He could be in the circus the things he knows to do."

"I will...I will not have a dog on the basin or in its engine rooms."

Rogers smiles at Blacky and rubs behind his ears.

"Did you hear that Blacky? Mr. Burt will not have a dog here. Well that's all right Mr. Burt, you don't have to. Horn and I will have him. Right Blacky? Right?"

Blacky barks and damned if he doesn't sound like the one arm fool.

"Take the filthy thing outside now or I will."

"It's cold outside," Rogers says smiling. "It's too cold for a wee dog, right Blacky?"

Charlie Burt's rage is such that he can't speak. Tiny growls come out of his stomach and escape his mouth. They form into scratchy words.

"You...you are breaking the...these are the rules. The rules."

Charlie turns and bolts back up the stairs.

"Poor lad, right Blacky?"

Blacky barks a "yes."

"Lots of guys lost something," I say.

"I wasn't talking about his arm, was I Blacky? I was saying 'Poor lad thinks he's boss, when he's nothing.'"

The pipe lengths are mostly done. Five lay on Rogers' cement floor and the last one's about off when Lowden shows and climbs down. He nods at Rogers and stands watching me. When I've got the length of pipe cut free, about eighty inches, I turn with it and see them standing together. Lowden with his sweaty shiny milky noggin and Rogers with his sweaty shiny black noggin. It's little wonder Bobby cannot know the world. Right now I couldn't make anything out of what's across the room, side by sweaty side. God might think he's got it right with Bobby after all.

"Reaming? You think?" Lowden says pointing with a pencil, like he's about to do something important. He'd like to ream the lengths, fit them back and charge for new. Lowden's got that idea the world thinks like a criminal and all his thoughts take a kind of low road. I wait a bit before answering because I want him hopeful and easy.

"No," I say finally, looking down the pipe's opening as if I'm checking for what I already know. "The bloody thing's corroded out."

"Still, a good reaming would ease the pressure and more than likely stop the leaks."

"It's ready to go. They all are. But if you like I'll ream them and put them back, and tomorrow we can come and put new ones up."

Rogers gives a laugh and Blacky barks. Lowden stares at me.

"I've forgotten more plumbing than you'll ever know, apprentice."

I nod.

"Mr. Lowden, you have forgotten a lot of plumbing alright. What are we doing? Shall I put them back? Shall I?"

Mummy would tell me we are in the world for a blink of God's eye. I don't want to spend my blink on Lowden. Jesus, Mary and Joseph. Lowden turns, as angry as Charlie Burt, and goes to the stairs.

"Bring the measurements. We'll get the lengths, only you can bloody well do it yourself. I'm a busy man."

Blacky stays with Rogers and we drive to the shop. I get them and cut them and walk back down to the basin balancing the damn pipes on my shoulders. I walk the long way past the Channel Lane Hotel. The same clerk is running things. His moustache and belly seem to have grown in the few days since I did the water closets.

"Molly around?"

"I beg your pardon?"

Jesus.

"Molly. She around?"

"Molly?"

It wouldn't be so bloody awful if God gave us another blink or two to waste on most people.

"Molly Reilly," I say.

"Ahh…Reilly. Reilly would be at the linen closet, or so she ought to."

He looks at me.

"Irish," he says sadly.

Molly walks by with an armful of wash, looking strong and new. This time she's got a black ribbon in her hair. I follow her down to the basement where one wall is lined with tubs and wringers. She don't say nothing while she drops her loads into the tubs. I don't either. Sometimes I need an invitation. Sometimes I need to feel I belong where I am. When they're filling with hot water and she still doesn't speak, I start to leave.

"Da's gone," she says, putting her hands into the heavy hotel apron. "I come home on my birthday and the place is locked tight. I go to the woman downstairs who owns it and she says he's gone and money's owed."

She says it all calmly like it's the end of a story I'd tell to Bobby. But then her face squeezes into itself and she starts crying, small crying with wee sobs. I watch a bit, almost like watching the pipes for moisture, but there's more and I go to her. I smell tea on her breath and sugar maybe. My hand moves to the top of her arm. I'm surprised because it did it on its own as if it's smarter than me. Now my other hand goes for her and there now, by Christ, if I'm not in a Molly Reilly hold, with my fingers moving in small circles and rubs. She brings her face in and lays it down onto my shoulder. I smell sweat mixed with oil soap and perfume. I've never smelled such sweetness. I've known other girls in service but none so close. Her coarse hair tickles my ear. I feel hands and arms sliding around me and holding tight. When Bobby's crying and he's got his face under my chin, I'm solid like a tree. I'm mama in the park, strong and true. But Molly Reilly's got me swaying in a breeze. I feel I would fall if we weren't leaning into each other.

"There," I hear myself saying. "There, there, Molly Reilly. Don't cry."

We stand like this until my hands begin to move over her back in circles that keep getting bigger. Tiny purrs come from her. My hands listen to them and the circles grow. It's like looking down an alley and seeing nothing on either side. Me, lost in what's at the end of it. Molly's head turns. I feel a brush of something against my neck, a brush then up to my chin until her mouth is onto mine and it *is* tea and sugar.

"I stayed in cook's room last night. She's gone 'til tonight."

I see her eyes aren't black at all. Green, or even emerald.

"I…I'm fitting up…the basin's got only two running…"

She takes my hand slowly, and pulls it onto her place. I stare at my hand and where it is. Her mouth is round and open enough to see teeth.

"The cunt," she says and we both look.

It's past eleven when Molly walks with me to the porch and my pipe lengths. She's holding my free arm with both her hands and whistling something. The desk guy looks through the window at us.

"I'm late," I say, to say something.

She just squeezes and keeps whistling. I stare at the pipe lengths, thinking of nothing and everything. I light one. Molly takes it into her lips and hands it back.

"Are we still flying a kite on Sunday, Shoe?"

I look at her face, her mouth and what I know.

"We are, by Christ, flying a kite on Sunday."

Rogers and Blacky are gone when I start to lay my tools out. Because of the order of them, on the cement floor, I can do the fitting without thinking. Or I can do it thinking of other things. I'm cleaning up when Rogers climbs down, holding Blacky and tossing his Tam 'O Shanter onto a tool shelf.

"We've had our lunch," he announces, and I see he's a little drunk.

"What did Blacky have?" I say, "And why, if you don't wear a shirt anywhere, do you wear that silly hat?"

"What did you have laddie? Fish and chips, wasn't it? And bitters? And I wear it 'cause my head gets cold. Are we done plumbing?"

When the last of my tools are packed, I stand up.

"We are."

I pick up Blacky, my box and walk to the steps.

"So you're fighting this bloody giant when? This Thursday or next?"

"What?"

"The bloody giant done Tom Ward under the light. I only seen a few but Ward was okay for a boatman."

"I'm not fighting nobody."

"Is that true Blacky? Is he fighting nobody?"

Blacky barks and turns his black eyes on me. He tilts his head like he knows something I don't.

"There's papers up says you're fighting."

"Not me."

"Hear that Blacky? Not him."

9

I fly a kite and Phil Gogarty lies on a table

Something has happened. I know it has, but, for the love of Christ, I don't know what. Bobby and Molly have the kite up by the big elm and Blacky is running in and out of its shadow. The kite loops and flutters, trailed by the tail I made from Mummy's torn yellow apron. Bobby pretending to be a gull. Molly looks at me and waves. I wave too, lying there on my side, feeling something but don't know what.

The McAvy went under the light again last Thursday. First Tom Ward and then a Rugby player from Blawith who came down with his father. I didn't see it. I'm through with that mob. Mr. Horn told me. Came home that night, called me a coward, told me The McAvy did it again. Told me he'd seen weakness. Told me how he'd bring him to heel himself but for a bad shoulder. Then he fell asleep at the table.

"Look Shoe," Bobby shouts and points.

Molly and him have got the damn thing a mile high.

"She's up there, Bobby Horn."

"She's...she's...up there, Shoe Horn."

The kite is silent and still above us. It doesn't seem held by the wind but set there by someone. Its tail hangs straight, like a dream of a kite or Bobby's drawing of one. Bobby's stopped moving, concentrating on the thing like it's hanging in the sky only because he's watching. Molly puts the ball of string in his hand and walks to me. I hadn't seen her since my visit to the hotel on Wednesday. I've thought though. I've thought over and over on it and hoped she still wanted to fly Bobby's kite with us. After church, we walked the long way to the park, going real slow past the Channel Lane Hotel. She was on the porch waiting in a white blouse and long brown skirt. She walked over and kissed my mouth. Bobby had run to his lookout. He didn't notice the kiss that said more than hello, setting me swaying again and stirred my thing enough to sit a bit. I took one out and smoked my foolish thing back down, where it belongs in a late morning. Now she's kissing again and it's back.

"I was mad, you know. I wasn't going to give you even one on the cheek," she whispers with a baby lick of my ear.

The bloody word chokes out of me.

"Why?"

She sits away.

"Because you didn't come by. Not once. Three days. And you and me."

"I thought about you," I said. It was true.

"Me or the cunt?"

Bobby looks over. Blacky too.

"What Shoe?" he shouts.

"Look how high you've got it, Bobby."

"It's high."

"It is lad."

"She's up with the birds."

"She is lad."

"Do you think Mummy's there and looking down?"

"Pay attention," I say pointing.

Bobby and Blacky turn back to the kite. I turn back to an angry Irish girl. I can't think of what to say or even what I should say. I don't know anything. She's got a sad feeling running up and down me. I'd like to leave now, so I stand.

"Why are you standing?"

I know the answer to this one.

"To get Bobby and go."

"Go where?"

"Well, I don't know."

"You don't know what?"

"I don't know anything."

She has turned me so I don't even know myself. I look at her in some shame for being me and for having thoughts of Cook's room. Molly smiles now.

"Look," she says pointing to my thing.

I sit back down so no one will see that it's stirred plenty all by itself. I'm looking around at anything else. She brushes her fingers over it. When I look at her she smiles, eyes wide and green.

"You know what I'd like, Shoe Horn?"

Her fingers make loops and feel wet.

"What Molly Reilly?"

She doesn't move her head a bit or pull her eyes off me. Her brogue is slow, clear and sweet.

"I'd like to take this into my mouth."

My eyes fall to her fingers. I can only imagine how dull my face must look. But my mind can see nothing else. There in her round wee mouth.

"Shoe! My kite! Oh...oh no!"

Bobby has let it go again, sailing toward the sea. Him and Blacky are after it. Molly is up and gone in a run too. I watch them, still somewhere off with my thing cuddled in that lovely mouth.

When I get down to the channel, the three of them are by the bridge watching it disappear. Molly points and Bobby laughs. Blacky's barking out his questions like a sergeant major.

"You got to hold on tighter, Bobby," I say, walking up to them. "You got to pay attention."

"I…I…Blacky was…he was chasing the birds…and…"

"So Blacky made you lose your kite?"

"No…no."

"So Blacky," I say to the wee dog, "Bobby says you're chasing birds when you're supposed to be flying a kite."

"Oh…oh…oh Shoe, dogs can't…fly kites."

We all laugh on that. Bobby picks up Blacky with a squeal and the dog barks and barks.

Molly's cheeks are fiery from her run. Some sweat beads over her eyes.

"Let's go walk on the beach," she says.

"It's too cold for the beach," I say.

"Not to just walk, and it's pretty too. Blacky can run all over."

"He runs all over anyway."

"Shoe…Shoe…he…Shoe won't cross the bridge."

Bobby points to the other side and keeps his long arm out.

"She's…she's there."

"Who's there?" Molly asks.

Bobby shakes his head.

"Bobby," she says. "Who's there?"

He so wants everyone to be happy. Another part of Bobby is his clear feelings of secrets. A secret is not a game or pretend. It's not waving to whoever you see or forgiving whoever's cruel. Bobby understands secrets and knows somebody, somewhere, has to be getting hurt for them to work. He hates them. He looks at me now, and the fool dog does too.

"Because…because…oh Shoe."

He's crying now. Secrets and islands and bridges roaring inside his thin body.

"It's alright, Bobby."

He comes to me and puts his face where he does. Him and Blacky under my chin. My good Christ is the dog crying too?

"You know what Bobby? I think Blacky's crying right along with you."

He moves his head away and looks up with those big red eyes. Then he looks over to the dog.

"He…he…he is. Oh don't…don't cry Blacky."

"See, Blacky's sad when you're sad and happy when you're happy."

His face goes wide with that, like he's discovered gold or something. He smiles and shows his teeth.

"I'm…I'm…I'm happy Blacky," he shouts and his friend shouts a bark with him.

"See," I say.

He puts the dog down and they march to the noise of drums and horns that Bobby makes. Molly stands with me, watching the guards change, a smile says she sees what I do in his halting, serious high steps that take him to places I dream of.

"I see the square," she says.

"What square?"

"Da took me to Buckingham Palace. I saw them change the guard in the square. That's where Bobby is, right?"

"Maybe. C'mon."

We walk up past the mongers back toward the park. I've got money for bangers and tea and some candy if they want some. Molly swings her arms. Her hand bumps against mine, but I'm not sure if she wants me to hold it. Bobby always grabs out like he's hooking onto something so he won't blow away. I know it's why he loves to hold The McAvy's great paw. But can Molly Reilly hold me to the ground? And do I want her to?

Bobby and me get hot sausages and a baked potato. Molly says the potatoes make you fat. Well, Bobby's not and I'm not. I'm getting smaller I think. Last night I thought I might disappear, lying there in my bed, missing Mummy. Last night I thought maybe she took me with her and left a guy I don't know, walking around, carrying the heavy load of tools with nowhere to go. Last night too, the Great Bitch was standing next to Mummy, whispering her filthy secrets, and Mummy just looking at me like a gull watching the beach. Yes, I thought I wanted to disappear.

"Albert."

I stop and turn to the candy shop. Addy Augarde is waving. Bobby says something to Blacky and to Molly also, but she's busy watching me. I wave a small one.

"Don't forget tea at 2:00. We'll take it in the parlor," she calls, and looks right at Molly.

"And bring that lovely brother of yours, if you like."

She steps back into her father's shop and we begin to walk again, carrying our lunches to the park. Now Molly's hands are not swinging against mine. I see them balled up. Petey Evans and that mob are kicking the ball in front of the Simpson Foundry's gates. Bobby hands me Blacky and rushes over to the little bastards. Petey starts to say something but looks up at me, thinking better of it. They've got coats set into goal markers. I count seven of the swine.

"How are you Petey?"

He looks at his shoes.

"Good."

"Got a game going?"

"Got one going."

"It's good we came along so Bobby can even up the sides."

Bobby is popping like a jack-in-the-box, trying to be still, waiting for the invitation. Petey looks up at me. He's getting bigger. I wonder if I'm really smaller or if I'm still dreaming. He'll be under the lights in a year or so and maybe see what's what. Not now though. He looks back at his shoes.

"You want a go, Bobby?" he says.

Bobby runs for the ball in his wild halting. I know it's like keep-away from him, but he don't. I'm trying to watch them but Molly's drilling holes in my head like a pipe reaming. That's all I know, I suppose. It all comes down to plumbing of some sort.

"Don't forget tea at two," she says.

"Look, Molly…"

"And bring that lovely brother of yours, if you like."

"It's just tea."

"I've got to go now."

"It's Sunday. I've got sausages."

She looks at me and brings her hands up to her hips.

"I'm not hungry."

We're looking hard at each other when I hear him.

"Shoe."

I hear the whisper of my name like a slap. I turn toward it and see The McAvy. The boys stop playing and stare. His shadow puts them in the dark until he passes. His shirt is buttoned to the neck and he wears the Sunday tie and cap.

"Good day to you, Shoe," he says, too politely.

"Good day to you, McAvy. This is Molly."

He nods to her, but she's backed up and lost her words. The McAvy can remove your thoughts by just being in your sight. He looks back at me, and puts the awful hands into his pockets.

"Shoe," he says in that whisper, "Phil Gogarty has fallen down dead."

The words hang over me and I feel Phil hanging there with them. The boys are playing again. I see them scurry but can't hear a thing. Dear Christ, what did The McAvy say to me? He whispers it again.

"Phil. He stood straight up at their Catholic mass, looked at his brothers, and went over the back pew. He was carried outside to the air but…"

I look up at the beautiful sky, watching my hard fists smack, one, two, three, onto the back of Phil's head.

"Well, he…he…he kicked my things and…" My mouth is moving but I say it so soft even I can't hear it. The words bounce around my chest then settle onto the bottom of my belly like stones.

"Shoe? Did you hear me?"

I look at him and it's true.

"You said that Phil Gogarty has fallen down in church."

"He's dead. Father Costello was there and said the catholic prayers. My mum heard it from her friends that seen it. They carried him back to the Gogarty place. They've got him dressed and clean in the parlor."

The McAvy waits through a bit of my silence, takes out a cigarette and holds the pack out. I take one.

"Molly smokes too."

He swings them to her. They're like matches in his hand. She draws one carefully.

"I…don't smoke much," she says.

"I like Three Castles," he whispers.

We smoke quietly. Something bangs inside the foundry gates.

"I had better go then. To Phil's, I mean."

"I'll stay with Bobby, Shoe. I'll bring him and Blacky back to the hotel," she says.

"Have you been, McAvy?"

"I have. With my mum."

"Then I'll go alone."

"The hell you will," he whispers.

Molly doesn't understand this. She cannot know the Gogartys or their friends. I don't say a thing to The McAvy. He knows the Gogartys are held together by that father leaving and always looking to put blame for things on others.

"Bobby!"

He looks over from his spot in the game and looks right back at the ball.

"Bobby!"

He looks at me again. He's going every which way in his play. I cup my hand over my mouth and go slow.

"I've got to go with The McAvy. I'll see you and Molly later at her hotel."

"And…and Blacky."

"Yes lad."

Molly kisses my mouth quickly like things have been decided. But what? If The McAvy notices he doesn't show it and we walk off quick and quiet until we turn by the public bath.

"So you know, Shoe, Tom Gogarty and that bloody cousin of his, the fireman, Arthur...they been going on about how you whacked the back of Phil's head."

"I did, too."

"You punched it, you didn't whack it lad. And you're not under the light to dance."

The McAvy slips his coat on and I do too.

"My mum got a letter from Donald the other day. He bought a house. He says it's got three bedrooms and two water closets. And you remember my brother, Shoe. He never liked to work like we do. He never took pride in what he did. And now he's got a mansion in America."

There's a crowd spilling onto the street in front of the Gogartys' place. Most have kept their Sunday clothes on. There's plenty of hard miners here. Those that work in creosoting timber too.

"Here he is," someone says.

The McAvy pulls himself even taller and nothing more is said. The street door is wedged open. The stairs up to the place are filled too and I feel the stares or think I do. The McAvy doesn't look at anyone, just the landing above where Liz is standing with that Father Costello, who's got a stout and a smoke.

"Hello Liz."

There's more to say, of course, and I do say it, only inside of myself. I say I'm sorry because I liked Phil at times. I say it's sad when a good worker like Phil falls over the pews. And if my lips could move, she'd hear it. She looks me up and down like Rudi the Russian did under the light, but I wasn't afraid of Rudi. Now she looks at the Priest.

"This is Shoe Horn."

He nods and drinks.

"It's a terrible thing lad," he says.

"It is," I say.

"The back of a man's head was not made to be whacked."

The McAvy leans in over my shoulder. His face floats there like an iceberg. Costello's eyes go wide.

"What did you say?" he asks.

The priest cannot speak, but I cannot enjoy it.

"Well, I'm sorry Liz," I say, and walk into the kitchen.

It's filled also, with smoke and people. The room beyond, where I see the box, is mostly empty. Above the whispers his mum speaks to him in moans and sobs from a chair at his head. When Mummy finally stared off at some spot on the ceiling, puffing herself out of all this, I sat at her head, too. Her lady friends had placed it for Mr. Horn but his "disappointments" sent him running. I remember I couldn't keen for her. And Bobby jerked about comforting everyone else, telling them Mummy had gone to God like he heard in church. It was his own small power over death. In the morning, when he finally understood that God was going to keep her, he clawed at himself and ran his head into the wall.

"Hello laddie."

I turn to the voice. It's Rogers in kilt, jacket, and tasseled stockings. I have to smile even if it's not the time or place. Christ, if he don't look the Scot, black or not. It's MacGregor tartan. He reads my mind.

"We're a sub-clan," he says. Then with a wink, "Sub-tropical."

I think I get it. Rogers nods over at The McAvy and turns back to his talk. I begin to walk into Phil's resting room. A hand stops me.

"What's this then?"

Phil's cousin in his full fireman uniform, white gloves and all, steps in front of me in importance. I think I remember him but I'm not sure. He's not tall or short, not fair or dark. It could be he wasn't really here, for all his plainness. But guys like this always are waiting for the opportunity of grand authority. Always need to tell you what's what. An apprentice meets more than his share of these wee men. But the kitchen settles at that.

"I've come to say I'm sorry Phil fell down."

"Oh, you're sorry are you? That's his mum in there with him."

"I know Phil's mum."

"In her parlor, with her boy. A boy that had been whacked in the back of his head. I know. I seen it."

Now even his mum has gone quiet. I hear some kids in the street below. I hear some gulls. Birds don't care. I want to be one.

"Arthur," The McAvy whispers.

"I didn't say you," the fireman says quickly with a step back. "I wasn't saying anything at all with regards to you."

The McAvy watches him close enough to set some sweat onto Arthur's face.

"If you seen it, Arthur," he whispers in his way that can be heard in the kitchen and down the stairs too, "If you seen it, then you know what happens when you get under the light. Phil knew, didn't he? He was great. I think Shoe got lucky is all. But Phil got in that bite on his throat, and that kick to his privates, and I thought he had him good when he tossed that sand in Shoe's eyes and kicked his mouth. Didn't you, if you saw? Didn't you think Shoe got lucky to take all those kicks and all that sand?"

I wait and watch with The McAvy. But lucky? I come up and break him down. Phil was twenty five or six. All you've got when you're old like that is sand and kicks. Lucky? Tom Gogarty comes in front of Arthur now, lighting one as he walks. Tom's what a Gogarty really is. Tall and hard, thin as wound cable, dark hair slicked full and back. He might be thirty but seems much older. Prison will do it, I'm told, and Tom's been there.

"Right. Phil beat him good. Didn't he?" he says looking at me.

When we'd finished, and the guys fighting after us were rolling around our feet, Tom walks by Phil with a snort. It's true. The Gogartys always fight with pins in their sock to stick you good. I knew it and didn't let him get it out. Tom was disgusted. He's still looking at me.

"Right? Phil beat you good."

Now I need Mummy to explain what's wrong with me. Why do I want to lay another Gogarty down? Why do I want to put Tom next to Phil? Dear Christ but I'm the great fool.

"That's right, Tom. I got lucky is all. Phil was great and I'll miss him."

"See," says Arthur proudly from behind him, to stay important in this sad room.

Tom shows a small smile. His teeth are like the inside of Rogers' corroded steam pipes, and his thin lips curl up to show them.

"Well," he says, "It's good of you to come, Horn. Phil's in there with our mum."

I nod and The McAvy and I enter the parlor. Phil's mum is stroking his hair and doesn't look up at us. I couldn't see them from the kitchen, but her ladies sit in a row on a bench against one wall, waiting for something or nothing. I don't want to stare at Phil Gogarty or what Mummy would say was the shell of Phil Gogarty, the spirit having long fled, but good Jesus Christ if he don't look better right here in the box than he did when I visited last. And it's not just the easy set of his mouth. Phil always had a slack-jaw, I-don't-care look. It's something else. Peace maybe? Finished with the whole Gogarty family piled up with cousins and brothers and all about to break something? Now she looks up at us. Her face is like a collapsed bridge. It doesn't seem to go from one end to the other.

"You came while Phil was at the kitchen table. Didn't you?"

"Yes, Mrs. Gogarty."

"He was alive then."

"He was."

She looks at him again. His beautiful Gogarty hair combed back onto the light blue pillow. His big hands folded together. Is that a sneer on his lips?

"He's not alive now," she says.

I wait to see if she's finished. I kneel onto the cushions someone has laid by the center of the table and pray something from the Book of Common Prayer Mummy made me learn when her friend, Mrs. Sutter, died of the flu.

> Unto God's gracious mercy we commit you.
> The Lord bless you and keep you. The Lord
> make his face to shine upon you, and be gracious
> unto you. The Lord lift up his countenance upon
> you, and give you peace, both now and evermore.
>
> Amen.

I stand and The McAvy takes my place. When he's finished I say it again.

"I'm very sorry about Phil, Mrs. Gogarty."

She looks up at me. Her head tilts a bit as if she needs to see me from some other angle. But there's more. Something is wrong in this room. Something is here and has my heart pounding into my ears. Was it here when I came to the parlor? It was only Phil wasn't it? His mum? Her ladies? Something is sucking the life out of this dark room.

"Annie," it croaks from behind me. "I came to you the moment I heard. Poor, poor Phil. He was an easy one. Anxious to get on with it. One tug, Annie. Do you remember?"

I cannot turn. I cannot speak. The Great Bitch has crawled across her bridge. Close enough now that I feel her terrible breath burn into the back of my head as she speaks. It steps in closer. Dear Christ her filthy black dress crackles against me. Still, I cannot move my legs. Her claw brushes now, across Mrs. Gogarty's forehead. The thick grey hair runs through its long nails.

"Tom was the hard one. Remember Annie? Tom came feet first. Tom came running. Like this one," it says, brushing the other claw, sweet Jesus, across my chest.

"This one came running, too."

10

I show Addy a toilet

I have never in my small and stupid life seen anything as crazy as this. Jesus! It sits like a bloody water closet, but the damn thing's got the reservoir *behind* it! *Part* of it! I'm trying to look like I understand, but I don't.

"It's French," Old Mrs. Strand explains.

Lowden nods and plays his hand. No one's richer than Old Mrs. Strand and her husband.

"Well, we certainly all look to the French for innovation in the trade," he says to her fat, red necklace.

"Ahh," she says.

The Fucking French throw their shit into the middle of the street. I've heard it twice, so it's true. Innovations my poor ass.

I got sent here before the bloody sun come up. Cleared out the perfectly fine water closet with its reservoirs overhead, brought it to the street by the time Lowden shows, and had just lit a smoke.

"Don't dawdle boy," he says right off, easing his small feet out of the truck. "There's work to be done."

There's lengths of heavy pipe in the truck and a cutter too big for my box. He's already in the place, too quick to soil his mitts. By the time I lay out the tools and pipes, he's explaining the process to the poor woman.

"What we'll do now, dear lady, is re-attach the main pipe fitting with the correct configuration to suit the new water closet."

"Toilet," she corrects. "It's French."

"Toilet, of course. This is a toilet, Horn," he says to me. "Soon they'll replace all the water closets in the Barrow, with Mr. and Mrs. Strand here in the lead."

The old girl smiles despite herself. Lowden has crowned her Queen of the Toilets.

"Now then, Mrs. Strand," he says with great importance, "What I will now do is talk young Horn here through the intricacies of joining the French "toilet" with our sturdy English pipes which, of course..."

I dreamed of Phil last night. I slept in the hard chair in Bobby's room and dreamed Phil Gogarty walked with me all around the Barrow, dressed in the suit his mum laid him out in. The bastard was still there when I woke up. Now he's standing behind Lowden and Mrs. Strand and they all look down on the plumber's apprentice. Lowden keeps going on. I can't hear him or don't want to.

"...and the essence, dear lady, of any plumbing problem is that with fearlessness and knowledge we can..."

I don't know much, it's true. What Mr. Horn hasn't punched out of me, the lights have. But I know when one pipe won't fit another and no fancy maneuvers or fast talking will make them.

"Excuse me, Mr. Lowden," I find myself saying.

"In a moment, boy, can't you see Mrs. Strand has taken great interest in our noble profession and I'm guiding the lady through a bit of it."

He turns back to her.

"Sorry, dear lady."

"I just thought you should know that the pipes are different."

"Different?" Mrs. Stand says.

"Yes, Mrs. Strand. The French thing..."

"Toilet," Lowden corrects.

"It's got a narrow shoot here. English pipes are wider at the neck.

"All dimensions are universal," Lowden sighs.

If he were looking at a horse and a dog, he'd say they were the same if he could make a penny on it. The fucking thing is fucked and he knows it, but knowing hasn't slowed him down. He puts his soft paws on his hips and rocks backward, shaking his head.

"When one attempts to teach the craft, Mrs. Strand, one must be patient."

He sighs again and looks up to heaven as if in prayer before turning back to his poor, stupid apprentice.

"A bit of history for you, Horn. For three generations the firm of *Lowden Pipes and Reaming* has served the Barrow with integrity and craftsmanship unmatched by other so-called plumbers with their shortcuts and shoddy work…"

I'm staring at him. Phil's staring at me. Mrs. Strand is staring at her shitter.

"…and, of course, it's only common sense to re-attach a series of varying size pipes while maintaining…"

Bobby would look at him and smile. He'd feel sorry for him because it's clear there's more than what Lowden shows to the world. There has to be. Can a man wear all he is on his chalky skin? Bobby would also give this poor Mrs. Strand a hug to last a week because he'd know she needs it. I smile on that and realize how tired he's made me.

"…female connection and the male. Simple."

Phil's lips are in the same snarl he wore in his mum's parlor, on the table.

"Horn?"

I'm tired. I'm so tired.

"Horn? Have you been listening to me? Horn?"

I look away from Phil to the silly Lowden and his fat, shiny head.

"Now see here Horn, you can't learn the craft if you don't pay attention."

I look at him and wait.

"That's better. Now, I was saying to simply fit a smaller pipe over the existing section of pipe."

I look back down at the hole in the floor and the pipe sticking up through it. There is only one way in plumbing. The correct way. It's why the work itself, when I'm alone and my tools are laid out in order and my hands think as well as my noggin, pleases me. It's true I hate lugging the box, but the particular steps of the craft give me a kind of peace. Leave it to Lowden to say there's other ways when there's not.

"Mr. Lowden, I was wondering if it might be better to run the correct size pipe up from the basement."

His baby face gets red and he turns to Mrs. Strand shaking his ridiculous head.

"The young," he says, and they both smile down on me. Dear Christ.

"Of course," I say, "If we ran a pipe up it would cost a bit and take a whole day, maybe two. I suppose fitting a smaller one over the larger pipe would save Mrs. Strand a great deal of money."

I don't know much but I do know Lowden ain't for saving other people's money.

"Now, that's true. Yes. Yes it's true my first idea was to save the good people some money because, of course, I knew that the way to make this installation a lasting one was to come up from the basement."

"Well, Mr. Strand and I both would like it to last," she says, wringing her fat fingers.

Lowden rubs his chin as if he's considering whether he should take their money.

"It...may involve some...expense."

"Mr. Strand always says 'price is not a problem.'"

"There's a lesson for you, Horn," he says. "The reason people rise to such high station is their understanding of quality, no matter what it costs."

The poor woman beams as if she's won something.

We decide that I'll remove the rest of the pipes and plop the new in tomorrow. I've got Blacky tethered to the gate and take lunch with him after Lowden leaves. I take water with my ham and buttered bread. Blacky too.

"Alright now, I'm going to slip your head off the rope, but it's going back in there when I go to the pipes. I can't have Bobby's dog running off and getting into trouble. And Jesus Christ, I'm talking to a dog."

"Albert?"

Addy Augarde is on the other side of the Strand's gate. She reaches over and pets Blacky, who looks, like he does, that she is the only one who loves him. I stand up.

"Addy. I'm very sorry to have missed tea on Sunday."

"Of course, Albert. Ronnie Manchester told me you had to go to poor Phil Gogarty's house because you hit him in the back of his head."

"Ronnie said that, did he? What else did he say?"

"He said that the giant is going to fix your wagon. This is a grand house, isn't it? After I study to become a famous actress I believe I will have several homes like this. Will you come and see me on the London stage? I will be able to give you seats for free. What's it like inside?"

"The house? Lots of rooms. Old fancy chairs and tables."

She rests her arms on the gate and stares at the bricks. Her blouse is tight over the hills. It's starting to stir again, so I stop watching her and turn instead to the house too.

"Is there lots of sun? In the rooms, I mean. The windows are so large."

"I didn't notice."

Addy's got yellow clothes on and a pretty blue hat. I can see her shoes laced to the ankles. I'm looking at her shoes, for the love of Christ, and my thing is rustling in the closet.

"I'm…putting in a toilet for Mr. and Mrs. Strand," I say.

"A toilet?"

"Bloody thing's a water closet, but it's French, you see, and you don't pull a chain or anything because the ball and cock assembly's right there in the tank on the seat itself."

Addy looks at me in her actress way, tilting her head one way, then the other.

"The what?" she says softly, and this time not like an actress.

"The…the ball and…cock."

Now the damn thing's doing a jig down there.

"Mrs. Strand has gone out for a bit. Do you want to see the toilet and maybe look at the rest on the way?"

"I'd like that, Albert."

I give Blacky the last of my water and ham. We look around the downstairs. On the second floor, it's only a peek into the bedroom. She follows me up to the third floor.

"There it is," I say, pointing to the crazy water closet.

"It's a what?"

"It's a toilet."

"A toilet," she says.

I take off the tank lid.

"See…this hole is where the valve seat sits. No chain. You're supposed to flip this flusher, it lifts the seat, the water pushes everything out, then the valve seat drops and fills the tank up again with water."

"A…toilet."

"And this is…the ball…and the…cock…that stops the water from getting too high."

She looks away from the open tank to where I am. The soft high cheeks have reddened as has the line of neck under her chin and maybe down too. Maybe down, and maybe her hills are coming red. I look now and she sees me looking. Things pile on top of one another is the way I see it…Phil, The McAvy, Mr. Horn, Lowden, Bobby, Molly…until it's like a swaying tower and one small thing more and the tower is down. That's my own complaint about me. I see that bloody overloaded tower as clear as day, but for the love of Christ, I keep piling more bloody things onto it. Addy Augarde steps in and kisses me easy on the mouth, takes my hand, and we walk down to the second floor.

By four I've got the pipes pulled, cut and stacked in the basement. Lowden hasn't come back and I don't expect him to, now that poor Mrs. Strand's got his hook in her mouth. I see her sewing in a little turn in the wall by the front door. A whole grand house and she's practically in the corner.

"I'm done for today, Mrs. Strand. I should be able to get your water…your *toilet* going by tomorrow afternoon."

She looks over her eyeglasses at me and gives such a sad look I feel sorry for her. I don't know why. She's got more money than the bloody King.

"Well, that would be lovely."

I nod and walk out to where Blacky sees me by the gate. His tail is going like the devil. I slip off his rope and off we go. The plumber's box is left behind in the basement. I know I'm not supposed to leave it, in fact, it's against the guild rules for an apprentice to ever leave a tool at the workplace, but for the love of Christ, I surely do not think Old Mrs. Strand is about to pilfer my saws and wrenches. Besides, I'm lucky to even remember where I've stowed them after my lunch with Addy. I'm sauntering. Blacky's sauntering with me. I light one and set my cap off to the side the way Dempsey has it in all the pictures.

It's only a few minutes past four and I don't have to pick up Bobby at Mrs. Bulmers until five-thirty or even six. Most of the time, if I can be there early, I'll watch him play awhile. Today though, it'll be the park and a good think. Or, at least a wonder. I look down at Blacky and he, by Christ, looks up at me like he knows I'm digging a hole big enough to fall into.

"I couldn't help myself is all," I say to the black thing and smile when I do. I don't believe I should be smiling, but the feeling of importance is on me. And it's pumping blood through me in shoots and tingles. Maybe I'm not getting smaller. Maybe I'm just beginning to grow. When I turn by the library, Ronnie Manchester's walking toward me. Is that Petey Evans lugging the plumber's box behind the dirty bugger?

"Why it's Shoe Horn. It's another apprentice like you, Petey."

I don't say a thing or put anything on my face, but the blood's still going around me in spurts I can feel. Ronnie's feeling strong too. Feeling tall. I can see it.

"It's not four-thirty and he's without his tools. See here Evans. Don't you go leaving your tools anywhere. You take them with you."

Petey looks at me and doesn't look away. I knew sooner or later the bugger would want a go. Who will Bobby play ball with? Christ.

"Got a smoke?" Ronnie asks.

"I do," I say and don't reach. "Did you tell Addy Augarde that Phil's dead because I hit the back of his head?"

Now Ronnie's face gets as flat as mine. The Barrow men give nothing away when we don't want to.

"It's known."

"I didn't ask what's known or not. I asked if you told her I killed him."

He looks behind to Evans.

"He thinks I'll turn my own head like Gogarty."

He turns his face back to mine. I see his hair is pomped and set. I never noticed how narrow his eyes are.

"What are you looking at?" he snarls, his hands opening and closing into fists.

"He's looking at you," Evans says with a snarl of his own.

"Be careful, Horn. You haven't got that filthy monster with you now."

I do a short one chest high, another on his thin lips and a half kick to his belly on his way down. Before Petey can raise his head, I give him a nose bleeder that sends him running back where they came from. I look down at Ronnie and light one. He's curled and rubbing his stomach. I'm enjoying the smoke and him down there. I'm even liking the wee noises he's making. The smoke, though, is bitter and I take it and look at it as if I've never seen one. I can't remember when I was without a cigarette or even how I began. The ham and buttered bread even tasted smoky in my mouth. I wonder what Addy thought? Or Molly Reilly. Molly smokes some, but her lips lick through my smoke mouth like peppermint or sweet tea. Addy's lips were spongy and wet. Softer arms than Molly Reilly, but not as strong. Molly Reilly *holds* you. You can't run from Molly Reilly. It's not a decent thing I've done and no one has to tell me that. But why do I feel so bloody good?

"The cunt, I suppose," I say to the cigarette and point myself to the park and a think. Blacky's walking beside me now. He enjoyed seeing Ronnie down there too, I can tell.

"See Blacky," I say when I'm sure no one can hear me talking to the bloody thing, "If you want to talk about others the way Ronnie was doing, you must expect what comes your way."

It's the best time of the day for the park. Some pigeons are on the grass by the water fountain and Blacky sends them flying off. We cross the big lawn to where Mummy's elm spreads low and thick. I stop when I see Phil under its leaves, watching me. Blacky stops and stares too. Can he see what I see? I close my eyes, open them and Phil's gone, leaving the tree to the living. But why is he showing himself to me? I lay myself down, under the great tree, smoke one and close my eyes without thinking a thing. When I open them again, it's dark. I pull my pocket watch and, by Christ, it's past eight. Bobby! Christ. Blacky's nowhere, the dirty little bastard. I give him some calls, running out of the park toward Victoria Hall. I'm halfway there when I see the cobblestones are shiny from rain. I feel myself now, soaked and cold. What great fool sleeps through the rain for the love of Christ?

When I come around the corner of the church, I see them standing under the awning at the top of Victoria Hall's steps. Only a small throw of street lamp gives Bobby, Blacky and The McAvy some shape. I hear them too, before they see me.

"…at least that's what Donald writes."

"America," Bobby says with wonder.

"He says I'd be almost normal," The McAvy whispers like he's talking into a hollow oil drum. "He says they like guys who work hard."

"America," Bobby says again. Blacky barks when he sees me, and Bobby and him run over.

"Where…where…oh Shoe…The McAvy…"

"I'm sorry lad, I fell asleep in the park."

He puts his face under my wet chin.

The McAvy walks down the stairs. As he's coming over, the rain stops. Even the bloody clouds are afraid of him. He's talking now.

"I was walking home and I see what's-her-name standing with Bobby, waiting for you."

"Mrs. Bulmers."

"I said I'd wait with him."

"Thank you, McAvy."

We've turned and are walking back down toward the sea.

"You're wet, Shoe."

"I feel asleep in the rain."

The McAvy nods and passes me a smoke. We walk slow and watch Bobby and Blacky march to his sounds and drums and horns. The McAvy points at them, leaving his hand up a moment before he speaks.

"The wee blind one, the one who doesn't speak, that wee girl with her head almost shaved, she was waiting for her mum too and going side to side, all shaky and such. Bobby just starts petting her like he does, and whispering like he does and, I swear it Shoe, she stood still and smiled."

Now I nod.

"It's true, McAvy. He knows. He knows things that can't be understood. He knows them all over."

"He knows them in his bones," he whispers to agree.

The other day I felt small and smaller. I don't anymore. I feel blood flowing and know I'm a big one for seventeen, so to see my shoulders as high as his stomach, to see him walking beside me as he is, in all that he is, makes me feel proud, I suppose, to know him. He's still looking out to Bobby, marching in high steps. Is that bleeding dog doing it too? By Christ, I believe he is. They both look back at us to make sure we're watching.

"It's not over with the Gogartys, Shoe. That Tom's a bad one."

I don't say anything but The McAvy nods as if I did.

"Something else too. She followed us out of the Gogartys'. Why would she do such a thing? Followed us right to the hotel and stood across the street in the dark, staring at Bobby in his spot."

The McAvy stops at the corner where he'll turn up to his mum's and looks at me.

"Why, Shoe? Why would Mary Corony follow us?"

I look down the dark wet street to where he still marches around a lamp, taking each turn in halting high steps, Blacky on his heels. I sing the rhyme The McAvy surely remembers and wishes to forget.

"Here comes Mary Corony,
Keep your eye on your family."

His great mouth opens a bit but nothing comes. Bobby waves and we do too. I smell the low tide and the mud it raises. Words scrape inside of me before shoving themselves into my mouth.

"She's the Dropper."

The McAvy walks away without good night. I see him fade into the mist moving faster than I've seen before. When I turn back to Bobby, Phil is with him, marching behind Blacky. Swinging his arms crazy like and stepping the same halting steps.

"Get away, you filthy bugger. Get away," I shout and run for them.

Bobby stops marching and picks up Blacky. They're both frightened to see me coming at them ready to go at Phil's ghost or memory. When I reach them, he's gone. It's raining again. Bobby's hair flattens around his big face.

"Don't…don't…don't be afraid," he says.

"I thought there was someone else marching with you."

He steps forward and puts both their faces under my chin.

"Don't…don't be afraid, Shoe."

"I'm not," I lie.

We walk home not saying anything. When we turn down the alley, Phil is waiting. I stop and Bobby stops with me. Poor Phil looks sad. It's as though being a Gogarty has taken too much from him. I know what I did. All of us know what we do under the light. If he's here for that, he's not the fair guy I knew. I light one on that idea and he stares back as if he'd like one too. I know he's in my head, but Christ I wish he didn't look so sad.

"Don't…don't…don't be…afraid," Bobby says in a whisper.

I turn to him and smile at my beautiful brother.

"I'm not," I say.

He puts his sweet face under my chin.

"I didn't…I didn't…mean you."

11

Onward Christian soldiers

Bobby's gone to the privy and Blacky's gone with him. He always wakes excited about the new day. The first thing he says is what Mummy used to say in her morning kitchen.

"We are waking to a happy new day."

"Aren't we Blacky?" he says. The dog shakes himself and smiles, curling his black lips over his teeth. Bobby shows his teeth the same and kisses the thing. It's still dark when they pop out back for the privy. I light one and pour scalding water over the tea leaves. He'll have something at Mrs. Bulmers', but I make sure his belly won't growl at her table with a scone and sweet cream. Mr. Horn comes into the house, sees me at the stove and sits awhile, not saying anything. I'm getting us off into the day and the bastard is just coming home. Must have slept at the bar, or the street maybe. He's drunk but not wobbly. I feel him watching, but there's nothing to say. He taps now, on the table. I put Bobby's scone on a plate with the cream and put a bit of cold pork pie on the corner of it for Blacky. I pour his tea and milk it with lots of sugar.

"Well, you've gone lucky, Boy."

I don't know what he means and I'm not going to worry on it. I put the plate and tea down at Bobby's place. I pour my own cup and fix it up.

"The shipyard has locked out all seventeen thousand. Buggers are mad as hell so take care if you're near the bridge. They're queuing up on Walney and marching over to the yard this morning. They'll be trouble alright. The rich take it and keep it. I've had my opportunities, but I wouldn't be one of them for all the tea in China."

Bobby comes in from the privy, talking to Blacky in his arms. That dog listens to him, feeling what he knows, believing in him.

"Here's your scone," I say quietly.

Bobby's surprised that Mr. Horn sits at the table and doesn't look up from his breakfast. I don't have to tell him who the bit of pork pie is for. He slips it down to Blacky.

"I was just saying how lucky Shoe Horn is."

Now Bobby looks up at him. The bloody dog does too.

"Is that a dog?" he says flat and low.

"He's...he's..."

Mr. Horn looks over to me and smiles kindly.

"Lowden and the others have agreed to postpone your go with the bloody giant. Union boss says they might be out ten maybe twenty days, so there's no money to wager. I've given the okay for the Thursday after the strike's over. That should give us time to prepare for the filthy thing."

"The...the...oh Shoe."

"Eat your scone or I'll be late."

"But...but..."

Mr. Horn lets a scowl go. "But...but...Christ. You got crumbs flying out of your mouth, you do."

Bobby looks at me, his eyes are wide.

"The...The McAvy?"

"They'll be plenty in the pot," Mr. Horn says to me, pretending Bobby's not there at all. "Winner take all if Lowden has his way."

Bobby's still looking at me. Blacky too.

"But…but…you can't fight the the Mc…"

"You shut your mug, you half-made little bastard."

I slam my fist on the table and stand over him.

"You shut your filthy mouth."

"How dare you?"

"Get your bag," I say to Bobby. "I'm finishing the Strand's toilet today and can't be late."

He's crying though, and it's not a good one. Crying from Mr. Horn because in his bones he sees The McAvy turning me to dust. I put my arm around him and turn him to the door.

"C'mon lad."

Mr. Horn's not done.

"You *will* go under the light with the beast. You bloody well will."

Bobby, Blacky and me are in the alley now, walking in the dark toward a Ramsden streetlamp. Mr. Horn is shouting, still in the kitchen, enjoying the sound of his cruel voice.

"You'll fight him with pins in your socks if you have to but you'll fight him."

His voice is a small echo when we turn up toward Victoria Hall, but we both hear him clear.

"You murdered Phil Gogarty and, by Christ, you can bloody well murder the fucking Giant too."

Bobby's gone down to sniffles, but I can tell he's thinking hard because his arms and legs are not going every which way. His head is hung and good Christ if Blacky hasn't hung his own mug.

"I…I…"

"I know, lad."

"I love you."

"I know."

"And…and…and…"

"And you love The McAvy too."

He turns and looks at me as if I've read his clean, wee thoughts. He hugs me, putting his wide, wet face under my chin.

"That's Mr. Horn being mean. We can't listen to anything he says because he's lost. Remember Bobby? He don't mean to be like that, but he's lost."

I pull his face away so he can see me.

"I'm not fighting The McAvy."

Bobby smiles that enormous kite flying smile and dances away from me. He picks up Blacky and gives him a twirl.

"See…see…see Blacky, shoe…shoe…We love The McAvy."

"The McAveeeeey," I shout into the early morning.

"The…the…McAveeeeey," he shouts.

Mrs. Bulmers is there with a hug for him. He runs to her, then to the wee blind girl, takes her hand, passes it over Blacky, and raises him to give her a kiss. The hairy little bugger changes her day, that's all. Now she knows what he does. How else to understand it? They all know, is what I mean. They all know in places other than the head and that's where the world falls apart, in the darkness of the awful head. I call for Blacky.

"Could you leave him with us?" Mrs. Bulmers says. "He's wonderful with them."

I look at her. Christ but she's a beauty in her age and heaviness. She's got to be as pretty…no, more than pretty…as anything I have ever seen. And I think it in the best way. All she does circles around her. Beautiful. It's true.

"Blacky understands. I think he knows," I say.

"I think he does, too."

"Bobby," I shout over to him, "Mrs. Bulmers says that Blacky's welcome to stay with you at Victoria Hall."

He stares with his mouth open, then gets it. He holds the dog up to the blind girl again and whispers his news. Something could pop right out of my chest if it hadn't run up to my throat.

"I've got…to go now Mrs. Bulmers."

"Stay away from the docks. They've locked them out."

"I know," I say.

She shakes her round grey face.

"It's '89 all over again."

I come onto the big road down towards the Strand's house as Ronnie Manchester comes into it from the other side, dirty little Petey Evans behind him struggling with his plumber's box. Mine's been left at Mr. Strand's. We're walking down either side of the street. They don't look at me and I light one to show I don't give a damn whether they do or not. After two blocks, I turn to where the mansions are and they continue on. I hope it's toilets for them, too, only overflowing with shit. Two police are standing by the Strand's door.

"I'm doing the toilets."

"The what?" a fat one says.

"I'm a plumber. I'm doing Mr. Strand's French water-closet. Toilet."

"Toilet?"

"That's it."

"Well, Mr. Strand's inside."

I knock on the door and an ancient serving woman struggles the door open. There's bags and trunks in the hall.

"Yes?"

"I'm the plumber."

"Come in then."

Mr. Strand is coming down the stairs, buttoning up his black suit vest. He gestures to the trunks when he's on the last step.

"Mrs. Strand is going to London to visit our son. Look lad, are you a union man? I don't mean anything, but they'll be parading by my house sometime soon in sympathy for the shippers and I wouldn't want you in the middle."

The old man is tall and wide but looks ready for a fight.

"I'm an apprentice in the plumber's guild."

"Then come back tomorrow lad. You don't want them to see you," he says, and pops through the front door to speak with the police. I look up to the second floor bedrooms. Addy frightened me yesterday, same as Molly frightened me in Cook's room on the couch and then the chair. Jesus now, I'm staring up the stairs to the bedrooms, only I'm thinking of Molly. I wish my thing was as true as I feel right this moment. I go to the basement for my box.

The sun has just now risen over the hills. Usually, for hours after I place Bobby in Mrs. Bulmers' hands, the streets are deserted except for other apprentice dogs. But as I climb towards the central train station and Lowden's place beyond, I'm passed by hundreds, thousands maybe, some with their Sunday clothes on, some in work clothes with clubs in their hands. Tom Gogarty and his brothers and cousins see me and cross over. Phil was the only joker of the whole bloody bunch who worked, so why in all good Jesus Christ would these guys be dressed to fight, carrying pipes and wood? And now, for the love of God, I'm seeing Phil cross with them, dressed as he was on his mum's table. All of them have their inky hair slicked back and shiny. Every one of them as thin and hard as nails. Tom stops in front of me and the others stop too. On either side the men continue down speaking in whispers.

"Horn? Is that you Shoe Horn?" Tom says with a snicker. He's drunk in the morning. I see that all of the Gogartys are. They've come for the fight. It wouldn't matter to them where their pipes fell, union man or boss, so long as there was blood. Phil is now apart but watching. I would say he's sad to have spent his time as a Gogarty.

"We're off to defend the working man, Horn."

"Well, that's a good thing, Tom."

He stares at me and the others do too. I speak, but I'm bent at the knee. If it comes to it, at least I'll take Tom down with me.

"How's your mum, these days?"

"My mum?"

"Is she alright, these days?"

He comes close. I can smell stale beer and cigarettes.

"She's lost her Phil. Did you know that Horn?"

I look around, but Phil has gone, ashamed of these relations, even though he's dead.

"One day he's mining, he's at the table, and the next fucking day he's over the back of the pews."

I nod but stay ready.

"Some fucking cheater punched him in the back of his head."

He slaps his pipe length against his open palm.

"Isn't it true, Horn? Isn't it true that some dirty fucking cheat....?"

"Shoe?" The McAvy whispers. Men look over on either side and slow. He stands behind me dressed for church, long hair parted in the middle and brushed into waves.

Tom keeps his snicker but is struggling to get the words back. The McAvy reaches down into my plumber's box.

"Can you help me a bit, Shoe? My mum's sink pipe is dripping."

He straightens up holding my big two-hander monkey wrenches, one in each hand.

"Do you think these would do the trick, Tom?"

Tom Gogarty has that mouth open but nothing comes out.

One of the others says from behind, "C'mon Tom, we don't want to waste time when the working man is suffering."

"It's true," says Tom, swallowing whatever bad taste had risen from his guts. "Fair pay for fair work. That's right, isn't it? That's what the Gogarty men are about."

He looks at me one more time, sees his quick death in The McAvy's wrenches and moves on, towing the other slick-haired dogs behind him like a bloody tugboat. The McAvy concentrates on their leaving. It's as if he has sucked their swagger out with his eyes. They'd better take care, I think to myself, he's taken the fight from them this day. He turns and puts the wrenches back in the box, picks it up like it's a pack of smokes.

"Where are you off to?" he says.

"Lowden's shop, I suppose."

"I'll walk with you."

The stream of union men continues. I turn at the crest of the hill and look down at the bridge. They're crossing it and filling the Walney Island side in queue for their march. Some others are forming them into ranks. The McAvy doesn't look back but knows what I'm thinking.

"You want to go with them, Shoe, you should. I'll put your tools at your door."

I watch the men. They're what I know, maybe all I know.

"Lowden…"

"You're part of a guild."

"I'm just a bloody apprentice."

The McAvy stops and I stop with him. He looks up the street.

"I was twelve and I had to stop school. That year my hands got like this and I started to grow into this thing I've become. Do you know how strange it is, Shoe, when everybody is afraid around you? My mum took me to the miller's, the iron works, the ship-break docks, shipbuilding docks, plumber's guild, wood lathe guild, three brewers. Everyone I met was afraid. Nobody had nothing for me, Shoe. Even Donald told me his friends wouldn't visit anymore because of the monster that lived with him."

The McAvy tells this without anger or sadness. He tells it hollow, as if he displays the sky and says, 'clouds.' Now he turns his face to me. It's horrible and beautiful all together. A thing so unlike anything that has ever been. I can't take my eyes away.

"Donald, before he left for America, he got close to my ear so my mum couldn't hear and he said…he said…'The Dropper should have dropped you when she had the chance.'"

"That…that bloody bastard."

"It's true," The McAvy agreed. "But Shoe, I would not be leaving my mum if I had a trade. That's all. Go. The tools'll be at your door."

He starts to walk again, the men on either side nudge each other or just stare. I watch him, then turn and join the flow to the bridge.

I'm somewhere in the middle. They've collected the clubs and pipes and piled them in the back of a big lorry. One of the men lining us up twelve across, dresses us at arm length apart from one another, explaining through cupped hands that we'll close and link arms as we approach the docks. I look front and back. I suppose maybe two or three hundred lines standing solid almost to Biggar Beach. Billy Crowley, who led the one in '89 and who can't breathe anymore, is wheeled to the front of the columns to cheers and whistles. The flag is beside him. The Baptist minister, the only religious one there, takes his place beside the flag, holding his bible. He's also a miner, so he should be here. One of the marshals speaks to a man in the first line who turns and passes it on that we'll sing "Onward Christian Soldiers" when we step to the far side of the bridge and those that don't know the words should hum. Rogers, for the love of Christ, in kilt, steps now in front of Billy Crowley, a huge drum strapped to him and begins an easy cadence. Boom. Boom. Boom. Some guy calls out to march in place, so we'll start smart. The feet drown Rogers' drum and, on command, the first line takes us out.

I wonder if it's as true for all of us as it is for me. This parading has, right off, cleared my little brain of whatever was lost in there. Jesus, two steps onto Walney Bridge, I'm proud to be in the trades, apprentice or not. I wish I carried that bloody plumber's box with me so the whole world would know it. I'd be carrying it for The McAvy, who should have a trade as much as any in the lines. And Bobby too, so he could stand with Molly watching me and know, in that mysterious way he knows, how it feels to be Shoe Horn. I look left and right. They might be thirty years older for all

I know, but each step makes them younger. Their faces fill with all they've seen. The first line strides onto the Barrow side and begins the hymn. There aren't many don't know it. It's loud and clear and carries its own echo at the rear. The marshals shout out commands to keep us together, but our pride is enough. When you want to march, when you bloody well *need* to march, the cadence pounds out of your heart. We pivot as one and smartly step toward the docks. The families, the strikers and other workers line the street, cheering and joining the verse.

> Onward, Christian soldiers, marching as to war
> With the cross of Jesus going on before.
> Christ, the Royal Master, leads against the foe;
> Forward into battle, see his banners go.

Addy Augarde is standing on a barrel in front of her father's candy shop. She's dressed like an actress today and pretends to not notice the men catching a glimpse of her and liking it. Her father's there also, along with the two Scottish women who work for him. They all wear huge brown leather aprons, covered with powdered sugar.

> At the sign of triumph, Satan's host doth flee;
> On, then, Christian soldiers, on to victory!
> Hell's foundations quiver, at the shout of praise;
> Brothers, lift your voices, loud your anthems raise!

We wheel now, close to the big shipyard. We show ourselves in order, then roll up the lane toward St. Mark's church before circling back to the locked gate of the big shipyard, so all can hear who we are and what we want. Behind the tall iron fence, several hundred men watch us, their flat faces giving nothing away.

"Strike breakers," the old man marching next to me wheezes. "Pay them twice what they pay us, just to thug it up."

Christ, there's Charlie Burt assembling them, the great one-armed fool. And he lives in this town. We pass Nuxhall, come in sight of the park, and turn around the church as if our column has wheels and pulleys. A loud cheer goes up from the little micks in their schoolyard. They've got those tough faces pressed into the fence wire and are waving with their fists for their fathers.

> Like a mighty army moves the church of God;
> Brothers, we are treading where the saints have trod;
> We are not divided, all one body we;
> One in hope and doctrine, one in charity.

We parade past the Channel Hotel. The funny little clerk and his funny little moustache lean against the railway, watching us with disapproval. Cook's there too, some other girls in service in their blue and white uniforms. I don't see Molly though and, it's true, I'm disappointed. I want her to see Shoe Horn as one of the strong hands and backs that spins the world. Ahead, I catch sun sparks off Rogers' noggin as he beats his drum. One of the marshals races ahead and raises his hand. The first line slows in place on his shoulder, marking time for the rest of us to follow. Now all the lines mark time.

> Crowns and thorns may perish, kingdoms rise and wane,
> But the Church of Jesus, constant will remain;
> Gates of hell can never 'gainst that Church prevail;
> We have Christ's own promise, and that cannot fail.

Hugh Landry, the shop steward at the ship-breaking dock, climbs atop of some wooden boxes set there as a kind of stage and raises his hands, lowers them palm down to indicate we stop marching. It's not an easy thing to do. Now that we're raising and dropping our feet in place, many have closed their eyes to the comforting thump. Rogers gives it three hard blasts on his whistle and it cuts us off, sending all eyes on Hugh Landry.

"Now lads, we…could have marched last year, and the year before, and the year before that. We could have closed it down to show we need to meet our payments. Instead, we sat at home counting our pennies, putting our trust and our hungry children in the kind hands of the owners of these businesses…"

I look over and see Charlie Burt swaggering on the other side of the tall iron fence, the goons in tow, toward the gate.

"…who the war has made fat and happy in their castles and their clubs…"

Well, good Christ, it didn't take long. They must have heard that strikebreakers are well paid because those great guys who stand for the working man…fair pay for fair work…the slick-haired Gogartys have joined up. Look at them for the love of Christ, sniggering with the rest. I see Phil now, this bright morning, clear as I see Hugh. He's on our side of the fence though. Is it because he's watching me? Or is it because Phil slogged it out in the mines with the rest of the working dogs?

"…and a working man works! A working man does not stand on dole queues! A working man takes no pleasure in relief work! Or hunger marches or any of the things they have put us to, in order to live like the bloody Kings they surely are not!"

Charlie Burt and the goons are at the gates. They are surely not opening them. A few hundred bully boys. Surely even a one-armer like Charlie can guess at thousands of angry men, out of cash and dangerous, listening to Hugh, not wanting to be disturbed.

"…our dads who remember '89 and some who are still here, still marching in '22, can tell you, we are brothers in the dream of fairness, in the dream of…"

I see Charlie Burt reaching to unlatch the gate. Even dead Phil Gogarty shakes his grey face.

"You there." Charlie Burt barks, stepping onto the platform. "You there."

Hugh Landry ignores him, as everybody does.

"The right to strike! The right to strike is God given. A man must have food on the table."

Now Charlie is shaking with his rage at not being listened to, not being accepted as the leader he understands himself to be.

"I said…I said…*you there,*" he screams and shoves Hugh from the platform. Charlie is pulled into the union men who kick and punch him. None of the goons move. They're not stupid despite being swine who feed on other men's sorrow. Right now they are watching the gate. It's as if they see the swarm now, clear for what it is and themselves for nothings. We are hot, so hot. Our marching contained rage and centered it on all true regrets, whether work or not. The feeling of the whole world wearing those terrible faces of Mr. Horn, and Lowden, and Tom Gogarty. But we're not marching now.

The gate had been open, the younger and hotter go through it and at the strikebreakers who begin to run. I push through, catch a tall redheaded bastard who takes a kick at me, punch him down hard. I see Tom turn on another strikebreaker and hit him across the back with his board and the other Gogartys join him, thinking to blend back into the buzzing hornets we've become. Arthur, the Gogarty fireman who called me a killer and made a claim of decency at my expense at Phil's wake, now comes toward me all friendly after hitting some poor goon whose back was turned. He reaches out the hand of union brotherhood. I bend it back until he falls to his knees and give the soft fucker a nose bleeder. He starts to cry and I'm not surprised. I see Tom has watched.

"C'mon, Tom. Come get yours."

He gives me the outrage of the guilty.

"We're here for the working men," he shouts over the mob.

"I saw you. We all saw you. You're known now, Tom, for the dog you are. C'mon."

Tom picks up a club from the ground without taking his eyes off me. That thin smile comes with the sirens and bells of the police. He steps in, feints then swings hard at my head. I get him three times on his right side and feel the ribs, he drops to his knees. The back of his head shows and I want to drive one through and out the other side. But Phil, the bastard, stands looking at his older brother with such sadness I cannot.

"Jesus, Phil, fair's fair," I say like a madman but let go of the back of Tom's collar. He falls and rolls onto his side, curling into his broken ribs.

The goons are down or running. No one knows what happens next, after the heat drains out of us. The yard is emptying slowly as the nervous police arrive. The shuffle of boots on cobblestone is the only sound, save Charlie Burt who has struggled back onto the platform of boxes and stands bloody, screaming through his tears.

"I have...I have the...one arm! One arm...you bloody, bloody...bastards!"

12

I am a liar and wish
Molly was one, too

The strike had been a one dayer, just to let them know what's what, but after the fight at the yard, old Mr. Thompson who owned both shipbuilding and ship-breaking and the docks to boot, locked out the union men and labeled their attacks on "the young lads who were mere innocents in the union thugs' obscene attempt to extort undeserved wage increases," as shameful.

"Serves them right," Lowden's saying to Mr. Strand as I'm loading my saws and cutters on his plumbing truck. "The problem sir, if you'll permit me to say it, is that the working man today is not keen on working, if you get my meaning."

Lowden's pleased to suck it up to a man of commerce who needs plumbing at home and industry. But Strand's looking at me. I catch the eye and look away.

"I think you underestimate the laborer, Mr. Lowden. I think you do so at your peril."

"Exactly my point, Mr. Strand. These are perilous times. There's nothing they wouldn't try for higher wages."

Lowden thinks this seals it. He sees "toilets" and radiators lining his pockets. Sinks. Steam-fittings.

"My point," Mr. Strand says, almost with a sigh, "Is that there is nothing without the laborers. They should be compensated and, I believe they should be compensated fairly."

Ha! I think, enjoying Lowden's small brain. What now?

"That's…that's *exactly* my point, Mr. Strand. These are the times to…to compensate the laborers."

Mr. Strand steps over to me, where I've just settled my plumber's box onto the bed of Lowden's truck. He pulls ten pounds out of his breast pocket and counts it before handing it to me, in front of Lowden.

"Here lad. I know good work when I see it," he says, turns and goes back into his house.

Lowden has not taken his eyes off the ten quid and I take my time re-counting it and folding it and slipping it into my breast pocket as if it's my expected due. I know what he's thinking. It's in his slitty black eyes. I've made sure some color of money peeks out.

"Mr. Strand," he says hoarsely, "Mr. Strand is an extremely generous man."

He'd like to snatch the notes right out of my pocket.

"That he is, Mr. Lowden."

Lowden stares like a hungry dog.

"And he knows good work when he sees it."

"Well, good…good…yes, I'm sure the toilet was laid competently. Now, see here Horn, I'm going to my club and I won't be going past your place, so you can pull off the box and carry it home. Oh and I've laid some new, bigger wrenches next to it. A lead pipe cutter too. So load them into the box and off you go."

The box is now ridiculous. Why not put a bloody sink into it as well? Why not a whole bleedin' water closet. Christ. I lay it down on the top step at Victoria Hall. Mrs. Bulmers hasn't finished yet, so I light one and listen to them singing their evening prayer. The voices wobble sweet and squealy. The cigarette tastes good. Phil leans against a column looking smaller and sadder.

"Chin up, Phil," I say.

We cross the road by the park for the long way home. Bobby and Blacky march ahead. Phil saunters with me. At the hotel, they rush to Bobby's lookout.

"Mo...Mo...Molly Reilly!" Bobby shouts. Blacky barks too, and I can hear their feet running to her. I swing my head around and catch her cuddling them both. It's lovely until she turns to me and I see in her eyes that she knows.

"Molly," I say.

She looks at me flat. She's not angry or sad. It's as if she expected I'd be the dog I've become.

"Shoe," Bobby shouts happily, "It's...look...oh Shoe, it's...Molly Reilly."

Molly turns back to them now for another kiss and cuddle. Says something I can't hear and walks back into the hotel. Bobby stares after her, then looks at me with his mouth open.

"Oh...oh...Molly's going...away. Oh Shoe...Molly's..."

Bobby starts to cry and flail about, punching his thigh over and over.

"It's alright, Bobby. Stop that now."

"But...but..."

"I'll speak with her...I'll speak with her but only if you stop that."

His fists clench with his sweet promise.

"I...I can...I can...stop. See?"

"That's good lad."

I leave Bobby and Blacky and walk into the hotel. The clerk's there at his desk, pushing letters or something into slots. He knows I'm standing here, but he reads each name slowly to himself and his lips move as he does. Finally, he looks up.

"Yes? May I help you?"

"I'm looking for Molly."

"Molly?"

Jesus, Mary and Joseph.

"Molly Reilly, she works here."

"Well I certainly am aware that Molly Reilly is employed here, but this establishment employs some three Mollys. All Irish."

"All Reillys?"

"Of course not."

"Because it's Molly Reilly I'm looking for."

"Shoe," she says from behind me.

I turn around and she's already walking out toward the side garden. I follow her like a child done wrong. Where's that bloody bully boy now? She stops at a stone bench but doesn't sit. Molly's got a red ribbon on the side of her hair by the ear. Even though I know what's what, I let myself into a pout. My lips hang and I'm feeling sorry for me. Poor wee me.

"How's Addy Augarde?" she asks me, quietly.

"Who?"

"The lovely older girl. That lovely older girl from the candy store who curls her hair or it would hang off her fat face like dead fish. How is she, Shoe?"

"Addy Augarde?"

She doesn't say a thing but watches me hard.

"Well, I don't know how she is. I haven't seen her in awhile. I was marching in the strike, you see, and..."

"Ronnie Manchester told me you fucked her."

It's bad enough to find yourself a running dog but to have some swine talking about it. Ronnie Manchester? And how should that temporarily living bastard know unless Addy told him? And what if my thing never stirs again?

"Ronnie Manchester said what?" I say to her so innocent I almost believe it myself. "He said I what?"

I put my hands onto my hips, hang my head and shake it side to side. Was there ever a poor lad more unfairly accused? Jesus, but I can convince myself of anything.

Now she's got her eyes squeezed and her face wrinkled in question.

"Are you saying Ronnie Manchester told me a lie?"

Phil Gogarty has sat on the stone bench between us. He looks at me as if he watched me with Addy in the Strand's bedroom. If he did, then he knows that pink skin couldn't be turned from. I almost ask him to back me, to say how it was her cunt and not poor Shoe Horn should be answering these hard questions. How's a small apprentice supposed to behave? She asks it again and waits. I raise my face and give her a good look at the honesty in my eyes. Her own face loosens and goes soft. She puts her hands over her mouth. I cannot resist this notion of decency.

"Yes," I say. "Ronnie has told you a lie. How could I do such a thing with her? I'm a working man, Molly. Do you think I have the time? What would I do, do the thing at my work? Take her to a room? What?"

Bobby told me a lie once. After Mummy had been taken, he'd gone for a candy and left Mrs. Bulmers frightened to death. When I told him he had scared her, he said he told her where he was going. I knew it was a lie. I said that Mr. Horn was the only bloody liar in our house and I cuffed him. I never hit him before or since. But Bobby needs to tell the truth. A lie would be just another thing for him to trip over. 'Always tell the truth,' I said.

Molly looks at the ground and sits next to Phil.

"Go home, Phil," I say.

She still doesn't look up but sniffles and says.

"What?"

"I said he's a liar. I said I'm a working man."

I see that Phil has gone. I take one out and light it and draw it deep. Maybe the smoke will drive the lying pinch out of my lungs and the vinegar out of my mouth. Maybe, if it's gone, it really wasn't a lie at all. Dear Christ, looking at the top of her curly head, I wish I had never touched, no, never *thought* of touching anyone but this skinny mick. She's gone to crying now and her breath catches in gasps. I brush my fingers over her hair.

"Don't cry, Molly Reilly."

Now I'm thinking that there's something to a lie. Or not a lie but really a story. Yes. A story that tells something but tells it in a way that someone else might not tell it. I would never be able to figure this out a year ago, but now I'm seventeen and my brain has grabbed hold of this idea in the way I grab a two-hander, or a hammer, or even a length of pipe. I don't have to trouble my mind, I just grab. So it's like that except my mind *is* troubled and I am, I suppose, a dirty bloody liar after all.

"I was…I was so angry with you…I…"

"That's enough now, Molly," I say. "Let's forget what he said or didn't say."

"But Shoe…Oh Shoe…"

I sit next to her. My cigarette is working on the lie and I'm feeling better. My guts are not so tight. I'm not so wronged now. I've got the false forgiveness in my mouth. I want her to be happy. I want her to be as easy as me.

"Ronnie Manchester…he…"

"He's a dog. I'll talk to him."

"He…"

"Don't fret none. He's just mad I took him down and his dirty little helper too."

"But Shoe," she says, turning up to me with such pain you'd think someone had whacked her. "When I thought you had…with that girl…when I thought that terrible thing…"

She stops talking and looks at her hands.

"What Molly?"

"I…I took Ronnie Manchester into Cook's room."

She whimpers, shaking her head side to side. I watch my fingers brushing her curls then pull them away and hang them tight and heavy. I can't bring a word to my mouth. Or a sound. I think of Ronnie Manchester and his narrow face and close eyes and the scraping noise his laughter sounded like when he first showed me those pictures of the cunt. But has she said it or have I only heard it, twisted around and back. Has she really just told me what I heard?

"What do you mean?"

What do you think she means you great dirty bastard?

Cook's room comes clear now. The blue rug with birds on it. The Indian lamp. The bed in the corner with the bench at its foot that Molly knelt on.

"What?" I ask again, but it comes out of my mouth like a cough. I'm choking on the bloody truth. When she can't answer, I turn and leave the garden. I want to run. I feel like Bobby must have felt when he asked me to explain a crow. I said, "a crow's a crow." But there was more and he knew it. The clerk doesn't look up from his mail sorting.

"Find her alright, did you?"

I stop and look at him.

"Who?"

"Why Molly Reilly. That's who you're after, correct?"

"After?"

He looks up now and knows I'm watching for the smile that will be his last.

"I meant…I meant looking for."

I watch him close a moment. If he has something to smirk about, he's swallowed it. I need to kill someone. I need to feel bone against my fists and knees. If I met *myself* in the lane, I'd have no mercy. My fingers, I notice, hurt from the blood filling them. I push through the hotel doors and onto the porch. Bobby runs to me. Blacky also but stops when he smells my mind.

"Shoe…Shoe…oh…Is Molly…is…?"

"Get the dog," I say and walk off the porch.

I never leave the house when Bobby's sleeping. When he was little his dream would wake him in the middle of the night. He'd wake up laughing. In Bobby's dreams animals would play with him and talk with him and let him be the leader. And he remembered everything about the dreams. The weather. The time of day. Even the smells, like strawberries or peppermint or wet dogs. He sleeps hard now that he has grown. He says sometimes he sees Mummy and sometimes clouds, but once he's sleeping he don't wake 'til I wake him. I don't know how I read the Cowboy and Indian book this night. Phil listens with him, sitting now, his head bent and eyes closed, as Pecos Pete ropes the tornado again and again.

When he's sleeping and Blacky's sleeping or pretending to, I light one and take it out to the alley. There's spit in the air, some from the clouds, some from the sea, so there's a salty sharpness to it as bitter as this bloody cigarette. Christ, I got to walk. I got to walk the picture of her in Cook's room, and Ronnie Manchester's sneer, from my poor head before it comes out my eyes. I go to the edge of the alley now, look up and down the street, then start for his mum's house.

I don't know why, feeling so low, so ashamed I guess, but I'm walking bully boy up the wet street. I've been a fool, so what is it gives my steps that roll, that sure-of-myself swagger? I feel the ten quid in my pocket and turn into Thomas' pub. It's filled with strikers re-telling the march and its ending. Some nod, but I don't. Let them keep their dirty jobs. Let the fucking ships break themselves apart and rust. I put a note down and take a bitter with a whisky. I drink it fast. When I turn back to the room, Rogers' sweaty black head is inches away. He's buttoned up now with a suit.

"Hello laddie," he says, seriously.

I nod. I got nothing to say. He gestures to the crowd.

"They're feeling bold alright. But wait if the lockout goes ten days. Wait if trainloads of replacements come up from London for the jobs…at half the price. They'll be angry for sure, but they'll be scared tomorrow. The last strike, you could hear the bitter flowing down their throats, that's how quiet it got."

I don't say a thing. Keep looking around. Some of Ronnie's cronies are here, but the filthy dog isn't.

"I got to go, Mr. Rogers," I say, and squeeze out onto the street.

It's a cold night. My shoulders and back feel the damp air. At the Mick school I turn up the small lane where his mum has her place. The little house has white windows, rubbed clean. "God Bless Us All" is chiseled into the brown door. Flowers spring from pots on either side. How does this good woman make a place for such as Ronnie Manchester? I flap her clapper and wait. She opens the door with my mum's smile. It's all rolled up and waiting. No one's a dog unless they bark. Except Ronnie, of course.

"Is that Shoe Horn?"

"Yes it is, Mrs. Manchester. I wonder if I might speak with Ronnie."

"Well, he's not here right now. But Ronnie's been courting a girl, you know."

"Oh?"

"Oh yes. Miss Dorothy Wickford. Do you know her?"

"No, I don't."

"Oh yes. Her father is Reverend Robert Wickford, rector of St. Mary the Virgin on Walney."

"Christ," I say.

She looks at me sadly.

"Sorry, Mrs. Manchester. I was thinking of something else. So they live in the vicarage?"

"Oh yes. Do you know it?"

"I know it."

A few steps from the bridge, I stop. I'm fairly soaked from the spray of this black night. The island rises and falls in fog on the other side. Why is everything so crooked? Why in good Christ can't a road someplace be straight and easy for once?

"Shoe," he whispers.

I turn to the half-open door of The McAvy's uncle's pub. He's standing stooped in the doorway, so his head doesn't hit the top. His apron hangs like a baby's bib. I don't say nothing.

"Come in for one," he says.

"I'm late," I say.

"Late for what?"

I don't say anything. Christ. Monsters in the doorframe. Monsters on the island. It's as if I'm walking through a soggy nightmare. I look down to the bridge and move toward it.

"Shoe," he says. "If I'm the monster in the doorframe, who is the monster on the island?"

Oh fuck yourself Shoe Horn! You're thinking out loud.

"McAvy," I say, "You're not...I was just..."

"It's fine, Shoe. I am what I am. But who else?"

I just look at him.

"Oh," he says and goes back inside. Maybe she'll pull my heart out and eat it while it's beating still. Maybe she'll hold my eyes on the ends of her awful fingernails, so I can see my own mind. I don't stop at my side of the bridge but stride on. I hear feet and turn. Nothing in the fog but my own pounding heart. I see her behind each girder. On her side now, I slow and will up the swagger, bold where I don't feel it, hot where the clammy spray sticks my shirt to skin. Here I go then. Here I go. I move where only three days ago ten thousand queued. Now I'm alone. I think of Mummy and her fat face and sweet voice all along the waterfront street and she's still filling me when I clap the vicarage door.

"Yes? What? What is it? What?"

It's that same priest from when I fixed the sink in the choir room. It's the same sour, painful pinched look he give me when I needed to ream the pipe in his bloody room.

"Excuse me, sir. I'm looking for Ronnie Manchester."

"Ronnie Manchester?"

Say it again why don't you, you bloody fool.

"Yes sir."

"He's with Dorothy, I believe. Yes. He came by. They went out."

He closes the door in my face. I'm not surprised or expect anything more. When Mummy died and I shook at her grave, the bloody priest from St. Luke's turns to me while I'm clutching Bobby, feeling ourselves sinking into the ground with our mum, and says; "Chins up boyos." I go to church for Bobby, so he knows that what he sees in Mr. Horn is wrong and what he sees in Mrs. Bulmers is right. But God? I know a game when I see it.

I hear his voice now. It's high and cocky. He's doing the talking as they step out of the fog under the light at the corner. I walk to the gate and stand behind the signpost of St. Mary the Virgin. They're at the vicarage gate when I step out. Ronnie drops her hand and starts to run. He's heading for the bridge and it suits me fine. I slow to get him good and tired. He crosses the street by Biggar Beach and I can hear his wheeze. He's throwing words over his shoulder.

"Nothing…happened…I don't care…what she…said…noth…"

I pull him down from behind by the collar.

"I've got…look here Shoe, I got paid…here…take it."

Ronnie's holding money out to me with both hands.

"For the love of Christ, Ronnie. You've been under the lights. You've had a beating before."

"But you're not going to beat me, are you Shoe?"

I see them in Cook's room. Molly on the bench, him sneering behind her.

"No, Ronnie," I say, the words rusty and cracked. "I'm going to kill you."

Ronnie doesn't think about it. He runs to the railing and over it. I hear him moan when he hits the black water. It carries him swiftly under the bridge and into the night. I hear him now, calling, sorry for the jump, sorry for the cold, then he's quiet. I stand listening. I hear scraping behind me and whirl to it, but nothing's there. This is a night full of ghosts. Christ! What's inside Shoe Horn? Where's the pleasure? I run off the bridge back to Walney toward the beach. I cannot see but a few steps in front, moving as fast as I can over these slippery cobblestones. I charge onto the beach.

"Ronnie! Ronnie!"

I don't hear nothing but the thick flow of the channel.

"Ronnie!"

I think I hear something. I think I do. I go into the slick water to my waist where the motionless beach meets the roil. Something is there. I feel it although I can't hear or see it. I lunge and grab and touch some hair. My fingers curl around it and I back out. In the shallows, I take his collar and pull him half up onto the beach. He's coughing and crying. Crawling now, I follow him to the soft sand. He rolls onto his back, leans to his side and pukes up water and lunch. I watch him and see that Phil does too. Ronnie Manchester on the beach.

"Am I a ghost too, Phil?" I say.

Phil Gogarty smiles at that.

"Wha...what?" Ronnie asks me.

I kick him in the face, and turn myself back to the bridge.

13

Bobby, The McAvy
and God too

This cold Sunday morning on the way up to St. Mark's for Bobby's church, The McAvy called from his mum's window.

"Shoe. Wait up."

The light was barely coming over the channel on this muted day with little sun peeking out behind grey clouds. Bobby looks at me with eyes wide and hugs himself.

"Blacky...Blacky...we...The McAvy says to...to...what Shoe?"

"Wait up."

"Wait up," he explains to the dog.

I've got a smoke working and take one out for The McAvy. He comes out into the wet street wearing his Sunday clothes. Bobby runs over and hugs him. His shadow throws the street dark again.

"Are you to church?"

"We are."

"I'll walk with you."

We smoke quietly. Even Bobby walks without a march or his horn noise. I'm grateful for the quiet because things have started to fall off the pile inside my head, hitting the hard ground and breaking as sure as the ships are broken at Mr. Thompson's breaking docks. I'm wondering if I can keep what I want stacked neat and clean, and the rest, let fall. Probably not. Things are crashing down and I'll have to just see what's left of my heap.

We pass the Catholic church of the Immaculate Conception. The McAvy doesn't slow.

"Here's your place," I say stopping with a nod to the yellowing building and its high stone bell tower.

"I thought I'd just walk with you and Bobby," he says in his echo of a whisper. "I don't care for that Father Costello."

We come to St. Mark's for the first communion of this Sunday. It's never crowded and usually old Reverend Clark gives it and gives it quick with a short sermon won't hurt your brain. That's when Bobby gives Blacky his orders.

"Now...now Blacky...you can't come to...to church...but God...God loves you so...so..."

"You stay and wait for Bobby," I say to the dog.

Bobby squeezes him and puts him down.

"I'll wait with the dog, Shoe, if you don't mind," The McAvy says.

"Why don't you come sit with us?"

"I'll wait on the steps."

"But...but..." Bobby says.

We wait. He's got something coming into his sweet mouth. Words somewhere inside, bubbling up.

"But...what about...about God?"

"What about him?"

"Don't you think...don't you...if you..."

The McAvy, God love him, won't let Bobby feel anything but pleasant.

"Sure I believe in God, Bobby. You got to believe in God."

"You...you do?"

"Oh yes lad, because he has to be, doesn't he? Because what would we be if he wasn't?"

Old Reverend Clark is as fast as ever. And as full of gibberish. His sermon has to do with a cat, a mouse, and a big stuffed chair that gets put onto a lorry and taken into the Lake District where a deer and some birds all have a go at the chair. The McAvy is waiting when we leave. Bobby runs down the steps, shouting.

"There's…there's a big chair by the lakes and…and…animals are all around it."

"Well, that makes sense to me," he whispers.

We walk smoking through the park. There's no wind for a kite and Bobby's sad. It's a good dark day for me though. I need one like this to sink a bit into. The top of Mummy's elm is swallowed by fog. Smoke drifts up from the damp grass.

"How's your friend?" The McAvy whispers. "The Irish girl."

"I don't know."

"I thought you were friends."

"I don't know."

We go quiet again and turn up to the cemetery. From its high ground it catches a small sea breeze enough to keep the mist at bay. Great crosses guard the gate. A statue of Mary with her baby Jesus welcomes you in. From the Barrow below, I hear the awkward voices of some congregation, raised in song. I can't make out the tune, but there's hope in their weak cry, or so it seems. The McAvy shrugs as if this long quiet had never interrupted us.

"It's just that she surely seems like a girl with sense."

I don't say a thing.

"I mean, Shoe, I hope you don't let her being a bloody mick worry you. They're not all as awful as we think they are. They couldn't be."

Phil is waiting inside the cemetery gate, standing by the virgin and child, his hands plunged into his pockets.

"What I mean is, I'm sure she's not like the Gogartys or their people."

Phil raises his head sadly.

"And when we had to go to Phil's, you trusted the girl with Bobby. I know that. I was there."

I look at him now. If you have never seen him or heard him, you could not imagine him. And here, by the old and crooked markers in their endless configurations, with his head the proportions of a marker itself, his hands like the shovels that dug the holes, you would think he was nothing less than the beast who guards the dead.

"I don't know," I say again, a whisper of my own.

Bobby has run into the cemetery, Blacky on his heels. He follows the stone path around the memorial to the great Queen, then goes onto the grass in a straight line for Mummy, where he'll sit and talk and laugh until something remembered makes him shake with tears and grief and rage. I don't try to stop it. He's Bobby Horn, that's all, and what he feels, he feels. How could we not come sometimes, to sit and be? To pretend she holds us once more against this world.

"Mummy," I say softly.

The McAvy looks over the stones, to the hedges of the field behind it.

"I don't know how long ago my head began to grow. It was the very first piece of me that went crazy. Even before these hands. One day I went to bed regular and woke up with this thing. I was ten or eleven. I ran up toward the lakes where I thought I'd live like the giant that St. Patrick raised up. Use the lakes like a tub. Eat deer whole."

The McAvy laughs at himself, but I don't. Living in the woods with a lake for a tub? For him? Why not?

"But your mum sees me all running and crying and catches my arm and brings me over to that...what was that tea and crumpet place that's gone now?"

"Boylston's," I say and remember how she loved to take tea there with Mrs. Crustler and Mrs. Plant and others.

"Boylston's, that's it. We had a pot of tea with lots of milk and sugar."

"Mummy loved milk and sugar."

"And scones with golden raisins in them. She didn't speak until the tea had calmed me and do you know what she said? Do you?"

Now his terrible face is beautiful. He can swing like the tide. I see over his head that gulls have followed him. They glide over us. I have never seen a gull over the graves.

"No. I don't know what Mummy said."

"She said…she said…'There has never been such a boy as you. You must be brave.'"

He smiles and shakes his head, great mop of black curls swishing up there like leaves.

"Will you come to her grave with Bobby and me?"

"I'd like that, Shoe."

"So would Mummy. Come on."

Bobby's holding Blacky, swaying in quick slices, telling Mummy old Reverend Clark's silliness.

"…They've got…right there in the woods by the lake…the chair now…dogs and cats…and…and…here comes this…this deer with horns…big horns…"

He holds out Blacky to the marker that reads:

GERTRUDE KIND HORN
1885 – 1919

ROBERT NELSON HORN
1904 – 1904

"See Blacky. That's Mummy. That's Mummy's baby."

He turns seriously to The McAvy.

"Robert…Robert Nelson…He was…he…he was…"

"He was our brother. You were named for him."

"Yes, yes," Bobby nods, then smiles like his face will burst apart.

"She had a…a great big face…right? A great fat, red face…and…and we would have picnics…and oh what did…what did she smell…like…Shoe?…What?"

"Honey and milk."

"Honey…and…and milk," he repeats, squeezing his happy dog.

"And Worcestershire sauce," I say, and by Christ I smell her too.

"Worces…Worces…"

"Worcestershire sauce."

Bobby turns to me and The McAvy, his hands outstretched, his smile gone. His mouth open but no words coming to tell his sorrow that has only grown. Oh Bobby, my sweet Bobby Horn. I know nothing and that's all I can put into your wee hands. He makes a noise, a moan I've heard every time we've come to her stone. He doesn't have to say a thing. He wants to sink into the grass, into her arms. I do too.

"That's enough, Bobby," I say.

His hands stay out to us. His face has boiled into angry tears. He brings his hands into fists and slaps them onto his thighs.

"I…I…I want…MUMMYYYYYY!"

He'll hold her stone now. He'll beg her to end the game and come back and bring wee Robert too and he'll share his dog, his bed, his smile. I know this is his way, but I must bring him here every once in awhile, for Mummy too.

"I'll…I'll…I'm a good boy," he's crying. "I'm…I'll do…I'll be a good boy if you…"

The McAvy moves to the grave and kneels next to my keening, pleading, weeping brother. He places a huge hand across the grass where her heart might be. He holds his face up to the stone and goes thoughtful, nodding, now and then looking at Bobby then back to the stone.

"…what…are . . ?"

The McAvy holds a finger up to his lips. The finger looks delicate and impossible and huge.

"…but…but…what…?"

The McAvy takes his other hand and gently wraps Bobby's whole head in it. Bobby stops crying. He stops shaking. The McAvy leans over and whispers something and Bobby leaps up with joy, grabs Blacky and begins to march. The McAvy stands and joins me. We light one and watch my brother marching to his noises. I look over to the great thing. He looks at me.

"I told him that heaven is a place of smiles. I told him his mummy is smiling on him."

I look back to Bobby, but I feel The McAvy's eyes haven't left my head.

"It's you she's worrying for."

The McAvy leaves us at the park.

"My mum thinks I'm at mass," he whispers, looking toward his street. Bobby marches ahead with Blacky.

"I'm gonna miss my mum because she's there, you know. It's good, but I've got to get out of here. Donald wrote my mum again. He's got the house you know. He's got it all."

Bobby and me stroll down toward the sea. I have tried to fill the days he's not with Mrs. Bulmers. Now I'm too filled with other things to even think about what to do. He turns and stops the parade.

"Can…can…"

"Can what?"

"…can…my lookout?"

Molly taught me, it's true. I knew nothing, but I understood, behind her in Cook's room, the mystery or something like it. Now I'm wondering about this sharp ache in my stomach. And Addy Augarde taught me something too. Long stretched words that came from somewhere inside her. "Shoe Horn," she said or I think it's what she said.

I nod and Bobby halts ahead, Blacky on his heels. I let him get out of sight. Christ. First, I leave him alone in Mr. Horn's house to find Ronnie Manchester, then I let him turn corners without me. And I don't care. I don't care about anyone except me. I'm about me now. It don't feel right and it don't feel good. It feels like Mr. Horn must, like a fly at his supper, eating 'til he's full and more. I'm sprouting little wings for the love of Christ. I turn the corner and stop.

Bobby's got Blacky raised up, displaying him like he does. The Great Bitch, her unmistakable back to me, has come in daylight, on a Sunday no less, to run her claws over the boy and his dog. I hear a laugh, low and hollow. Bobby points and waves with a fat smile and the thing, dear Christ, the thing turns and looks at me, a wicked smile still. Can she be in the light? I look up and, of course, the sun has been swallowed by the gloom of this Sunday, otherwise, she'd turn to flame. She floats to me, Bobby close on her long, brittle, black skirt.

"I was…I…I was…"

"Bobby Horn has shown me Blacky," she says like a scratch on the back of my neck. "And Blacky has told me what good care you take of both. Is it true, Mr. Horn?"

Something jars me. I know what it is and I can find my voice.

"I'm not Mr. Horn."

"That's…that's…he's…"

"That's…my father," I say to the thing with shame. She looks deeper and I drop my eyes.

"Yes. Yes. You're Gertie's child. You're Albert."

"He's…he's Shoe Horn," Bobby announces from behind as if I were King of England. I look up past her to my happy brother. He cannot know. And he should not.

"We lost Robert. He came too slow although I leaned and pushed."

She pulls my eyes to hers.

"You came running. No pushing for you."

Phil has come up behind her. I can't read his face. He's flat as the high tide.

"And Phil," I hear myself saying, "Phil came running too."

She smiles at his name.

"Phil was a good one."

Phil smiles on that or I think he does.

"I pulled them all…all but this one," she says pinching Bobby's cheek. "Gert closed the door. Gert had Mrs. Royles, who was not a Mrs. at all, and who had just begun. I knew how she carried that it would be a special one. And I was correct wasn't I?"

She steps close to me. She dropped Mrs. Gundy's when she closed her eyes. She dropped the Bamford's girls. Both. Dangled them by their toes in front of their mothers. Laughed when she let them go. I've heard from others, so it's true. I see my brother falling like a tea cup, spilling himself on the way to the floor and see the Bitch rise like a gull, spread wings and screech.

"But this one gives more than he gets. Much more. Am I correct Albert?"

My mouth has gone dry again and she smiles at my silence. Somewhere I see Mother putting the chair against the door. Somewhere I see her crawling back to her bed.

"Am I correct?"

"He does," I hear myself say.

"He does," she agrees, turning to Bobby and holding both claws to his face. "Much, much more."

We are at the hotel and Bobby's lookout before my hands stop shaking enough to light one. I draw too hard at the match, tasting flame. Bobby and Blacky are at their place, staring out seriously at whatever they see when Molly comes onto the porch, smudged and in the heavy leather coal apron. Her hair is tied back under a white cloth, smudged also. She's thin, so thin. I stand at the bottom of the steps watching her. Phil has gone up with Bobby. He turns and watches too. She stops when she sees me. Am I thinner myself, eating only lies and sadness?

"Hello, Shoe," she says softly.

Molly looks as if she might be blown out to sea. What holds her to the porch? The heavy apron, I suppose.

"Loading the bin, are you Molly?"

"He's drunk again, so yes, I am."

I stare at her.

"I'm strong."

"I know."

Bobby runs to her for a hug and she gives it, her eyes still on me.

"You...you...didn't...you didn't...go."

"No," she says to me. "I got no place to go."

"Shoe," Bobby shouts in his joy.

He runs off the porch and puts his face under my chin.

"Molly...Molly...Oh Shoe..."

She comes down the steps halfway. It's cool, and streaky sweat has dried in swirls about her cheeks and chin and flattened her white scarf. Crazy black hair curls free from the cloth and wiggles in the damp breeze. Even Phil cannot take his eyes from this wire of a mick. My heart catches and pounds. I want to hold my hands out, my arms, so she can be here, in this grab of Bobby. I want to, but Ronnie stands in my head behind her, and Addy Augarde turns her white face onto the Strand's pillow. Forget it, something says to me and Phil, by Christ, nods yes. Yes. Forget what's past. Raise them up. Spread out your long fingers to her. Take her in. This is the only thing will save you.

"I can save myself," I say to her, with a stranger's voice.

Phil walks off the porch with a shake of his head and turns up toward his mother's house.

"It's true. I did it. I was at the Strand's. Addy Augarde come by and I couldn't help myself. She took me more than I took her.

Her face on the Strand's pillow, calling my name, maybe, from her stomach."

I didn't speak it though. The words dropped out of my brain down to my feet. Legs gone heavy with the lie still clamped inside myself. Molly's head hangs and a sob comes once. The wee thing could fold into her apron.

"I thought," she says to the ground, her words like feathers floating off the birds, "I thought you had been with her. I thought... I..."

Bobby raises his head.

"Who?...who?...been...been..."

I don't know much. I know pipes and wrenches. I know I can lay them down under the lights. I know my brother, who's staring at me now. I light one. I'm my father's son after all.

"Well," I say, convincing myself that a lie can be the truth, "I wasn't."

14

Maggie and her trick

The McAvy is going under the lights again. I haven't seen him since the cemetery and he never mentioned that Piggy Brady from Crummock Water up in the Lake District, who lifted full grown cows onto his shoulders at fairs, had decided to come down to the Barrow for some easy money. He came with a crowd of farmers who queued up behind Lowden, the odds maker. Lowden kept glancing at the corner where The McAvy always showed, dressed for church, buttoned as his mum would have him, because he liked the bets placed before they saw what he was.

Piggy Brady was thirty-seven and, to him and his cronies, in his glorious prime. He'd been the King of the Lakes since he took that circus guy at Grasmore in '04. Piggy also brought down his wife of twenty years and his four children who danced to some piper with their mother pointing and laughing. It was hard not to like Piggy. He was no braggart or bully. He came to do for his family and his friends. There was a charm that loomed within his violence and threats. An ordinary guy, who had a gift to lay them down. A fleeting gift that would be gone before he knew it could be. He accepted that, I suppose, as long as he didn't see it coming.

Coming as clear as the line of day. Coming like a wave comes for that baby in the sand. Coming.

Piggy played in the circle under the light with his children while he waited. They did this thing with a balled up sock. They didn't kick it exactly, but lifted it so each could balance it on a head. His little girl was the best. She caught it every time on her forehead, flipped it up to her crown and threw it back into their play with her nose. The farmers laughed and clapped and many out-of-work dockworkers did too.

"Here, Maggie," he said, "Catch this."

Piggy lifted one a mile high and Maggie moved side to side to get under it. The sock was out of sight for a second then fell back into view. How could she get this one? The wind swayed it and swayed with it.

I'd done pipe cutting all day at the Taylor's place because the Mrs. had finally glued up the works with flour, butter, and what looked like a blue coat with a high crinkly collar. Well, she put a cat down there once, why not a bloody coat. I got to Victoria Hall early enough to watch them chase Blacky about until he let them catch him. I lit one and Mrs. Bulmers sat next to me on the steps. Phil too. Bobby runs over for a hug and runs back to his play.

"He's growing tall," she says.

I watch him, going this way and that.

"Yes," I say.

The blind girl is in the center and Bobby never forgets to touch her and whispers to her as the rest swirl around. But Bobby gets angry lately, and more easily disappointed, as he does now when he can't catch the dog.

"The older Bobby gets, the harder it will be," Mrs. Bulmers says, seeing what I see. "It's only natural that he'll want to do and understand things he never will be able to."

Phil has strolled over and is standing next to the wee blind girl who turns as if she sees him. Which she can't, I don't think.

"Special children become special grown-ups. Bobby's not too far from that. He has to have training so that he'll have order. Order will be everything."

I look at her. She smiles and pats my back.

"It's getting time to love enough to let him go. There's a school on Quince Island."

She struggles up with an "oof" and claps three times. They run over for the day's final prayers and songs. Bobby doesn't want to pray or sing. He halts about.

"Bobby," Mrs. Bulmers calls.

"I...I...don't want to."

"That's alright. But don't you want to hold hands with the rest of us?"

"I...I...I...no!"

He shouts and starts to hit his thigh. He throws back his head and great tears spray out of his eyes. I see him alone now, flailing about at the world. Did I think Mrs. Bulmers was forever? Blacky stays with him, but I don't move from the steps. I'm watching as if he wasn't mine no more. The others begin to say their prayer, holding hands in a circle, Mrs. Bulmers in the middle. Bobby starts to march in defiance, his feet slamming, his arms pumping to the drum and trumpet sounds he makes.

"Yes," I say, softly to my smoke, "My pile is falling."

Now they begin their song of praise for the lovely day and the coming night. Bobby stops and listens. A smile spreads over his teary face. His green eyes sparkle and he lifts Blacky and runs to the circle. His voice is high and hard as he adds it to theirs, holding hands with the blind girl and putting Blacky down so he can join fingers with the wee mongoloid. He shakes and smiles. Mrs. Bulmers is right. There's order in the prayer and song. Something known, I suppose. But what else in the hard and silly world will line up for my Bobby Horn so that he can grab on and understand and live?

Mrs. Bulmers kisses him goodbye and we walk down to the channel, the plumber's box feeling heavier with each step. We hear them under the lights and Bobby runs ahead, Blacky close behind.

"Stay where I can see you," I shout.

"I…I…will."

"Bobby! Do you hear?"

"Stay…stay where I…what?"

"Just don't run so fast."

When we turn the corner, Piggy Brady has lofted the sock.

"Here Maggie," he says, "Catch this."

The crowd laughs and points at the sock still rising up. Bobby rushes over and jumps up and down to see over the men. The sock begins to fall back to earth and she's swaying side to side trying to get perfectly under it. Her hands are clasped behind her back and she's squeezing her face watching the thing come down, down to her forehead, when she sees something on the edge of her sight. Something that has come around the far corner. Something impossible. She drops her sight and the sock flops onto the cobblestones. Now Piggy Brady and the rest turn and see what Maggie has seen. The Barrow men know and have seen before, but still there is a part of each that can't believe and are as surprised as the farmers.

"Jesus…God…" I hear Piggy mutter as his wife squeezes his arm and gathers in her youngest.

"The…The…McAvy," Bobby shouts halting to him.

Bobby hugs him like he does. The McAvy smiles and holds his hand and together they walk under the light. Bobby looks about as if he's become part of the thing itself. The McAvy glances at me with flat eyes. He's never cross, thank Christ. Maybe that's what saves him and us. When he gets to Lowden, I see Mr. Horn for the first time, looking thin and more of a ghost than Phil ever did. Just when I think there is nothing else he can possibly do to shame himself and me, he plasters a knowing smirk onto his mug and lets a dirty laugh out. The McAvy ignores him.

"I thought we was third up," he whispers.

Lowden still hasn't found his voice, so Mr. Horn sways in.

"You're the only ones up. You and Piggy Brady. So you can stop trying to scare everyone with your great ugly mug."

The McAvy says nothing on that. His mug is a lot of things but not ugly. I would say it's impossible is what it is. He turns to Lowden.

"What's the winner's pot?"

"I would...yes I would say...uh...fourteen pounds or so."

The McAvy nods his shaggy head and walks over to me, still holding Bobby's hand. The crowd watches him in low mutters.

"I've got thirty-nine pounds. I've got more than enough," he whispers as he makes certain he's buttoned up like his mum would have him.

"Donald bought an automobile, Shoe. A car, for the love of Christ. And he'd need one because America's so bloody big."

"America's...bloody big," Bobby repeats.

I see myself going around America in my own automobile, my plumber's box on the seat next to me, people waiting outside their big houses for the plumber to save them. I see my house, too, and the easy American work that gets it.

"C'mon then," Mr. Horn's reedy voice pipes above the murmur, "We're busy men."

The McAvy shakes his head sadly.

"I'm sorry about your father, Shoe. It's a harder world for some than others. My mum always says that and it's true."

"C'mon, you bloody thugs, c'mon," Mr. Horn shouts.

"Piggy's back is hurt."

We hear her quiet voice together and turn to it. Piggy Brady's wife has come over to us, wee Maggie in hand.

"What's happened was he tried to lift some stones out of a field yesterday, and his poor back went pop or something."

"Are you a giant?" Maggie asks.

"Shush now," her mother says with a pull on her arm.

The McAvy says, "I'm bigger than a giant. And giants are slow. I seen one once in a circus. Their hands and feet are too big and so they're slow. What's your name?"

"I'm Maggie."

"I'm McAvy."

He bends and they shake.

"I'm Bobby," he yells, jumping up to The McAvy, "I'm…I'm…a great good guy."

Piggy's wife smiles like a mother at my Bobby Horn then looks back onto The McAvy.

"Piggy's got us, and now he's got this hurting back."

I look over to Piggy who two minutes earlier was laughing and lofting socks and throwing grabs and punches at the air. He sees me and looks down to his big feet. I'm thinking first you look at your feet like Petey Evans, then you raise them up when you know you can lay guys down and then, before you know it, you're look-ing at your feet again. It's a funny world alright.

"Well, Mrs.," he whispers, "It's not right for a man to go under the light with a bad back or bad anything. I'll tell Lowden to call it."

"Piggy's…Piggy's worried about the wagers his friends have made."

"Mummy," Maggie says, pointing at The McAvy. "It's bigger than a giant."

She pulls the child close to her.

"He's worried if there's no fight, they won't get the money back."

The McAvy looks at me. I shrug, but I know that if Piggy was about to fight me, his Mrs. and the kids would be still laughing and the socks still flying.

"Mr. Lowden," The McAvy rumbles with a wave of his hand. "A word here."

Lowden looks uncomfortable but starts over with Mr. Horn rolling importantly on his heels.

While they're coming, The McAvy turns back to me.

"My uncle said I mustn't come clean up at his pub again. Said I made the customers drink less. I said I'd come after they left if he liked. He said he didn't like."

"Yes. What is it?" Mr. Horn spits from behind Lowden. The McAvy ignores him and speaks to Lowden.

"Piggy Brady has a pain in his back, Mr. Lowden."

"What sort of pain," Lowden says like the idiot he is.

"A great pain that…"

"Pain my ass," Mr. Horn snarls, "He's seen the fucking thing and now he's lost his nerve."

"There's a lady here and Maggie too, Mr. Horn."

"What of them," he slurs.

"He means your dirty mouth," I say.

"How dare you?"

"Look," Lowden says, "Wagers have been placed. Piggy knows the rules."

"I've got a great pain, too," The McAvy says, rubbing his ear. "It's an earache or something."

"So what are you asking?" Lowden says getting his voice back strong at the prospect of losing money.

"I'm saying there's not going to be a go. So you have to return the wagers."

"The hell he does," shouts Mr. Horn, swaying like a blade of grass.

The McAvy gets close to Lowden. He's sized him up good.

"It's the right thing to do, don't you think, Mr. Lowden?"

Lowden feels the bills all fat in his pockets. All the farmer's money. But he feels The McAvy too.

"Well…well, I suppose we…"

"Mr. Lowden, a word here," snarls Mr. Horn.

Lowden's glad to have a reason to move away from The McAvy. Mr. Horn whispers and gestures. The crowd watches and grumbles. Piggy Brady picks up one of his kids and watches too.

"Well...Mr. Horn, who I believe you know, has suggested a compromise of sorts, that will allow me to announce the...cancellation of Mr. McAvy versus Mr. Brady due to mutual discomfort, and to return what monies have been wagered."

Mr. Horn snorts and smiles. Bobby picks up Blacky as if to protect him from this bloody villain, our father. I look at him and the wasted devil gives me a sour smile.

"As is well known throughout the Barrow and its environs, there's another match of great interest to all."

Lowden looks at me. The McAvy raises his hands to his hips and hangs his head, the great shag of hair slowly shaking left then right.

"Are you its boy?" Maggie asks Bobby, pointing to The McAvy.

"No...no...I'm, I'm the...McAvy's friend."

Lowden has grown bolder.

"A match to take place two weeks from today—here—eight sharp."

"That will give me enough time to train my boy," Mr. Horn says, loud enough for all to hear. "And he'll bring the filthy thing down when I teach him all I know."

"It will easily be the biggest purse," Lowden says to me. "Half the Barrow will come."

"Look, I'm not going to..."

"Who'll hold the money?" The McAvy whispers over me.

"Myself and Mr. Horn here," Lowden says.

"Yourself and someone else."

Mr. Horn's face gets red and he clenches his bony fists.

"Ten years ago I'd break you myself," he utters.

"Who else?" The McAvy asks.

I see Rogers' black head shining in the crowd.

"Mr. Rogers," I say.

Lowden turns.

"Who?"

"Mr. Rogers," I call.

162

Mr. Horn spits.

"A bloody Watusi for the love of Christ."

Rogers walks out of the crowd. Blacky runs to him. He picks the thing up and carries him over to us. Bobby smiles a huge one to see the two black things together.

"That's…he'…he's…Blacky."

"I know, laddie. He's almost as black as I am."

"Are…are…are you a…Watusi?"

Blacky barks.

"Blacky says I'm a Scot."

He hands the dog to Bobby. Nods at us.

"How can I be of service, gentlemen?"

"Why don't you…" Mr. Horn begins, but I speak over his slurs.

"The McAvy and me want you to hold the purse we'll fight for."

If Rogers is surprised, he doesn't show it.

"When would that be?"

The McAvy looks at me when he whispers.

"Two weeks from tonight. Eight. Here."

"I'll be here," Rogers says.

The McAvy turns to Lowden. There's something in his voice. Something as far away as America.

"Give them their money back," he says and walks away.

Bobby's excited about something, but he don't know what. I'm trying to read the Cowboy and Indian book to him and he won't quit moving around, squeezing my arm, wanting to speak but not having the words come. It's making him angry.

"I…I…I know." he shouts.

"You know what?"

"I…I…I know that…that Pecos Pete lassos the…moon."

"And some stars."

He looks at me like he's heard it all before, and he has.

"I...I know!"

"Well then, it's a waste to read anymore and let the words fall all over the floor so I'll have to mop them up after you're asleep."

"Oh...Oh Shoe. Words can't...can't..."

"Sure they can. You drop them when nobody's listening and they'll fall on the floor and sometimes some break, but that's okay."

He looks over the side of his bed.

"Well, you can't see them, Bobby. Words are nothing you can see, but they're down there."

He gets thoughtful, I know, when he crinkles his face up as he does now.

"I'm...I'm scared."

He looks at me. I got nothing to say.

"I...I...why am I...scared?"

Blacky crawls up from the bottom of his bed and puts his hairy face on Bobby's chest.

"I don't know why you're scared, Bobby."

"I'm...I don't..."

"Everybody gets scared."

"They do?"

"Sure."

"Do...do you?"

"Sure."

"Does...does...does..."

"Yes Bobby, even The McAvy gets scared."

"He's...he's a...big one."

He thinks a bit. I see his eyes getting heavy on him. He taps the Cowboy and Indian book, wraps his arms around Blacky and is asleep before Paul Bunyan and his big blue ox walk out of Minnesota.

I have tea and cigarettes at the table in the dark, thinking about the pile of my life and how the more that falls from it the more fool things I stack back on. Thinking that tomorrow will be the same, up with the fools before the sun, Bobby to Victoria's Hall and me to

Mr. And Mrs. Strands for more French "innovations." But if it's the same, why does it feel I've never been here before? Why do I dread the day and the week and the year?

"I'm Shoe Horn," I say to the glowing tip of my cigarette.

There's a knock on the door so soft, if I wasn't sitting in the dark, I wouldn't hear it. It's a brush really, against the wood. I go through Mummy's parlor and open it. Addy Augarde's back is to me, looking out at the alley.

"Addy?"

She has come down here, down through the alley to this dark Horn house. She seems surprised to see me.

"Shoe?"

"You know it is."

We stare at one another. I'm thinking of the lie that got wrapped around me and how what happened at the Strand's couldn't have really happened. Or how things that happen don't really happen. Phil's standing next to her. He's looking down and behind her. Creamy white all over. Soft, Christ Jesus, so soft.

"I'm…I was…would you come for tea?"

"It's after nine."

"I meant this Sunday. Two?"

"You shouldn't be here now. It's not safe."

"But you don't walk by anymore."

"What did you tell Ronnie Manchester?"

"Ronnie?"

I nod.

"Oh. Are you upset at that? Is it a secret?"

A secret? Jesus, Mary and Joseph. A secret? How the bloody hell shouldn't it be a secret? Is it something to talk about? There were sounds coming out of that room and Molly's too and oaths and promises. How would you explain such noises?

"Ronnie came by Pa's shop to see about a walk, but I told him I was in love. That's all."

In love? Dear Christ. In love? Addy steps forward and lays her head onto my chest. Her hair smells sweet, as sweet as the sugar bags stacked high outside her father's candy shop. Powdery and sweet. Phil has not taken his eyes off her backside. I gaze down too and stir, my hands dropping closer. When I have her completely held she raises her head and looks at me. They're wet and red.

"You don't have to love me because I love you."

Phil's gone, thank Christ. I squeeze my eyes tight. I see Molly in Cook's room, and see her fingers grabbing the pillow, her little face pushed into it. Jesus, Shoe Horn, where do you think you're going? I let my hands move in circles, a boiler to stir me more. Only the streetlamp at the end of the alley clears the night. But someone is under the light, watching. Hooked and old. A shadow maybe. What sort of clothes are on that bent thing?

"Can I help you?" I shout.

The shadow unbends with great effort into the shape of a man. Is that Phil standing with him? The thing lights one and a face of bone and leather flares. I wait. I've said enough. I've said too much. Mummy. Molly. I pull Addy tight. The shadow draws its cigarette and pointing at me spins sad, dry words down the alley.

"It's where I lived, if you can call it that."

"...if you can call it that."

"It's true," Phil says.

"And I never let him walk down alone. I'd say, 'Bobby! Bobby! I'll finish my smoke first!'"

"It's true. I saw it."

We had been the same size. He could be three of me now. His suit is the same one his Mum put him out in. His hair is thick and black and slicked back. Is he talking now?

"Phil Gogarty," I say.

He looks at me with eyes flatter and darker than I remember.

"Shoe Horn," he says.

He isn't smiling.

"So you're back with me. And you're talking. Or am I talking to myself?"

"I'd spit if I could."

"I can hear you Phil."

"How do I sound?"

"Young."

"I'm not."

I take a last puff and drop the smoke. We both watch it fall and blow down the alley. A man walks by and I don't care if he thinks I'm talking to myself.

"The place seemed so bloody big then Phil. The circle up to the park, Victoria Hall, the Docks, the bridge, the fucking light at Nuxhall. I walked the whole thing in an hour. And on these stick legs for the love of Christ."

He don't say nothing.

"Ahh hell. I never should have come back."

"Why did you Shoe?"

"Why did you Phil?"

"I didn't go anywhere. I've stayed is what. I waited for you like I think I was supposed to. I miss my mum."

"You should have come with me."

"Things were good, were they?"

"They knew good work when they saw it. I worked it in Boston and worked it in Providence. There was always work for a plumber. I had my own truck. I had my own shop."

I stopped talking and looked out at things I had and those I didn't. A little rain started. I couldn't feel it and only saw it in the wet cobblestones. I didn't care. Phil points down the alley.

"The days always fall down is what I've seen. That's not your house but it is. That's not your alley but it is. This can't be my town but I've seen it crawl past me. Mummy calling for her mummy, Tom weeping in his cell, Liz off and back again, off and back again, lipstick the color of blood. They have come and they have gone, and I can't feel the sun or smell the salt from the bay."

He starts to walk away.

"C'mon boyo," he says over his shoulder.

I don't move.

"I don't want to Phil."

He turns now.

"C'mon boyo."

"No."

"You should have come sooner. You should have and could have but a dog's a dog, right Shoe? We have things to finish."

"I don't want to finish anything."

My insides are roiling. I catch myself wanting to weep.

"Might as well weep, Shoe," he says reading my heart. "Might as well weep for all I know and all you'll never know."

"I know plenty you fucking dead Gogarty."

He's at my face before I see him move. He puts a hand on my chest. I feel the weight of the dead. The rain falls harder.

"No Shoe," he says with almost a smile. "You don't know shit."

15

Addy visits me and
the Gogartys piss on me

Bobby runs ahead, stops, runs again, stops and begins to cry. Blacky sits and looks up at him. I take my time, not only for the heavy plumber's box, but all my thinking has put a spike behind my eyes. Addy had fallen asleep by the time Mr. Horn crawled home. I lay with her leg over my stomach, smoking in my little bed, pushed into a corner off the kitchen. I heard the bastard fall in the hall, cursing the loose rug, or the chain on the door that made him drink until he pissed himself and then tripped him when he came to his house. He went quiet. I imagined him leaning against the red wallpaper Mummy hung when her own mum and dad came over from Warrington when I was small. I took my last puff and heard him sliding to his room, heard the bed springs squeal. I wouldn't have cared if he looked in and saw me. I'd say, yes you dirty beggar, I never promised not to fuck. Or a visit is what Addy calls the silly thing. But then I suppose no, I wouldn't care to see him embarrass her. But I got Bobby in the privy and while he dressed and marched with Blacky, we "visited" again, her hair spilling down my face. And it *is* a silly thing, for the love of Christ. A silly, easy thing. Then why, if it's so easy, do I wonder all the way down to her father's shop, before I put Bobby, if I'm alright at it? Bobby marches. I carry the heavy box, Addy on my arm.

"I might not be an actress, after all," she says, shyly and not like a girl been to Blackpool for acting lessons.

"No?" I say, to say something.

"I think I'd be a better mother. And wife, of course. I'm a very…I'm a nice girl."

There's another language that comes from her…Molly too, who I know I shouldn't be thinking about, for the lies I've told. But this language might as well be French, how confused it leaves me. Shouts and orders and pledges. Whispers and murmurs. Words though. Lots of words in starts and stops. Addy finds my ear with her round mouth. There, me under her softness. "Yes," she whispers and "Yes, Shoe, yes." Molly turned her head and shouted "Come on Shoe! Come on for the love of Christ!" But I'm silent with both. Or mostly. And Jesus it *is* silly, but it's turned me into this lying dog. Listen.

"Well, here we are Addy. I hope your father won't be worried."

"He's at the lake."

"Ah."

I light one.

"Bobby!" I shout. "I'm seeing Addy off."

"Oh…oh…oh Shoe there's the…moon," he says, pointing up for me and Blacky and Addy too.

"It is lad…well, Addy…uh…look, I don't think…what we…I mean…"

"I would never talk about it."

"It's just that guys like Ronnie Manchester…"

"I only said I love you."

She stares up at me. She's soft, it's true but very pretty. Her eyes are watery.

"But just because I love you doesn't…doesn't mean you have to love me."

She keeps her face at me. A tear comes, but she doesn't dab at it.

"Look Addy," I say, "Am I good at it?"

"Good at what?"

"Visiting."

Addy looks down and doesn't speak. Christ! I'm no good at it! This easy, silly thing and I'm no good at it!

"You're good at it," she says, to her feet. "But Shoe, it's nice to *look* at who you're visiting."

I am seventeen and the fucking rules are everywhere. Look? How can you look?

"So I should look?"

"It's a nicer visit when both are looking."

So they're looking while I'm not. Should I say I bit my tongue on the visit?

"Well, thank you for telling me that Addy," I lie.

When we get to Victoria Hall, Bobby has stopped running and is bawling at the bottom of the steps. Does he know that The McAvy will be killing me in two weeks? Did he hear that loud promise Addy lifted from her chest in my bed?

"What?"

"I...I...I'm mad!"

"Yes?"

"I'm very...I'm mad!"

"Mrs. Bulmers is waiting for you, lad. She's got boiled eggs, I'll bet."

"She...she *always*...boils eggs."

He sits down on the steps, draws his knees to his face and cries harder. Blacky nudges him, but Bobby pushes him away. Blacky squeals like his feelings have been hurt. Bobby sees it right away, scoops him up for kisses.

"I'm...oh Blacky...I'm...sorry."

I sit down with him and wait.

"I...I don't...I'm too big for...for here."

"You think?"

"I want...I want to...to be a plumber."

"A plumber," I say surprised, though I'm not. "Why would you want to spend your life in a water closet?"

"I…I don't want to…but there's, there's…what?"

"Sinks?"

"There's…there's sinks."

"And pipes?"

"Oh…oh yes…pipes."

"And bathtubs?"

"Bath…bathtubs with…with claw feet."

"But mostly water closets."

"No."

"Yes. And there's poop in them lots of times."

"No."

"Yes."

We're quiet for a bit. The lockout is ended today while the workmen and the bosses talk. I'm to be at the shipyard with Rogers in his pipe room, and I want to get there before the boys start in. But I want Bobby to get himself out of this. Mrs. Bulmers is right. I can't wait, can I?

"But…but…oh Shoe…I want to be…I want a job."

"A job?"

"A…a job…and…and carry a…a lunch like you."

"You got a job."

"No."

"You…got…a…job," I say punching each word.

He stands and sniffles and crosses his arm for proof.

"What…job?"

"You got *lots* of jobs."

"Lots?"

"Sure. Blacky's one job."

"Blacky's not…not a job."

"No? Well, he'd still be crying in that alley, wouldn't he, if you didn't get him and take care of him like you do. Who'd do that job of taking care? Who?"

"I…I do."

"And who would make sure the wee blind girl…"

"Bird…Birdie?"

"Who would make sure Birdie has fun and gets to pet Blacky and get his kisses?"

"I…I make sure."

He stands and laughs.

"And…and kites…that's a…a job."

"See?"

He grabs my head for a squeeze.

"I got…I got…I…"

"You got to go in and help Mrs. Bulmers with Birdie and the others?"

And he does. But as I'm walking down from Victoria Hall, hearing them, hearing Blacky talk too, I know I can't be tricking him much longer. Order, Mrs. Bulmers said. Training. I'll take a stroll over to that school on Quince Island soon. I'll tell them what he knows and how he knows it in his bones.

Rogers is in his pit in the same old pants with the black belt wrapped around them. Shirtless in the damp cold place. He's pulling wheels to open spigots when I climb down.

"Give us a hand."

I get the other side and pull while he pushes.

"Closed them up when we went out and the damn thing's rusted in a week. It's a fucking comedy down here," he says with a toothy smile.

"Well, you're back," I say.

"For awhile, laddie. I don't hold much hope though. Your job's across the way. Big water intake pipe is done. I told them a year ago. C'mon."

We climb out, cross the yard, climb back down into a bigger hole, and stand looking at the heart of the shipyard. Building and breaking don't get done without this fat pipe. Cold water sprays from every connection. Rogers takes two out, gives one to me and we smoke quietly listening to the hiss of the water.

"How do you shut it off?" I ask.

"I don't know. I been here twenty six years and never had to."

"Well, you have to."

We follow the pipe into another room and another and come to a ladder going down deeper still. There's a lantern hanging on a peg, so there's no light save the oil. Rogers shakes it to see it's fueled, lights it and hands it to me.

"It's a hole in the ground," I say.

"It stinks too."

"What's it like down there?"

"I never been down."

The ladder is metal. Something gooey covers each rung. I count forty steps down before I feel concrete. Or packed earth. Either way it's slimy and slick and smells like a dead clam. I swing the lantern and follow the pipe to where it begins at a great wide spigot. I give the wheel a pull, but it don't move.

"Mr. Rogers?" I yell.

"Yes laddie?"

"I got it, but it won't shut off. I'll need grease and oil and my two hander wrench."

It takes about an hour and a half. Finally it squeaks an inch and I know we've got her. Rogers and me don't speak the whole time. It's a nice quiet in the cold and dark. Rogers don't need to say anything to know he's with you, comfortable and easy. Sometimes he hums a tune and I hum too.

"Well, I'd better call Lowden and give him dimensions."

"There's a telephone at the gate."

"Shit," I say, shaking my head. "Charlie Burt in the morning."

"Not for long, laddie. He's with the strikebreakers. We seen him. We come back, Charlie leaves. I'll walk over with you."

Across the open yard, the boys come through the gates, lunch packs and pails, cleats over their shoulders for the slippery work. Rogers waves and they wave back.

Charlie Burt is looking out of the gate house window. It's covered with the spit each boy shoots at the glass, Charlie behind it. I am seventeen and what I know could fold into a lunch pail, but I know that there's thirty thousand working men in the Barrow and they haven't forgotten 1888, let alone last week. I leave Rogers with them and go into the gatehouse. Charlie doesn't speak, doesn't look at me. He's watching them. He's wishing it was two weeks ago when he knew what he knew and thought he was smart.

"I've got to use the telephone for yard business."

He doesn't answer, so I use it to call Lowden. The filthy bastard wants to go to his club. Can't it wait, he says.

"No."

"Well, Christ!"

I tell him what size and where I'll be. I can hear the spit slopping against Charlie's window when I hang up. He still hasn't moved. Before I leave, he gives a little laugh, and speaks to the globby glass.

"I saved them. I save them all, do you know that Horn? I gave the Kaiser my bloody arm for them."

I can still see him smirking with Tom Gogarty. I don't say anything and open the door.

"The fucking giant is going to kill you good, you little shit. I hope the fucking thing rips *your* arm off so you'll know."

I walk out and over to Rogers.

"I'll be cutting the pipe now."

All morning I turn the cutter, do a ream as best as the rotten connections will let me. Rogers is in and out, running here and there, tightening, loosening, oiling, cleaning. He's the engine's engine, and a part of each pipe, each boiler, each bloody cable that serves up power to the shipbuilding and shipbreaking. He's never tired, while me at my lunch can barely chew. He sits next to me in the sun outside the basement door.

"Where's Blacky?" he asks, drinking stout from a pail.

"With my brother."

"He's a good one."

He offers a sip of stout and I take it.

"You haven't said how The McAvy is going to kill me."

"I was thinking about your dog," he says in his thick brogue, then laughs. "Besides, I don't need to tell you, you already know."

We both laugh and I don't know why. Last night I dreamed The McAvy threw me up to the gulls. I flapped my arms and flew to America, away from everyone, until I stood alone among strangers. Not known. Not Shoe Horn. Just someone there and away from here.

Lowden doesn't come until afternoon, leaving me to struggle with the heavy piece, so we can get the water flowing. When I get to Victoria Hall, it's dark. Mrs. Bulmers and Bobby are sitting with Blacky. He's crying again, shaking his head and hitting his legs. She dabs a cloth at his face and sings something. Phil is sitting next to him shaking his head too. Bobby raises his gaze to me and, Jesus Christ, he's covered with red and black bruises. Both of his eyes are puffy and black. He runs off the steps to me.

"Oh…oh…oh…Shoe, they…they…"

He slams his face beneath my chin and squeezes me for his life.

"Bobby…"

"They…they…hit me."

"Bobby…I've got you. I've got you," I say soft, thinking, Bobby first and then them. I look at Mrs. Bulmers who has come down the steps.

"Bobby had Blacky out to do his business before we took our nap and that damn Petey Evans and his bunch jumped on him."

"They had…they had a…a…ball and I said we'd play…we'd play…"

"I know Bobby…"

"We...we'd play...me and Blacky but...but Petey, he said he... they all just...oh Shoe, look, I'm bleeding."

Good Christ even under the light we know when to stop. I take the damp cloth from Mrs. Bulmers and touch the swelling cheeks and nose.

"Who?" I ask him.

He looks at me and his wounded eyes narrowed.

"I did...I did my job good."

"Who?"

"I...took care...of Blacky and...and Birdie...I made...I made sure..."

He's not going to tell me who was with the little fucker, but I can guess Taber and the fucking little mick. I dab at his face a bit more.

"Alright, Bobby, let's go home."

His halt is bigger and I see why. His left knee is as swollen as his face.

"Does it hurt to walk?" I ask behind him.

"No," he says, smiling over his shoulder, forgetting bad things like he does.

Phil walks too. He's thinking and doesn't look at either of us. I light one, but it tastes like shit and I throw it down. We turn by the bridge for Mr. Horn's house and Bobby's bed and his supper and his Cowboy and Indian book. I get him in a bath and float a boat in it. Then some bread and cheese and potatoes. I finish the book, but he makes me start it again and read until his legs go quiet and he sleeps the sleep of the just. I've left him alone once before for Ronnie Manchester and I leave him again. The blood's going. Phil walks fast to keep up. I turn up out of the alley toward where I know Petey lives behind his father's bakery. Mummy loved his tarts and I am after his boy.

I walk around back. It's dark in the place, so I go back to the street, smoke and try to think. I can't, of course. Not when the blood's hot and I'm hot. They're always cruel in their games. I know it and have wiped dried blood off his face and clothes before. This is new. I didn't think Petey and those boys of his were smart enough to plan a cruelty. It's quiet tonight. I hear voices and lean out of the light. It's Petey and Taber. I don't see the fucking mick, but he can wait, although not for long. Petey stops and lights one, the match glowing me out of my darkness.

"Shoe!" Taber shouts when he sees me, but I'm on them too fast. I can smell the beer they've had and see it slowing them. I see my Bobby too, bruised and cut and know it wasn't no game done it. Each goes down with a nose bleeder. I haul Petey back up and lift Taber over with a kick in his stomach. I slam his chest with my fist, and again he falls and I raise him up.

"Your face will look like my brother when I'm through."

"No!" he cries, covering it.

"And I'm not going to be through for a good long time."

"It wasn't us," he says, crawling away.

I walk over him but give Taber another kick. He moans and vomits. And he should, the fucking thing. Petey stands and tries to run, but I only have to walk fast to catch him on the far side of the street.

"No…it was…it was Tom Gogarty paid us. He paid us."

The information circles my head but too slow to do Petey any good. I give him two in his stomach and one good drive at his jaw. He might be dead, but I don't care. I start to the Gogartys', then stop. Did I hit Petey too hard? I walk over to him and he struggles up and starts to run again. I guess I didn't do it too hard. Or hard enough. Or I don't have much left. I grab him.

"Take Taber home and you go home too."

He's crying now.

"I will. I promise."

I watch them leaning into each other, moving like drunks. I look for Phil, but he's gone again. The blood's still going as I cross the street and walk the lane that leads to the Gogartys. I stand on another corner in shadows, watching their place and knowing that

Petey has told the truth. These are the men who would take after Bobby to avenge themselves. These are the strikebreaking guys
who are all for fairness to workers. Christ Jesus. What do I know?
Is that Phil staring now out his window? Is it? Come on then, Phil,
send them down one at a time. Arthur and Tom and the three
cousins and I'll slick the bloody bastards back as slick as the Gogartys' hair. Come on.

I hear one before I see him. No. It's two coming down the
street. It's two of the cousins. They're smoking and slurring. I don't
care if there's three. I'm hot. I'm so hot. I don't need to tell myself
to cross the dark street and meet them at their door. The legs go
and I follow.

"Who paid Petey Evans to hurt my brother?"

They stop and look at each other, then me. They get up the
Gogarty sneer.

"Who?"

"Who's his brother?" The taller one says, laughing at me.

"I think he means that crazy fool."

He begins to laugh too and imitate Bobby's halting steps. I
drop him to a curled up ball with two hits and a kick. The taller
one backs up a step and doesn't try to help the one who's down.
Now I turn to him. Words I need to say are in the blood in my
fists. My plumber's fists. He looks behind himself like he's waiting
for someone to help him. When he don't see no one, he balls his
fists and circles to his left. I don't have no time for this dance and
go right at him. One of his punches gets my cheek but all of mine
get him. Face, shoulder, chest, belly. He turns like he quits. Like
Bobby maybe turned to quit their dirty little game. I let this one
quit like they let Bobby. I kick and punch until he's on the street
with the other. A couple of drunks watch from the other side. I
see Tom at the windows.

"Come down, Tom. Come down for yours, you bloody coward."

Tom says something and disappears. In a moment the front
door opens and Tom comes down his steps. He's got a blackjack

and I'm not surprised. That third cousin follows with a stick. Another too, his fireman coat open and his face closed. Liz stands in the doorway, Phil beside her, watching me in sadness.

Tom and the big one circle in opposite directions. Arthur just stands, his thumbs in his belt. I wouldn't worry about that big faker if he had a gun, which he might being a Gogarty. Tom don't say nothing. He just watches like he could see through me. He's wiry and prison hard, but he don't work either and likely had some drinks this night. The big one has circled closer. I see the hope in that. I draw him closer still by keeping my eyes on Tom. I hear the rustle of his pants and turn low and fast, driving out at his gut. He lets an "oof." I turn him now so he's between Tom and me and take him down by his face and chest. Tom has just watched like the last ones. Do the Gogartys enjoy blood wherever they find it? Even their own? When he gets to one knee, I kick his kidneys. He'll stay there awhile, I know. Now it's Tom.

"My brother's eyes are banged shut, Tom. His lips are red."

"My brother's dead. You killed him."

I look over to Phil, a step behind his lovely, fierce sister.

"Are you angry with me, Phil?"

He shakes his head and looks at his feet. I look back to Tom.

"He's not angry. He knew about going under the light."

Tom points at me with the blackjack.

"He's crazy, Liz. I told you."

"Come on then, Tom."

I watch Arthur to be sure the fool won't come and he don't. Tom smiles and moves closer.

"You're a fool, Horn. You're a bastard and a fool."

He's moving open to whatever I give him and I'll give him plenty. What does he think? He can just walk in and give me the blackjack? Jesus, Tom, who's the fool? I set my feet. I'll take him chest and arms and rise up to his face. I'll change that pointy nose too. I take a step and feel the air behind me move before the broom handle slams the back of my head and knocks me down. I turn my head up and Liz gives me another, this time across my mouth.

"That was for Phil," she says, dropping the broom handle and walking back inside. I see the twirling blackjack come hard onto my shoulder. I'm curled on cobblestone when Arthur kicks my face. The last thing I see is the tall one I took down early. He stomps my head. And I'm in my dream of Bobby and Walney Bridge. This time Addy and Molly stand with Mummy and Mr. Horn.

"No," I shout. "No Bobby. Stay here with me."

"Run, Bobby," I hear Molly shout.

"Run," screams Addy.

"There he goes," says Mr. Horn.

But Mummy only reaches out to me. I want her to say something. Anything. To hear her voice. Bobby halts faster and faster. I see the Great Bitch now, calling from her side, long bony fingers cupping that brittle mouth. Is that a song? Is that a part of a song I hear filling the bridge? Is Mummy singing it too? Yes. And Mr. Horn is piping it out on his coronet.

"Bobby," I shout, "Don't listen. Don't listen."

I see him folding into her black crackly gown. I see my brother vanish into blackness and I follow. I follow Bobby Horn into blackness.

It's dark and moonless when my good eye flutters open. I smell dampness and piss through the sticky blood inside my nose. I push onto my back trying for a deep breath. My lungs feel papery, refusing to fill. So they've pissed on me. Liz brought me down and they pissed on me. When I'm on my feet, bent and holding my guts to keep them from dropping out my ass, I look up at the Gogarty cave. There are no lights on. There are no lights anywhere. Even the bloody streetlamps are not burning. Some moon comes through the drifting sky, some stars too, and their glow bounces off cobble-stones until I can see a twinkling way home.

16

Molly and me get clean in a
postcard full of bubbles

Some dirty little mick has poured cement into every water closet. The big facility on the second floor that has seven of them is filled with water because the main outtake pipe exploded. It's not right I should be standing in shit, after being pissed on last night. Christ. I can hear the big priest, the tall one with the giant belly, yelling and cursing at the boys in the school's dining hall where he's got them.

"…and if you little buggers think they'll be no consequences for your actions…whoseever actions they are…think again! Now come forward and accept punishment you…"

I turn my ear off to the bloody mackerel snapper. He'll wait a long time before one of those little bastards owns up. Jesus, but my head pounds and the small of my back hurts so much I forget my ribs ache with each breath. I got to Mr. Horn's, then must have fell asleep in the hall, or passed out. I was on the floor when Lowden woke me, pounding on the door.

"Jesus, what happened to your face?" he asks when I open up.

I don't say nothing. I'm good at that. His truck's lights cut through the alley blackness like flames. His bald head gleams. Even though I may be dying, I'd love to crack that shiny egg right open.

"Well, now, see here Horn," he says when he sees I ain't talking, "There's been trouble at Mary the Redeemer. Water's everywhere and…"

I know it's not time to work, even for an apprentice. Lowden takes any job, any time, as long as *I* do the work. Dear Christ, the Gogartys got me good. That fucking Liz up from behind with the stick. I feel the back of my head and watch the silly fool's mouth go.

"…And…And, now Horn, are you listening to me?"

"I don't feel well, Mr. Lowden."

Now he takes a good look at me. I see those blinking eyes roaming over my face. If I can't work, then that would leave Lowden to do it. I don't know much, but he ain't going to do it. He's thinking. He smiles, then gets a serious look on his face that turns into a frown. I smell like Gogarty piss and I don't care.

"Now lad, it's a difficult life alright and the plumber's lot is often hard and cruel. But that card, that plumber's card is a sunny day, if you get my meaning."

He watches me and I watch Phil coming down the alley. I can't clear my head enough to say, "I can't work."

"I'll have to wash. I'll have to take my brother early. What time is it?"

He pulls on his vest chain and his watch rises to his hand.

"Four o'clock."

"I'll be there at five."

"That late?"

I close the door on him, take off my clothes and put them in a ball on the back step. I take a pot of water, get Mummy's palm oil bar too, and wash off the Gogarty night. The small kitchen mirror catches me. Christ but I may be forty. I may be dead and not know it. Bobby's hard to wake up and stays sleepy after the privy.

"C'mon Bobby."

"I...I..."

"C'mon."

"No...no...no..."

Blacky and I look at him. His bruises have come blacker. Bobby looks angry. He halts around the kitchen. I'm buttering bread, letting him go. When he stops and sits at his place, he looks at my mug for the first time.

"Oh...oh...oh..."

"Eat your bread, lad."

Mr. Horn steps into the kitchen, holding his wrinkled self against a wall.

"Here...what's all this...noise, you dirty buggers."

"...Shoe's...Shoe's..."

"Ah Christ...speak like a man...and...Jesus now, what the bloody hell happen to you?"

"I got...Petey..."

"What?" he says to me. "What the hell happened? You've got a match coming, you great fool."

He pushes himself off the wall and half falls to me, catching himself and swaying.

"I asked you a question, you fucking fool."

"Bobby. Eat your bread. Drink your milk."

I pull my pants on and drop suspenders over the Lowden Plumbing shirt. I look hard at Bobby and he begins to eat and drink. Mr. Horn turns and sits at the table shaking his head. He's asleep in the chair by the time I pull shoes on. It's not until I begin to lace them do I feel the broken finger.

And so here I am swimming in shit at Mary the Redeemer, finger wagging loose, pulling out globby mounds of wet concrete. By noon I manage to get most of it on the wet floor in front of each water closet. I've got the outtake pipe half reamed when Lowden speaks from the doorway, the big belly priest next to him, listening.

"...Ah...here we are then. As you can see, Monsignor, we have evacuated the areas of concrete, well before they could set hard.

Then we proceeded to ream the pipe-to-porcelain connection. Finally we will remove a section of the intake pipe and replace it with a brand new length."

"We? *Intake?*"

"I don't know what gets into them. I honestly don't," the priest says in a high voice.

What gets into them is *them*, the potato-eaters. I'm hungry but didn't bring bread or cheese. Not that I could chew it. At lunchtime, I'll try to find a bit of sun.

"Can we be flushing by vespers?" the priest asks.

This outtake pipe will need welding. This pipe will need a miracle for the ancient thing not to turn into dust when I take the cutter to it, let alone thread another piece in.

"I think I can extend my guarantee of evening flushing on behalf of Lowden Plumbing," Lowden says.

"That would be lovely," the priest says and walks back to the dining hall.

Lowden's quiet in the doorway. When I turn to shake the reamer, I notice he's got a cloth up to his nose.

"Well...I suppose I'd better be...now what are the dimensions on that intake?"

"Out-take."

"That's what I said. What are they?"

I tell him and he leaves. I don't care. I'm ankle deep in shit and why have Lowden add his own to it. At lunch I walk out and smell the sea haze, which is sweet and salty at the same time. Mary the Redeemer is around the corner from the Channel Lane, so I walk over, sit on the top step, and light a smoke. If she don't see me and come out, will I go in and ask for her? I don't know myself. That's why it's so hard to see through the big problems. Mostly, I just don't know. But now I don't have to. She sits next to me and looks out over the sloping rooftops where I look, to the green and brown sea.

"Can I have a puff?" she asks softly.

"You can have a whole one," I say without looking at her.

"Just a puff."

We pass the cigarette back and forth in silence. The smoke can't cover all those good smells that jump off Molly Reilly and float up my smashed nose. I might be as black as Rogers for the bruises, but she doesn't say nothing about them.

"I dreamed last night we were somewhere," she says so soft it might be to herself. Her hair is under some cloth. Her skin is dark where it bunches under her eyes.

"We were somewhere and it was like we had both just been born only we looked like we do now. Except I had bigger...you know...these."

She brushes the back of her hand over her chest.

"They're very...nice like they are."

And I'm stirring in a storm of Molly.

"So because we were both new, both babies, only we looked like now, we didn't...we hadn't made...mistakes. We hadn't been... stupid or...or jealous or any of those things and when we got into the warm tub..."

"We got into a warm tub?"

"With bubbles like the kind Miss Ella Drabo is in on a post-card I seen. We just got in and rubbed the bubbles all over each other and...and felt each other so clean and so new."

She went quiet and looked at the sea again.

"Then what happened," trying to seem only a wee bit interested.

She looked at me and still didn't mention the closed eye and the flattened face.

"Everything," she says, "Everything that can happen, does happen."

Molly Reilly reaches over and rubs my thing. Squeezes it.

"Let's be just born, Shoe. Let's be clean and new."

I look at her eyes. I feel her hard fingers.

"Yes. Let's be new."

Molly walks with me to the mick school. I'm late by an hour. She'd raised her face from Cook's pillow and didn't try to muffle her shouts and cries. And me neither. It was like Mr. Horn, The McAvy, Bobby and all the rest passed through me and out my mouth in a kind of yowl and for a bit, not long enough, but a bit, I was clean.

"Well," she says at the school entrance.

"Well," I say.

She kisses my mouth and holds me. Holds me as hard as Bobby does.

"I love you," she says.

It's as if I'd wrung out the lies.

"I love you, too."

She puts her hands to her mouth in surprise.

"I got to go and get them flushing."

"I got to clean some rooms."

We both got to go but ain't moving. Some sun breaks through the hazy day like a promise. But a promise of what? She kisses me again and we're gone. Before I can say "bloody hell" I'm back in shit. The length of pipe I measured for Lowden is leaning against the door along with the welding torch and fuel. "Here Shoe, do it all, I'll be at the club." The dirty bugger. Ahh hell, I just don't care. I grab the pipe and think of Cook's room, and the whole place smells better.

I leave the micks flushing away and go for Bobby. The bloody box must be getting heavier, even with switching it from hand to hand, my shoulders feel pulled down to the ground. On the corner, across from Victoria Hall, I see him, standing next to a lamp and nearly as tall. He raises his hand in a small wave and I know he's been waiting. Waiting for me? He steps off the curb and we walk slowly in some silence. I can't tell if it's a good silence or something else. Another thing about The McAvy, you cannot hear his breathing. You cannot hear the ocean of air he takes with each breath. So how can you know his thoughts? I take one out and offer it. He takes it and I take another and we stop to light.

"I talked to a guy says he can get me on the *Madagascar*. It's a Cunard. I'd be an assistant in the boiler. I'd be a coaler. But it'd be only for a few weeks. It gets into Boston.

"Boston?"

"Boston," he whispers.

We go quiet until Victoria Hall.

"It's a city too, but I can walk out of it. It's big. America has room for a big guy."

A big guy? Room enough for The McAvy? It's like he can't be. He just can't be.

"Look Shoe, you'll take me down. That's it. I got enough and you can take me down and keep the pot."

Take him down? Christ but I am not my father's son.

"Cheat?" I hear myself say.

"I got enough."

"I don't need to cheat. I'm bloody Shoe Horn. I'm known."

The McAvy looks at me. I can't hold it and look away. What's inside of him? I'm afraid to know.

"I'm growing," he murmurs. "I'm eighteen and I'm not stopping growing. I'll grow out of my mum's house if I stay. I'll break through the roof. I'll sink the whole bloody Barrow. I've got to get to America. But Shoe, I got to be careful now. I feel like I'm getting stormy. I can taste it in my mouth when they look at me. I won't be able to walk away soon and somebody will die and you know it."

I look up at him. It's true, he's bigger. His hair falls wet, almost to his shoulders. Has he grown out of his curls too?

"You know it," he whispers, words rising out of the deep well.

I watch him move back down toward his mum's. He's not hanging his head to make himself smaller as he's always done. He's straight up and something more, something I can read in his shoulders and swing of arms. He *is* a storm and he's ready to come ashore.

"He's…he's…a big one."

I hear Bobby, turn and…Christ Jesus. I step back, almost stumble. He stands at the top of the steps by the door. In his hand is her hand, the long claws wrapped like snakes around his fingers.

"We've said our prayers," she utters. "We thanked Him for our lovely day."

"And…and…we…we…"

"We sang."

She keeps her eyes on me, moves the awful head to Bobby and kisses his hair. Bobby claps and runs down the stairs to me, Blacky on his heels. His face is buried beneath my chin and I hold him, looking up at the thing. Hold him as I've never done. She smiles a wicked smile. Phil comes from the shadows. He stops and she turns her look to him. Can the thing see Phil?

"She can see what she wants," I say.

She turns back to me.

"See what, young Mr. Horn?"

She steps off the top of the next step. I step back, still clutching my Bobby Horn.

"Where's…where's Mrs. Bulmers," I say, my voice different and high.

"Inside. In her rooms. Victoria did not feel well today."

"And…and the others?"

"Home…except for Birdie. Where her father is I cannot say. But Birdie is with me now."

Her rasp sprays into the dark street. She points at us.

"I brought his bruises down."

Bobby pulls himself off my chest with excitement.

"She…she…Mary did…did magic."

"I can do the same for you," she says, her awful teeth catching the streetlamp. She takes another step down. Then another.

"We have business to conduct, young Mr. Horn. You know it. First, I'll bring down your bumps and bruises," she takes another step. "And then we'll have our little chat."

I step back, grab Bobby's hand and pull him away toward home.

"Tomorrow then," it calls after me. "Or the next."

Through the streets sloping toward the docks, I watch the sky above me for her flight. Her black flowing flight. Mummy said she'd seen it. Seen it swoop and turn, an awful night bird watching the houses of mothers. Waiting in the firmament or under the street for Bobby and the rest.

When he's washed and in his bed, I begin the Cowboy and Indian book, so low he can't hear.

"I...I...can't hear you, Shoe. What...what about the...the blue...ox?"

Phil sits and listens to Paul Bunyan's ax drop trees all over America until Bobby is snoring. I close the book and look at the dents my fingers have made in its cover. How many years? How many times has it been spoken out? He knows the bloody thing by heart, can speak it back to me, each word coming as if he's just heard it, his eyes wide and clear. But now I see what I take to be clear isn't clear at all. It's him trying to line the world up into what he knows, like stones in a brook, so he can step from one to the other and be dry and safe and sure. I brush his hair to the side and see that his fat face has a smile. He's off somewhere with Mummy, I suppose, maybe under her elm listening to the birds, while she butters bread and tells him the words to each of the bird's songs.

"Tomorrow at lunch, Phil, I'm going to that school Mrs. Bulmers told me about. The one on Quince Island."

I laugh.

"Christ, I'm talking to a ghost."

Phil laughs too only I can't hear him. His laugh drifts off his face because he knows more than I do. I begin to weep in great grabs of air. I weep until Phil has gone and I have spread myself onto my bed. My tears telling me the truth of my lies.

17

I see the doctor.
I see the bitch.

"Where have you been?" Lowden demands, silky white hands on his woman's hips. "It's past two. Mrs. O'Connor called to say you didn't return. You walked away."

I don't even look at the fool and begin to lay the tools out for the afternoon.

"I had some business. I'll stay the extra hour. Tell Mrs. O'Connor her shit will soon be flushing into the Irish Sea."

"Shhh," he whispers, closing the door behind him.

"Look, I had business. I needed to go somewhere. I'm back and I'll give you the extra hour."

He watches me slide the bowl into place. The bloody woman had used twenty pounds of newspaper to wipe her ass.

"Well, I suppose that will be sufficient. Yes, yes that will be sufficient. Don't want to work you too hard. I'll have money riding on your strong shoulders in a few days."

I look at him. Money on me? On what? On what time I'll crash back to earth after The McAvy lifts me up to the stars. I look back at my wrench and shake my head.

"Your father tells me he's been training you quite hard, giving you hints and skills that will baffle the great thing."

I snort. Mr. Horn lives only in his drunken head.

"Last night at Greel's Pub, he demonstrated what he referred to as "Around the Horn," a boxing move he developed just for his boy."

Lowden exhausts me. My back aches like an old man.

"Mr. Lowden, I can't work with all the talking."

He looks at the water closet and pretends interest.

"You've certainly got this in hand. Tell you what. Only one more today and then you can get back to training. The vicarage of St. Mary on Walney."

Walney. Jesus but I am turning to dust.

"Do you know it? The Reverend Robert Wickford apparently severed the intake pipe with a shovel while burying a cat in his backyard."

The day is sunken with heavy grey clouds. The Great Bitch has made a day for me. Lowden's still going.

"...from near and far. Police are going to rope it off. You and the giant. That's what we've been waiting for."

When I don't answer him, he puts his silly hat back on.

"Well, I'll be going now. Inventory. Shop work. I envy the time you spend with the craft. No such luxury for the proprietor."

He waits a bit. I feel him watching and thinking.

"So...the vicarage. Know it?"

Walney Island. This dark day.

"I do."

Walney has disappeared under a fluffy quilt of fog. Colors glow through in puffs of shop signs. It's like I'm crossing the bridge into a fairy tale. It's like this in my dreams of Mummy and Bobby. The Great Bitch calling and him running to her. Mr. Horn and Mummy watching me from their side of the bridge, watching me chasing him, calling him out of the blackness. Or trying to.

Now I'm thinking how at lunch I walked to Quince Island, which is not an island at all, to the Special Children's School Mrs. Bulmers had told me of. The tall red brick building was also called the Armory and was used to store weapons during the Great War, in case getting Charlie Burt's arm wasn't enough and the bloody Krauts came to the Barrow for more. Now it smelled like boys and girls.

"Can…can I help you?" a heavy girl says. "I'm…I'm…Janey."

She half shouts it with a fat smile. I smile back.

"I'm looking to speak with somebody about my brother."

"What's…what's his…name?"

"Bobby."

"Is…is…is he like me?"

I don't know Bobby anymore. I don't know the things that play so completely through him. How he sees the birds and shouts at them, to square up and fly together. How he says that Mummy's elm isn't an elm at all but another great Mummy, swaying and swishing over all of us. But what I know is the flower he is. Big and full and true. A rose hanging over all of us.

"Yes, Janey," I say. "He is like you."

She hugs herself and gives it a squeeze. I can't stop myself from one too. I hold her and feel the things she knows so deep inside herself, the same as Bobby.

"I'll…I…I'll get Dr…Dr. James."

She halts halfway down the corridor and disappears into one of the rooms. Order, I keep telling my small brain. Mrs. Bulmers is right. I've seen it too, how any change, anything not done over and over, sets him marching and shouting and crying these days. Janey comes back into the corridor holding the hand of a tall, thin, towheaded man about thirty or so. He's wearing dark pants with a white jacket over a white shirt. She's talking and he's listening with a smile. She points at me.

"This…this is…Mr.…Mr.…."

"Thank you Janey, you're very helpful."

"Thank you…thank Dr. James."

Janey gets a serious look and walks back down the hall. The doctor holds out his hand.

"I'm Dr. James."

"Shoe Horn," I say, and we shake.

"My office is on the second floor if you don't mind following me."

Right before the stairs I see the gymnasium through open doors, hear their squeals and watch a ball kicked and chased. Dr. James stops and watches too.

"Dr. Henry Gray, our director, has developed a theory that play is inseparable from training. It brings balance to the arduous task our students face daily."

I look at him on that. He smiles.

"Everything we take for granted, they must *not* take for granted. Come."

He's quick and up the stairs, like a goat. He waves me into a small room. The walls are heavy with books, his desk piled high with paper and scraps of paper. He points me into a chair.

"Forgive the room. There's never enough time to tidy up."

He lights a cigarette and I do too.

"Now, I gather you had something you needed."

"Uh…well, yes, Doctor. Mrs. Bulmers over at Victoria…"

"Wonderful woman. Accomplishes small miracles."

"Yes sir, that's her…see, I'm an apprentice…plumber…and Mummy's gone…dead…and my father…well Doctor, my father's always drunk and Bobby's up with me early and I get him to Mrs. Bulmers then work and bring him home. I'm not the cook Mummy was, no one is, still he's fed good. Lots of bread and butter and beef and…and fish. And I read him to sleep. Oh and he's very clean, he's not at all a dirty lad. He can do his privy."

Their shouts and cries and laughter drift up the stairwell and by his office. I smile at the sounds.

"And…and he loves to play. He plays nice. He plays hard."

Dr. James smiles too. Then waits for more.

"Lately…lately Bobby's angry easier…"

"About what?" he asks, watching me close.

"About anything he doesn't know. Mrs. Bulmers says 'training.' She says 'order.' "

I look at the Dr. and feel the words coming out of my heart.

"And she says it's time."

The doctor stands and looks out the windows to the sea.

"It's time for you too, I'd say."

I start to stand.

"No, I can do it…I just…"

"Right now, I'd say you're living half of your brother's life for him at the expense of half of yours. It's very common. But it *is* time to change it. What Mrs. Bulmers sees, I'm sure…and, of course, I don't know your brother…but what she sees is a special child becoming physically a man. Am I right?"

I nod. He knows.

"It's difficult enough for a normal man, let alone one whose acquaintance with this bitter world is purely and decidedly innocent. A world not willing to contemplate that there is great truth in their clean minds."

"What he knows he knows in his bones."

The doctor smiles and nods.

"Yes, he does. I'd like to meet Bobby."

I stand now.

"I can bring him by. Would Saturday or Sunday be alright?"

He looks through the piles of his bits of paper and nods.

"Shall we say Saturday? Ten in the morning?"

I stop in the doorway.

"Uh…how much would…"

"The students live at the school. Did you know that, Mr. Horn? Your brother would only have visits fortnightly, but he'll get used to it. And slowly he'll come to some recognition of the world through which he must move. So to answer your question, it would be expensive but for the charity of Mr. and Mrs. Strand."

"Mr. Strand?"

Now I'm crossing the bridge to Walney in the fog. Dr. James was clear and I play his words over. Mr. Strand and his sad wife? How can anyone even understand such a thing? I walk to St. Mary's vicarage and allow my legs to bully boy out. The plumber's box feels lighter. The fog is lifting and so, it seems, am I. I give it three hard knocks and wait. A pretty girl, her hair in a bun, opens the door. She got on a sky blue dress and flowers spread on the color. She smiles, then suddenly stops, and looks at me cold.

"Yes," she says.

Why are the girls angry or sad? All the time, angry or sad. Molly, Addy, Christ even Liz, but I suppose Liz was angry without a question. The back of my head throbs where she got me.

"Lowden's plumbing," I say with a flat face. "I've come about the dead cat." ·

She'd like to close the bloody door and I don't blame her. This must be Ronnie Manchester's girl, the Vicar's daughter. Well, he didn't bloody drown, did he?

"Alright," she says finally and steps aside.

I follow her through the hall and kitchen to the garden. She smells…Christ, Horn…you'll be cutting and welding, leave the smells, you dog. Leave the lilacs and roses and…what?…all of it to Ronnie for the love of Christ.

"There," she says pointing.

A small hole filled with water and mud is bubbling off to the right of the garden path. Grass swirls in the center of it. Something pink too. Petals? Petals from that fat rose there? I look at her and don't speak until she looks back at me.

"I'll need your telephone."

"Why?"

"It's got to be shut off. The water. It's in the street somewhere. Lowden will know, if the bloody beggar can move his ass to shut it."

She steps back.

"Your language is foul," she says with a sneer.

"Right."

"I don't like your words."

"Then show me where the fucking telephone is and I'll shut my dirty yap."

Her little white hands ball into fists. I've never hit a girl, but I think I might lay this one down if I don't get to the phone. We stare at each other a moment before she shakes her head.

"This way."

I follow her to a room off the kitchen. It's got books and a desk. This must be her father's room. Jesus, I can smell his pipe tobacco and French water. All I know of him is the silly man at the church and the vicarage door, but I hate him and don't know why. I ring up the silly Lowden.

"It's me. We got to shut off the water from the street, but I don't know where."

"You don't know where?"

"I don't know where."

I can hear the lazy bastard thinking.

"It's…it's nearly four-thirty."

I don't say nothing. I want to beat him. I want to beat her. I want to pound the whole Barrow into the ground.

"Look, Horn, it's late in the day. Seal it and get it in the morning."

It's true. Lowden has forgotten it all. The pipes. The connections. The flow of the bloody profession. He's got the pride of a clam.

"I can't seal shit if the water's running."

"Don't use that tone with me."

I put the phone down.

"Mr. Lowden says your father has ruined everything. He says the cat has destroyed your water and everything else. He says what your father has to do now is pray that the water from the street will shut itself off or else your house will float to America."

I spit the words out so fast I can barely hear myself say them. She looks at me as though she knows I'm a lying fool. But there's more. She sits and puts her face into her hands. Jesus. I wait a bit for a word or something that don't come.

"Look…uh, look, what I'll do is see what's in the street. See if I can find some turnoff."

When she still doesn't speak, I walk out and start looking. I've only had something like this once before, but the owner knew where the shutoff was and had it off before I even got there. The vicar, Reverend Wickford, is not that kind of man. He's too busy trying to say "work and pray" a million different ways. Ahhh. A metal plate on the far side of the street. I pry it over and see six shutoffs. Which is which? I wrench the first one and walk back behind the vicarage. The water's still bubbling out. I get it right the third time. After the water goes down, when it's only a mud hole, I wash off the pipe to see. It's a gash the size of a penny. What was the old beggar using to dig his dead cat hole? A bloody pick-ax? I'm thinking I can clamp it and hope it'll hold. When it's done, I turn it on. It's holding good.

"It's done," I call into the house from the garden door. The sun's going fast. Another afternoon murdered. It seems this job took minutes not hours. Or maybe that's what happens when days are a blur. The tools are packed into my box and I give the bloody pipe in its mud hole one more look.

"So it's done then," she says from behind.

"Right," I say to the hole.

"And what do we owe?"

"Lowden will give a bill. He's got to do something."

I look at her now. A good long look and she don't mind. She knows I'm looking. Her hair's out of its bun. Long, brown and straight. One pink ear shows. Her green eyes are wet and red.

"Well, Miss, sorry I was rude."

I pick up the box and start around to the side of the house and the street.

"May I…would you like a cuppa before you leave?"

No miss, I'm thinking. My head is full of Ronnie Manchester and Molly. Poor me. I don't want your fucking father's tea.

"I would like a cuppa, Miss. If it's no bother."

We're quiet while she steams water and pours it over the black leaves. We take it there, in the kitchen. I'm dirty with mud, and my face is marked black by the Gogartys, but she don't ask.

"My name is Dorothy," she says, watching me put a mountain of sugar and an ocean of milk into my little cup. The thing feels like an eggshell.

"I'm Shoe Horn."

She nods and sips.

"Ronnie says that Shoe Horn threw him off the Walney Bridge."

"He jumped."

"Jumped?"

"That's what they do when they got to pay up. They'll always jump if they can."

"They?"

"Guys like Ronnie."

She looks at her cup and goes quiet. I should too. I should finish it and shut my mug. But I'm Shoe Horn and I'm not the guy I wished I was.

"He jumped and I ran to the beach and pulled him out. It's true. He's a beggar, Ronnie is. But you've seen him and listened to him, so you know."

That's made her a little angry.

"He's a plumber. He's not an apprentice."

"It's true, he is. And I haven't heard anyone speak against his work, so I suppose he's good. That's only plumbing though, and it's a bigger world that needs getting…acquainted with," as Dr. James told me and I think I understood. But I like the word. Acquainted. She gets a frown up over it.

"What a curious thing to say."

"You know, Miss, because I'm an apprentice doesn't mean I ain't a good plumber. I mean, there's more right?"

"Oh yes. I could *sink* into my books."

"Well Miss," I say, "I read a book every single night. I haven't missed reading a book since, well almost five years now."

That's no lie, and Pecos Bill will back me on it. Babe the Blue Ox, too.

"Ronnie has told me he reads, too. When I ask him what, he tells me he has forgotten."

I laugh. She wants to too but fights it. Her eyes can't lie though.

"Well Miss, you can ask me and I won't have forgotten. I promise you that."

"I believe you."

Why, I want to ask her? I'm a lying dog and more. I asked Molly to bring Bobby to the hotel tonight because I'd be late. I imagine her walking slowly back to the hotel, Bobby proudly marching ahead. I can even hear Blacky barking to his horns and drum. No, don't believe me.

"Thank you then, Miss."

"Dorothy."

"And you can call me Shoe."

"But what's your real name?"

"That's it."

"I mean…"

"Well…I guess I was called Albert. But that's not my real name. My real name is Shoe."

I'd a soon as be named for that mud hole I spent the afternoon in than carry Mr. Horn's name the way I carry the bones he's broken. Christ but my days are as if they have happened to some other poor fool and I have just watched him with pity.

"So…you and Ronnie are to be married I heard. Heard it from his mum. She's a nice lady. She is."

Dorothy gets red and looks away.

"I met him in the park. The one here, on Walney," she says. "Things have happened quickly."

"That's how most things happen," I say wisely, "That is, to those I have been…acquainted with."

She nods, stands slowly and goes to the sink. She knows I'm watching things move on her. The kitchen is full of her now and it smells of Mummy's clean linens on a line, drying in the buttery sun. Yes. That's Dorothy. On a line in the sun. It's time to leave. I know it and she surely does too.

"My father's up at one of the lakes," she says looking above the sink and out a window to the garden. "He likes to write his sermons in a rowboat. He says the gentle splash of oars inspires him."

He's a fool. I've seen him thinking at his desk in the church while I reamed his bloody pipes. Smoking a silly pipe and talking to himself. Good. A rowboat's what he needs.

"Is your mum with him?"

"My mother is in a hospital. Father and I pray for her daily. She…she hears voices."

A nut, I'm thinking. Well, me too, though I haven't seen Phil for most of the day and it's just as well.

I stand and she turns.

"I'm nineteen," she says with a half smile.

I'm seventeen. I don't know a Goddamn thing.

"I'm nineteen, too."

I step to her and put both my hands onto her waist. She's not surprised. Yes, I don't know a thing. She leans against me, kisses my neck, my jaw, my lips. She's muddy with me and don't care. Dorothy takes my hand now, and leads me up the stairs to a large bedroom. Pipe tobacco and French water and lemons swirl together.

"This is my father's bed," she says working her buttons.

Father's bed? And the sun sinking. And the Great Bitch waiting. No one has to tell me that I should lace back up my boots, grab
my bloody box and run. But her dress is open now and she's full
and beautiful. Father's bed? Hell…

"I don't know if I'll marry Ronnie. I don't know," she says at
the door.

I've got the box and I'm ready to go.

"I liked the way you kept your eyes open when we made love."

Made love? You can make love? Her dress is only half buttoned. Her hair is like she's been on the beach in the rain.

"It was very romantic, Shoe. Did you feel how romantic we
were together?"

Dorothy Wickford screamed her father's name. Just threw
her head back at her moment upstairs and screamed the old fool's
name. Romantic? Jesus!

"Yes Dorothy. It was very romantic."

She sighed and opened the door for me. I checked my pocket
watch. If I stepped out, Bobby would only have been at his lookout
an hour or so. I hope Molly has fed him. Did I tell her he likes lots
of butter on his bread? He'll tell her, maybe. Phil steps up with a
shake of his head and walks with me. The fog has gone, blown away
by a cool breeze. The night is clear. Phil shakes his head again.

"Look," I say, without looking at him, "If something happens
and a guy knew it wasn't a good idea for it to happen, after a bit it's
like it never really happened. That's my idea. So nothing happened."

The bridge with the moon hanging over it is like one of Bobby's drawings. I stop and light one and look at it. The Barrow
seems beautifully clean in the distance. Houses short and square
rising in order up the hills to the parks and churches. But I hate
it. I hate it so. Mr. Horn and Lowden, the Gogartys and the rest.
The Barrow does the living, not you. Phil watches with me. I
point across the bridge.

"It looks clean."

He looks at me. Shoe Horn, fool and liar and apprentice.

"It's not clean."

"It's true what you say," she rasps from the place Phil stood.

The Great Bitch is an outline against the moon. She crinkles even standing perfectly still. The yellow eyes hold me. I cannot speak.

"The world is not the unsullied thing we wished it to be when we were wishing."

She steps closer. Why can't I feel my legs? Why can't I take my eyes off its dark and horrible face?

"But I am much, much older than young Mr. Horn and he should still wish. If…he wishes. Isn't it extraordinary how your sweet brother…how they all make the world cleaner, moving through it with lives and thoughts pristine? I have watched you. Are you clean too, Mr. Horn? Can anyone but them be so? I see the others. Ones I took small and hard. Ones long and thin. Some with hair of gossamer, some with none. Mothers muttering prayers or curses. Fathers walking, waiting…or running, running."

I can feel her so close to my face the words pinch my cheeks.

"They have sealed me in shadows with their songs…But, I can do the necessary errands in darkness. I can finish what's begun."

I open my mouth. Nothing comes.

"We need to speak…of Bobby."

Bobby. Yes. That's it. It's what I've always known. Mummy too. It's Bobby the thing wants.

"I…take care of him."

Now I feel my legs and step back. Finish what she's begun? It's true. It's all true.

"You can't have him!" I scream and even the gulls go quiet in the night. I hear my voice hit the metal on the bridge and fall back onto me. I'm running toward it and shout it back at her once more.

"You can't have him!"

18

Bobby visits a school and
Blacky visits his friends

"Where's...where's Blacky?" Bobby wonders, as we walk. He missed him at breakfast but didn't say anything.

"C'mon Bobby, we've got business at ten," I say.

He smiles at that.

"We...we...we got business."

"Right."

"On...on...you said...Quince Island."

"Twice right."

We walk across the street and along the channel. He's not marching he's thinking. Me too.

"It's...it's not...not a real island...is it?"

"Why Bobby Horn, you know everything."

"No...no I...don't."

He runs ahead and chases some gulls strolling the walkway. He makes growls and they flutter up to the sky. He watches them while I catch up.

"Do...do you...do you think Blacky's visiting his friends?"

No Bobby. Ahh Christ no.

"Maybe that's it. Blacky and his friends."

When he fell asleep last night, I took my smoke outside. The damn house is stuffed in the smell of hot lead from the shop next door. I've left him before so each time is getting easier. I walk to Blin's Pub by the water, have a pint, smoke a bit, even see Ronnie Manchester with his cronies. Dorothy's too good for that dog even if she does shout her father's name in that tobacco bed of his. I'd like to tell him that, but he's not looking at me and I don't care. I have another pint and a bit of whiskey and smoke one home to Mr. Horn's cave. The door's open, I can see it from the lamp at the end of the alley. Mr. Horn, home from training his boy, in his crazy stout-soaked brain. Christ. Well, I'm thinking at least the bastard can't give me a sleeping whack. My mug hurts to the touch as it is. The kitchen is lit up so maybe I'm not so lucky after all. I hear water and muttering. Mr. Horn's at the sink cleaning something. I sit and watch the bastard. He might know I'm there, but he don't turn around. His black coat hangs on bony shoulders. His head seems large from behind but that's because it sits on a neck so thin it's like a pink twig. He's shaking, all of him, shaking. The thing he's working clings and clangs in the sink. He speaks in that high squeak without turning.

"And how's my boy, this evening?" he slobbers quietly.

I don't say a thing. There's nothing to say. I am what I am. A dog. An apprentice. A liar.

"Mr. Lowden has told me that a certain Mr. Strand has given you a certain sum. For work well done, he said."

I light one. Money. I've hidden what I got. For me and Bobby. I know Mr. Horn has been looking. Now he's given up and begging. He turns to me, drying his hands. He's never more disgusting than when he's pretending to be temperate and kind.

"Well that's excellent. Good fellow, Strand. Played rugby with him in the park before he got unlucky enough to make a great success of himself. Money and more money. It's all those buggers can think of. But there are other things in life that a man should be acquainted with."

He pauses and folds the cloth as if I'm waiting. Acquainted?

"Mr. Lowden, your employer, has told me that, with the talk that's about of the match, the kitty could rise to seventy-five, even a hundred pounds. They'll be coming from everywhere to watch you defeat the beast."

He's excited now, pulls out a chair, sits across from me. I light one and watch him, swallowed as he is by the chair.

"So here's the approach we'll use," he says, wringing his veiny hands. "You'll turn over to me what you've got squirreled away and I'll place the wager with Lowden. We'll divide those winnings and the prize money per our apprentice agreement."

I look at him. He's bloody serious. He visits Lowden every fortnight for most of what's due me for plumbing and drinks it up. I can't speak. My father.

"Well," he's nodding and smiling. "It's settled then. Let's shake on it."

He holds his trembling hand out and all I can do is stare at the thing.

"By Christ you will do as I say!" he shouts, banging on the table. I smoke and watch. Just because it's my life doesn't mean I have to live it. I'm as dead as Mummy to cries and threats. Suddenly I'm old. I'm not seventeen at all. My heart says I'm a hundred.

"You will stand up, you bloody fool, and you will get Strand's money and the rest. It's for…your own good."

I don't move. It's like a dream. A silly dream and I'm inside it.

"Stand up now, for the love of Christ, or by God you'll get what the filthy thing of his got."

I look at him. What did I hear?

"What?"

"Get the money. I won't ask again."

"What filthy thing?"

He straightens his back as well as he can. I can see through his chest to the wall, or think I can. I ask it again.

"What filthy thing?"

"You bloody well know."

Now I come back to the room and myself. What's that on the cuff of his sleeve, peeking out from beneath his coat?

"What's that? What's that on your cuff?" I ask him quietly and slowly.

I stand now and walk to the sink. At the bottom is Mummy's long kitchen knife that curves at the end. A scrub brush lies next to it. Black-red spots have splashed on the white sides of the sink. One spot is lying on Mummy's faded flower curtain. I look again at the spots on his cuff.

"Get the…get the money…" he says with nothing behind it.

I run to Bobby's room and open the door. He's still sleeping, a smile on his face.

"Blacky?" I whisper and listen.

Suddenly Bobby is the dog and the dog is Bobby. Is Blacky with him in his dream of Mummy and her elm? Of kites and beef and slabs of her sweet butter on his bread. I shake my hands and my shoulders. I need all of Shoe Horn now. All his welts and bruises, all his lies. I turn and Phil is in the doorway. He looks at the hall floor and I step out and follow the ghost's eyes. The black-red spots spread across the wood toward the back and Mummy's overgrown garden outside. I close Bobby's door moving on old man legs, following the spots.

"Blacky," I whisper again.

I take a lamp, light it, step out into the garden.

"Blacky…Blacky."

My eyes are closed tight, adjusting to the night lamp with its orange glow. When they're open I see the spots on the slate path to the privy.

"Blacky? Where are you Blacky? It's Shoe. C'mon now, Shoe ain't gonna hurt you."

There's more spots on the privy door. I open it. The dark spots are splashes now on the privy floor.

"Blacky," I call like a fool, for there's nothing in the small room but flies.

"Mummy," I whimper.

The seat lid is closed against the smell of our waste. A spray of the awful color shows itself in a line of dots across it. I stare at the wooden lid; the old grain looks like a smile in the light of the lamp. A twisted and cruel smile. This night I truly believe the privy lid laughs at me. I reach out and raise it up. Can I move the lamp slower? It's as if some great hand is holding it from a dangle over the seat hole. When its orange glow is there, my head moves after it. The light spreads down into Horn shit and piss, and Blacky too, on his back, mouth open forever in a last bark. I stagger and catch myself. Outside, against the brick wall, Mummy's tools lay where she left them. I take her hoe and fish the sweet thing out.

"Oh Jesus, Blacky." I say to the night.

I lay him on some ivy and hoe a deep hole under it. When he's lying in it, I try to think of a prayer, something, to be said for this black thing that understood Bobby and the others. But nothing comes. Nothing. The dirt seals him in a hole under ivy.

Phil has not come into the garden. He watches from the door. Behind him I hear Mr. Horn in my room, searching for all I've got. Now I know he's taken enough.

"No more promises, Mummy."

His sounds are louder with each step. His grunts and swears. My bed's been turned. Both of my pants have been thrown on the floor, the pockets inside out. He steps up to me shaking with rage.

"Give me…give me your money, you bastard."

I punch him hard in the face. He's too stunned to scream. He crawls to a corner of the room. I walk into the kitchen for the knife. When he sees it in my hand, he makes a sound like a baby makes when its stomach is empty.

"I want to kill you."

"No…"

"I want to kill you and shove your filthy murdering ass down the privy with the shit, where you belong."

"No…no…you, you promised your mother…"

I go across the room and kick his knee, then his shoulder. He's weeping now. Weeping like the fucking baby he is. I pull him from my room by his hair and into the alley. I raise him to his shaking feet. Slap him hard, slap him again. I drive his back against the sooty wall.

"Look at me."

He shakes his head, still crying and gasping.

"Look at me."

He stops his head and looks. Blood drips from his nose and lips. Tears and panic fill his red beggar's eyes. I point to the house.

"The place was Mummy's and now it's mine and Bobby's. Never come back. Never come back," I say with a hard backhand to help him understand.

I rush him like a bum from a pub, down the alley to the street lamp. I slap him once more, sending him off the curbing, half into the gutter.

"Live there. Live in the gutter. Live in the street. But never, never come back or I will take the knife you know so well and cut out your fucking heart."

His sobs and gasps follow me and Phil back down the alley. I can hear them still. Hear his half gurgle "please, please." His vinegar voice echoing here, in front of the school on Quince Island.

"C'mon lad," I say to Bobby who has stopped at the bottom of the school steps and squatted.

"I…I…I don't want to do…no…business."

"But it's *your* business too."

"What…what is it?"

"What's what?"

"This…this place."

I squat down with my brother and push his wild hair away from his eyes. I know he needs what's here, still the feeling churns inside me that I am giving, just giving my brother away to clear a path out of here for Shoe Horn.

"It's a school."

"A…a…school?"

"When I visited the place, everybody was running around this gymnasium, playing and laughing…"

"What's a…a…?"

"A gymnasium is a big room where you play."

"Like…like…Mrs. Bulmers' room?"

I squeeze his shoulder.

"You're a great good guy, Bobby Horn."

He stands with a smile.

"And…and you're…a great good guy, Shoe Horn."

It's Saturday but the rooms are full and the gymnasium is loud with jumping feet and voices. We climb to the second floor and Dr. James' office. He's coming down the corridor the other way and we arrive at the same time. We shake. I touch Bobby.

"Dr. James, this is my brother, Bobby Horn. Bobby this is Doctor James."

"You can call me Bill, Bobby."

Bobby smiles then thinks with his whole body.

"This…this…is a…school."

"Yes, it is. Would you like to sit in my office?"

Bobby nods and we follow him into his room of books and paper.

"What do you enjoy the most, Bobby? What do you like to do more than anything in the world?"

Bobby crinkles his face. Smiles.

"I…I like to…to march with…Blacky."

I should have killed my father. I should have.

"Show me. Show me how you march."

Bobby jumps up, stepping high to his drum sounds and his trumpet honks.

"I'm…I'm changing…the guards."

"Yes, I see that," the doctor says and damn if he doesn't get up and begin to march too with sounds of his own.

Bobby's not surprised. Why isn't the whole bloody world marching? He marches into the hall with Dr. James high stepping behind him. Janey, the girl from the other day, sees them from the end of the hall, opens her mouth and halts down to join their march. After a minute the doctor stops and laughs. Bobby and Janey stop too. Their laughter drowns out the feet from the gymnasium below. Janey hugs Bobby and they both hug Dr. James. The rules of order are as simple as his believing their marching is not just good but necessary.

"Would you like Janey to show you the rest of the school and our big field outside?"

"Can...can I...Shoe?"

"Sure."

Janey takes the most important thing in this whole bloody world by the hand and they halt to the stairs. We watch them until they're gone.

"No one, of course, understands why He made them as he did. But part of it must be the joy special people bring Him."

I nod. He leans against the wall, his arms folded, watching me closely.

"Victoria Bulmers thinks you're going to America."

I look at him, my mouth open a bit. He smiles.

"She's read your mind, hasn't she? Most of her charges do not have the facility to order their lives but Bobby has. I've just seen it and so has Mrs. Bulmers. Actually Mary mentioned it to me earlier this year when she placed the Packard girl and also young Ramsey Scott."

"Mary, sir?"

"Mary Corony. Do you know her? She certainly knows Bobby. She's even visited the Strands on his behalf. When we met earlier I couldn't place the name, but Mrs. Bulmers informs me Bobby Horn is the one."

"The Dropper…?" I mumble.

"Sorry?"

I'm cold, but is it fear or is it shame? Christ Jesus. Mary Corony?

"She an odd one, Mr. Horn, there's no doubt about it. Mrs. Bulmers tells me Mary had birthed half this town until some sort of rumor drove her into her house with the shades drawn. She only comes at night but…but it's astounding really, she *knows* who they are and where they are. She sees them falling and tries to catch them all."

Christ Jesus. Can The Dropper be The Catcher? I can't speak.

"Are you quite alright, Mr. Horn? You're pale as a cloud. Come sit down."

"I'm fine," I mumble, but follow him anyway back into his room.

Doctor James lights one and offers one to me. I wave him off, take my own out. Come on, Shoe Horn. You're here for Bobby. Worry about your own lies and foolishness later.

"Can my brother come here?"

"Everyone agrees it's the best thing. Would you like me to tell you what will happen? How we'll proceed helping Bobby discover his place in this world?"

You've come for Bobby, Shoe Horn. Bobby first.

"Yes, Doctor James, I want to know."

"How old is Bobby?"

"He's fifteen. He's sixteen April fourteenth."

"Mrs. Bulmers says he knows his numbers to one hundred. She says he can read a first primer."

He knows? He reads? What?

"More than likely you're surprised at that because while there's no question of Bobby's affliction and dependence upon you, some of the things that occur at, let's say, Victoria Hall, are in a way…in *their* way, personal and private."

I nod. I understand him. Maybe.

"Through play and repetition we will help him build upon his numbers and reading, until the purchasing of food or buying a cup of tea will not seem the immensely impossible things they must seem now. He'll be able to read street names, perhaps even enjoy stories in books for boys. And certain work, comforting in its repetition, is a real possibility."

I have read *Pecos Bill, The Great BIG Cowboy and Indian Book.* That is the only book I have ever read and I don't enjoy it. Not now. But work? Work for Bobby? A lunch pail and smile?

"We believe in repetition of life. Everything at our school is aimed to recreate the familiar. To set boundaries that the pupils can recognize and move within. Boundaries that they themselves can station for the world they will exist in. Even our play is a kind of order."

Dr. James puts a hand on my shoulder.

"When Bobby comes for his first day in this school, it will be the first day of his new life. He can no longer rely on his brother to do for him what he *must* do for himself. Once he's here, his life… whatever it shall become…is his."

He's clear. My brother can and will learn to live without me. But can I live without him?

"I understand doctor. Thank you…When would he…?"

"Go home and collect his things while he's with Janey. He'll cling and weep all day. They all do. The only order he knows will be gone. But after a day or two he'll begin to find a new structure. And it will be inside himself."

His small trunk has his clothes, his Cowboy and Indian book, the picture of Mummy with me and him on a wee boat. A picture, I remember, Mummy's own mum took one summer. A small box with a clip of her hair. I stop on the way back to the school for candy at Addy's father's and put it in the trunk as a surprise. She's nowhere and I'm glad, I think.

When I pass the gymnasium, Bobby calls my name and runs out, sweaty and happy and gasping. Janey's right behind him.

"We…we've been…we've been playing good," he shouts and puts his face where he always has, under my chin and squeezes hard. Janey, God bless her, squeezes him from behind. My Bobby Horn, held tight all around.

"Can…can I…can I play some…some more?"

"Sure."

"Thanks…Thanks, Shoe."

"Thanks, Shoe," Janey says too.

They run back and I continue up to Dr. James' room.

"His things," I say, holding the trunk.

"Just set it down," he says. He's writing something and seems miles away.

"What…what do I do?"

Doctor James looks up now.

"Come back in a fortnight."

"A fortnight?"

I'm standing there, the trunk still in my hand. Bobby Horn's trunk. His clothes. His pictures.

Doctor James puts his pen down and stands.

"Don't be afraid, Shoe."

We stare for a moment, then I put the trunk on the floor.

"Should I…do I tell him?"

"Come back in a fortnight. It's better if I explain it."

The place smells like chalk and the sea. Good smells. I look once more down to his trunk. A piece of rope holds it together. We don't have much.

"It's the right thing," I say.

The doctor smiles.

"It's the only thing."

19

The giant and the boy

She sleeps curled, half on me, some black hair in my mouth. It's still dark, but I should get Bobby ready for…No, it's been three days. At least today I remember while I'm still in bed. Yesterday I was up for half an hour before I stuck my head into his room and remembered. The day before, I made buttered bread for two. I slide under her leg, then down and off my bed. She makes a noise, turns and curls deeper into herself.

My money's in a can wedged under the sink. I pull it and empty the bills onto the kitchen table. Twenty two pounds. It's what I got. I'll need more. I told Lowden two days ago that Mr. Horn gets nothing for my apprenticeship. Nothing. I told the fucker that if I didn't receive the full amount, I'd quit. And I meant it. Mr. Horn came to the door begging, pretending he did not understand what has happened. I drove him down and out of the alley. My alley. He's dead to me. I hate him.

"I hate him so," I say to the money.

"Who?" she says in a wee voice, rubbing her eyes like a child.

"Molly, good morning," I say quietly.

I don't get up and she don't move from the door. After I finished up at Coyne's Brewery, reaming a clogged vat of ale, I tried to drink it all up. I even left my plumber's box with the brewery's watchman, having enough difficulty lugging myself through the streets. I light one and keep watching her. Finally she floats into the kitchen and sits across from me. I had stood outside the Channel Lane Hotel shouting her name.

"Molly Reilly! Jesus, Molly! Can you bloody hear me?"

I call again from the middle of the street, wobbling there, my hands on my hips. She doesn't come and I turn down to the sea. Near the shipyard I hear her running feet and voice at the same time.

"Shoe. What? What is it?"

I stagger but catch myself. Molly holds my arm in her two strong hands.

"I threaded my fucking reamer through a vat full of ale and still drank the filthy stuff."

She's turned me.

"Where?"

I point toward Ramsden and my alley off it. Half way there, I stop and grab her shoulder sloppily.

"I'm...I'm Shoe Horn...I'm known."

She takes my arm back. We turn down the alley. I stop again.

"Bobby's at a school. Bobby's at a school."

She looks at me, waiting for more.

"He was...he needs to be...there for a bit. It's the only thing. It's the only thing."

We go into my cave. I stand drunk in front of Molly Reilly. I can smell Bobby in the house and those smells drive my tears. I bury my face in my hands. She comes to me, and lays my head onto her small shoulders. I weep for a moment and then she's all I can smell. Her sweat and her rosewater. Is that coal in her curls? I push her down onto my bed. That was last night.

Now she's sitting across the table. She wears my blue shirt with Lowden Plumbers spelled on the back. I don't remember much. Her shouts though, her cries too. I was rough, I think, and wanted to sink into the little girl and be lost awhile. She yawns and a smile comes.

"I love it when you're behind me."

Now I smile.

"Yes?"

"I wish I could watch you go. I like being on top of you too."

I don't remember who was where. I'm on my bed and then I'm awake.

"Do you remember what you said when I was on top of you? Do you?"

What I said? No, I don't remember what I said or anything else for the love of Christ.

"Sure, I remember."

She gets up, comes around the table and kisses my mouth.

"You said, right before, you shouted, 'We're going to America.'"

I smile but think that Bobby is in the school. He's still mine even if I can only see him every fortnight. He's still mine even if they're teaching him to be his. I've got twenty two pounds. Where can I go with twenty two pounds?

"When?" she asks.

Molly has a serious look and speaks as if confessing something bad.

"I've got twenty-seven pounds and some. I've got a bit Da left with his note. I've got wages."

She's wide awake now and her cheeks spread redder with excitement. She sits on my lap. I'm always surprised at how slight she is. With her face into a pillow shouting out muffled orders and promises she might be bigger than me. When I don't say nothing, she looks at me hard and serious.

"And I'll work too, Shoe. I'll work harder than anyone you know. And we'll have babies and everything we ever wanted."

Molly pulls the shirt over her head.

"America," I say. And carry her back to my bed.

Lowden's shop is on Brimley Lane across from the Brimley
Auction Rooms and next to the seed store. It's five-thirty and the
lout's still not here. I left Molly sleeping, picked up my plumber's
box at the brewery and got here a half hour ago, sitting on the curb.
There's some sun coming up under the fog. This is the best time
in the Barrow because people can't spoil it. They're asleep mostly,
giving this part of the morning to the birds and the apprentices. It's
the only time when air has sugar in it. Sugar and sea. Mummy said,
"Sweet smells are the rewards of the early riser." I could have used
another bit of sleep though, the fucking ale has left my head filled
with bubbles and pins. A dog, bigger than Blacky, walks by slowly
in the middle of the street. The thing stops and looks at me.

"Good morning, Mr. Dog."

The thing smiles, it does, and teeth flash. The tail goes side to
side in a wag that nearly whops its ribs.

"Horn's the name," I say, "Shoe Horn."

"And he's a friend of mine," a bottomless voice whispers.

The dog and me turn to it at the same time. The smile goes
and the wag, too. The dog steps back but can't stop looking. And
if the mutt can wonder, well, he's wondering. The McAvy walks
down the middle of the street toward me. His cap sits square on
his head. The long hair still flat and falling. He's buttoned and
creased the way his mum would have him. Everything swirls in
my head but The McAvy. It would be like being confused by the
mountains or the sea.

"Good morning, Shoe."

"Good morning, McAvy."

He sits on the curb with me and holds his hand out to the dog.
The dog stares from across the street. The gulls that follow The

McAvy glide overhead pretending not to notice him. He is as big sitting as I am standing.

"I like the morning, Shoe. I like this time."

"Yes."

We don't smoke. The smells are too good and the air too clear for anything but being here. His clothes seem smaller. The dog slowly moves closer.

"I stopped sleeping last Christmas Eve," he says, to the dog as much as me. We both look at him.

"My mum had made a sweater for me. It didn't fit. That was when we knew it was coming again. The growing, I mean. I stopped sleeping. I don't know why."

The dog is a foot away from his outstretched hand, if it really is a hand.

"But I like walking at night and morning. I pretend I'm walking away."

The dog moves close enough to let the hand that could crush its head with two fingers, roll gently over it.

"Bobby?" he asks.

"He's at school. Not Victoria Hall."

He looking at me now.

"It's a special school on Quince Island. I can't see him for awhile. The doctor there says I must let Bobby learn to do for himself."

"He's a good lad."

"It's true."

I feel him thinking a bit, see long, beamy fingers scratch the crown of the dog.

"Yes," is all he says.

Lowden's truck pulls onto the curb and stops. The door opens but he's seen The McAvy sitting next to me and stays in the truck, pretending to be busy.

"Boston. Working coal on the *Madagascar* to cross over."

He stands and I do too.

"Then I'll just walk out into America."

His smile is far away and he follows it as the dog follows him. Before he turns the corner, he holds his arm up in a wave without turning. I wave to his back. Surely such a thing can see from behind. I watch The McAvy vanish, and the gulls floating after him.

"Well, lad, he's gone is he?" Lowden says getting out of his truck. "Look here, these are the announcements of the match. They'll be all over Barrow-in-Furness and into the countryside too. Looks like the two of you, don't you agree?"

The cardboard had a drawing of a giant in skins holding a club, growling at a small, neat young man holding a bible. It don't look like us, it looks like another lie. Above the time and date is written:

THE MONSTER and THE BOY

I give it back.

"Keep it for a souvenir."

I keep it out to him until he takes it, unlocks the shop door and we go in. The place is piled high with water closets new and used, sinks, pipes, tools. It's comfortable to be around the things that wait to be placed by me or guys like me. I always feel satisfied being in this room…until Lowden speaks. His voice can scrape the pride out of your heart.

"Alright then, let's see what we've got for Horn," he squeaks to the paper he holds. "There's the Bamford foundry on Keats Street… Let's begin there…some thing-a-ma-jig is acting up…then it's all homes. The Taylor's…"

"Aw Christ," I mumble.

Lowden looks at me. I look right back. What's that old Taylor woman done now? She's flushed a coat, lost a cat in her tub and stuffed a spoon down her bloody sink. He's reading again.

"Let's see…the Taylor's as I've mentioned…then across town to the Gogartys' for a kitchen sink that's…"

"What?" I say, "Where?"

Lowden knows them, the dirty bugger, and knows me too. But there's money to be made with sink troubles and he surely is not going to turn down money. Or do the filthy work himself.

"I'm sure you'll have no trouble Horn, and we wouldn't be very decent plumbers if we left them to struggle alone with the thing, would we."

Sure, they couldn't go to any of the other plumbers around, like the one across the street from their bloody house. Christ!

"There's more on the list," he says holding it out.

I'm already beat, just lugging my box to Bamford Foundry. Lowden's thing-a-majig is a pipe that's let go and scalded a bloke yesterday. The man who points it out to me says it went with a pop and took the shirt right off the poor bastard. Half of his skin too. It's still hissing and firing steam.

"Why ain't it off?"

"What?"

"The bloody steam. Why ain't it shut off?"

"Well, I suppose it ain't off because no one shut the bloody thing off."

Jesus, Mary and Joseph.

It's past one before I'm kneeling next to poor Mrs. Taylor. I don't ask why or how she managed to get her arm into the water closet bowl, but she's snaked it in like a reamer until it's wedged tight. Mr. Taylor's sitting on the tub's edge, smoking and talking.

"...and so I simply stood toe to toe with my competitor and uttered the phrases I would become famous for in the Wood Pulp Company. I looked straight into his eyes..."

"Oooo," Mrs. Taylor puffed out when I tried giving her forearm a bit of a wiggle.

"Did that hurt, Mrs. Taylor?"

"It tickled," the old girl said with a smile.

Mr. Taylor cleared his throat.

"...so I've got him stared down, this far from his cruel face and I say, 'I hate to disillusion you, my good fellow, but it is the

Wood Pulp Company of Barrow-in-Furness that truly produces the finest stationary in England and its environ.' Well, ho ho, the poor fool had been crushed. Couldn't say a word. Congratulations flowed like fine champagne."

"Mr. Taylor, could you pass me some soap?" He grabs it off the sink and hands it to me.

"Sometimes a man must stand for his beliefs, even if it might be an unpopular stand. You have to consider 1905 when I tell you they were perilous times for the Wood Pulp Company in particular and fine paper stationary in general. Linen stationary! Ha! And I said it, chest out and proud."

I've got the soap thick on my hands so the water in the bowl won't wash it off for a bit. I'm working it a finger at a time over the crazy woman's wrist. I'm thinking Bobby wouldn't even have thought of doing what she's done.

"Who's Bobby?" she asks with a sad smile.

There it is again. Talking my thoughts out without knowing it.

"My brother…wiggle your wrist, Mrs.…wriggle…"

It takes me ten tries with the soap and one with a handful of grease to rescue her and enough time for Mr. Taylor to bring me all the way up to 1917 when he told Lord Beaverly, face to face, man to man, that his purchase of the Wood Pulp Company's Letter Paper Excelsior was not surprising, considering how extraordinary the Beaverly Line had always conducted themselves. When I leave I feel half my brain remains on the bathroom floor.

It's past four. I light one, take Lowden's paper out of my pocket and try to see my way out of doing the Gogartys'. I stare at the list of sinks clogged with rotten meat, water closets overflowing with shit, intakes and outtakes all ripe for reaming. So why do I feel I must show at the filthy mick's cave? Phil is waiting on a corner and walks with me. The sun is low and hot. The clouds have burned away. It's a good day for what I know I must do, but only after I do the terrible sink of the Gogartys'.

I knock loud and wait. I hear the stairs. Liz looks at me with flat black Gogarty eyes. My lips aren't fat anymore and the swollen ear is almost regular, but my eyes are bruised from the beating and the back of my head still throbs from her stick.

"Good afternoon, Liz."

"Is it? I haven't been out."

"I've come about your sink."

There's something reddish about the Gogarty men, Tom and the rest, but Liz is as white as Mummy's linen tablecloth. It makes her long black hair seem blacker. Blacker even than Molly's. When she speaks you can't help but notice how wide her mouth is.

"Well, the sink's clogged, it's true." she says, still not inviting me in.

There's nothing to say and nothing to do. I look at Phil, then back at Liz.

"Look, there's a mick plumber right over there," I say pointing. I'm not angry. I'm tired.

She snorts and steps aside.

"It's the kitchen sink."

I squat and look at the connections for where and how I'll get in. I lay out the tools I need and she watches from the door. After my sleeves are rolled, I stand.

"Look Liz, I've got to lie on my back to get hold of the parts that need working."

She watches me. What's that I smell in the house of Gogartys? It's olive soap and I can smell it on her white skin from across the room.

"See Liz, I want to make sure I won't be stomped."

"Stomped?" she says with another snort.

I want to be serious but I feel a smile coming. "Stomped," I say again.

She pushes off the door, crosses the kitchen to the parlor saying, "I'm the only one home and as much as I'd like to, I promise I won't stomp you."

It's a twenty minute job. I'm wrenching the parts back in place after the ream when she kneels next to me and lets her head under the sink, next to mine.

"Will it work?" she asks me.

"It will."

It's olive soap and something else. Lemons for the love of Christ. Liz Gogarty is olives and lemons.

"I'm sorry about the stick."

I stop wrenching and look at her face so close to me and so beautiful too. She gets a little smile or a sneer, I can't tell.

"I mean to say, I'm sorry I hit you, but I'm glad I did too."

"You got me good," I say with a laugh.

"How old are you?"

Her breath is warm, almost hot.

"I'm twenty."

"You're seventeen."

"Then why'd you ask?"

She looks at me curiously.

"I wondered if you'd lie."

"Well, I did. I do."

"I'm twenty five."

She moves her head closer to me. Her breath is hotter. Her smell fills my nose.

"Did you give it a good reaming, Shoe?"

Christ Jesus.

"I did."

Now there's something on her face I've never seen.

"Did you ream it hard?"

"Yes, Liz. I did."

Her face goes flat again.

"C'mon then, you bastard. We haven't much time."

* * *

Stars twinkle. You're lucky to see them clear six or seven times a year. A falling star, sparking yellow and gold, sprays itself across the night. I heard Rogers say, out of the blue, that each star was bigger than the sun. I should have told him he's a fool. Nothing's bigger than the sun, you fucking shiny African who might be a Scot. But I let him think he knows because I like him. But he don't know. He can't. They're *stars* for the love of Christ. They're but a twinkle over the water. Over the great ass Shoe Horn and his pile of lies, struggling to the alley with all of Lowden's tools.

I lay the box by the door and walk back out. Because nobody's around I sing "Molly Malone" for Bobby, only I sing it to the empty night, the bully boy's not in me, not at all. I wish he was though, because that guy's never sorry. His nerve is something to brush against. Mummy called it impertinence. Maybe. But I'm sliding and I'm changing. I stop and smoke one all the way down on my side of the bridge. I have lived my life in this bloody place and never seen Walney so fucking clear. The park by her side of the bridge is glowing in the moon. The cobblestones lay flat and dry, like a drawing of a road. A wide level picture leading somewhere. But where? If she slinks in shadow, where must I look? All the world spins in my head.

Phil is waiting for me on Walney. I don't look at him or say anything because he's still a Gogarty and wouldn't understand that if something happens, even if you didn't want it to happen or even expect it to happen, then nothing really happened. It's the way liars look at the world and I think Liz believed the same thing, in between her threats and cries. So I'm clean again. Or as clean as I can be.

I walk the streets looking for a shadow, listening for a crinkle. The stars and the moon are vanishing in fog now. The streets get wet and slippery until you feel with each step you're falling back onto yourself. The bridge is ahead of us so we've come a circle without even knowing it. I'll come back tomorrow. I'll keep coming until it's settled and *that* ain't a lie. Phil stays on Walney, watching until I get to the middle of the bridge. I turn to him.

"Look, sometimes things that happen didn't really happen. Do you understand me, Phil?"

But he's gone as quick as he came. And what would he care about the lies I tell myself anyway? I liked it better when Bobby filled my time. Now I think about Shoe Horn and he's not a guy to think too hard on.

Light's coming from the house, and I smile to think of Molly, home from the hotel, maybe fixing a cuppa for me and her. But it's the girl smells she fills the place with that's got me stepping faster, feeling clean. Yes. Clean and good too. I pop in the door, turn to Mummy's kitchen and stop. Addy Augarde and Molly Reilly at the table with cups filled. They look at me, expected and not. Addy's eyes shine wet and red. Molly's burn wide and hot. I have always fallen back on Bobby, but Bobby's gone. I am that dog whose tail wags past his nose.

"I'm not a dog," I lie to them.

"There," I say, pointing to a corner, "There's where Mr. Horn took my front teeth when I was twelve…and that's my black old blood on the wall by the stove. Mummy saw it. Mummy knew, but that's why there was Shoe Horn. To stand and have his face changed by his father. To have it flattened and swollen and changed."

It's as if I'm alone in the room saying the things I need to hear.

"He would say, 'What are you looking at?' He would say, 'What are you thinking?' And my mummy would say, 'You've upset your father.' There." I point to the glass by the sink. "My head through it, glass in my eyes, lips, and Mummy shouting, 'Stop upsetting your father.' "

I look and remember. And the next morning while the filthy bastard slept and Mummy hummed a tune over her stove, I went to Mr. Connor's, bought a pane, and put it back in. On the table, between Molly and Addy, is Lowden's announcement. The giant in skins, the boy clutching the bible. Another great lie, only this time on the table. I tremble and lock my fists.

"Bobby Horn!" I hear myself howl. "Bobby Horn!"

20

Mr. Rogers sees
a naked giant

His head is bowed and scabby and he shakes it slowly side to side without so much as a sound. His thin, dirty fingers open and close but not in a fist. There will be no more fists now that no one stands between him and the bloody world. Past his shoulder the sun begins to burn the fog. I would like to reach into my box for the big two hander and take him off the doorstep with it. What I know is hard and true. Mummy's arm through his, strolling fast to the church he helped mason. He'd stroke the bricks and mortar each time as if it were a lovely girl. There were kites to fly and balls to kick, stories too. He would sit on my bed, his breath only beginning the sharp stout, and tell me how Luigi, the great dago stonecutter, made a kite of marble and flew it up to the clouds. And I would fall asleep to their soft voices in the kitchen or Mummy's singing or the sad, clean pipe of his coronet, played with a towel stuffed inside. Then the hand reaching into his neat tight vest and rolling a first cigarette across the kitchen table. Teaching how it's held, how it's lit, how smoke is held deep and let out through the mouth and nose. I didn't like it until I was ten. Until I understood something about the smokes and always looked at the thing after a puff or two.

When did I wake to his growls and curses and slurs? When did I see him look at his pale of stout like a lover, licking his lips after each deep slosh? I was back from the park with Bobby. I was twelve and Bobby was Bobby. Mummy's nose was bleeding at the sink. Was she crying? He walks to us and stops. The punch drove me against the wall, the second to the floor. The kick in my heart put blood and teeth out of my mouth and he was gone. Gone to the pub. Gone from the world. Bobby ran to Mummy, weeping at her sink. She held him close, turned that sweet fat face to me and said, "You've upset your father."

I step aside and after a long moment he moves, a stranger, into the house and to the big room where he stands staring at what was his.

"I'll smoke in the kitchen now, then I'm to my work. Don't come in while I'm here. Ever. Don't be here when I come back. Ever."

I close the door behind me, have my smoke and tea, then lug the fucking box to the shipbreak yard. At the yard house is the announcement of the match. Inside, Charlie Burt is putting his things in a sack, talking to himself. His eyes are red with great black tea bags of skin under them. I watch him a moment, scooping things off the top of a desk.

"They've sacked me, Horn."

I nod. He waves a piece of paper at me.

"I come to the yard house and this was on my chair. Get out, it says. Serve the King, give the arm and get out."

He looks at me as if I might have something to say. Well, I don't. I don't care about Charlie Burt. I don't care about any of them. I'm dry as a desert.

"Say something you bastard!"

"I'm plumbing the shipbreak with Mr. Rogers, but I wasn't told where."

This is what keeps Charlie Burt alive, to know something you don't. He smiles and looks me up and down.

"Look at you."

"Charlie, tell me where Rogers is."

"I said, look at you. A lout. A fool. A bloody apprentice to a fool. I could smell you when you opened the door. Did you know that, Horn?"

He's talked himself around the corner of the desk. Yesterday, last week, a man would say these things and I would feel violence spread through me like blood. Now I'm only tired. Now I have the memory of anger, nothing more.

"Charlie…"

"Mister," he demands. *"Mister* Burt."

I don't care what he thinks. I'm wondering if Bobby's scoring goals with people like him, who knows what he does in their bones.

"Where would Mr. Rogers be, Mister Burt?"

His smile has become a sneer. I feel something but don't want to. I want to keep Bobby's fat face in my head, if I can keep anything.

"That's better, Horn. A man doesn't go to war and give the arm to have some bloody apprentice, some bloody half-worker take first name liberties. I've a good mind to give you a beating you'll not forget."

I put the box down. Now I do feel something and it's spreading through me fast. Stop it Charlie.

"Yes. I say what you need is a lesson on how to respect your betters."

The nose bleeder sends Charlie back to the desk. As he falls his one arm sweep his things off, spraying them about the room with his small treasures.

"Where would I find Mr. Rogers, Mr. Burt?"

He's pushed himself against the wall, holding his bleeding nose.

"I've got…I've got the one arm, you bastard!"

I start over to him.

"…He's in the twelve block basement! He's in the twelve block basement!"

I step back to my box.

"Thank you, Mr. Burt."

There's another announcement of the match wired to the gate, and another on the first block building. Everywhere I look The McAvy in skins and me with a bible. Some men nod and smile. No one has smiled before. The monster and the boy. I pretend I don't see them and turn up to twelve block.

"What's it?" I say stepping down into the basement. Mr. Rogers has got a furnace door open and it's not cold or damp like everywhere else. He's got a teapot and cups on a table. Looks like a plateful of scones too.

"Tea time, is what."

He pours two cups and points to a chair.

"These scones are the closest this bloody town has to the real ones. It's the raisins, laddie. If they're not soaked first in warm milk, they're like wee pebbles for breakfast. Put some butter on too."

We load our cups with milk and sugar and a little tea also. The scones are warm and the butter melts nicely. We eat in the quiet. Mr. Rogers and me are good in the quiet, not worrying why the other ain't speaking or what he's thinking. He laughs to himself.

"What?"

"There's no plumbing problem today."

"No?"

"I told the company I need something done and they called Lowden. So they'll be paying you for having tea with the bloody African from the highlands."

His eyes grow serious.

"I was coming to work two days ago. It was maybe four in the morning, but I don't have no watch so I couldn't be sure. It was when I walked toward the Auction Rooms on Kale Street. They keep their own big lamp burning in front of the place at night. It glows, that's all. I see something or think I do. Something I've seen before but had trouble fitting it all inside my old noggin. I stayed out of the light and moved closer to the glow."

Mr. Rogers puts a piece of scone into his mouth chewing in thought. After a wash down with the tea, he looks at me.

"It was the great thing…your friend. His clothes were in a pile on the walk. He was as naked as a baby, except he's no baby. I stood in the shadow and watched him throw punch after punch at the air. Sweat was coming off his head like a waterfall. And for the love of Christ, this man who seemed as tall as the lamp, danced and punched as quick as a cat…or quicker. He was still cutting the air, high and low, when I moved on. I could think of nothing else all bloody day. I couldn't work. That night I couldn't sleep."

I had told Bobby sometimes words fall onto the floor when you don't listen. Sometimes they float over your head, too, and if you look up you can see them. We both gaze over each other's head.

"And his dance was in anger," he finally adds. The basement engines cut into our quiet. I stand and nod, pick up my box and walk back into the chilly morning. At the gate, I squat against the wall and take the list from my pocket that that loafer Lowden handed me last night. I haven't looked at it. First on the list are his best customers, by Christ, Mr. and Mrs. Bloody Christ Taylor! What's the old girl done now? The hand in the bowl cannot be topped. After that, the firehouse. They're all a bunch of micks, so, of course, everything's plugged or leaking or overflowing. I walk past the Channel Lane Hotel. I'm early on the rounds thanks to Mr. Rogers and maybe it would be nice to sit and smoke a couple down on the steps.

Molly didn't cry as Addy had, at least not so's I could see. They got up and left the house together. Addy leaning into Molly who patted her back as if she were a hurt child. That night I missed reading to Bobby Horn. I missed Pecos Pete and Paul Bunyan too. It's easier to lasso the stars than make some lies seem not like lies at all. Phil sits next to me now.

"You see what it is, Phil? It's not that some things that happen, don't happen. It's that if they happen and you don't have the *slightest* why they're happening, then…aw for shit's sake, Phil. Nothing happened. Nothing ever happened."

"No?" she says above me.

I turn and look up. She's in her coal apron again, the dirty cloth over her hair. When I stand at the foot of the stairs, she moves closer to the lip of the porch so my head must tilt up to see her eyes.

"How's Bobby?"

"I don't know. He's at the special school on Quince Island. I can't…they don't let me see him but each fortnight…I haven't seen him yet."

Her face shows nothing.

"It's…it's the only…He's there so he won't need me…so much, I mean…"

"I thought it was you and me. I thought it was something we didn't have to say, it was just there like the birds and the sea. I dreamed a whole life, you know."

I don't know, Molly. I don't know a fucking thing.

"I know," I say.

She gives a laugh on that.

"No you don't, Shoe Horn. You don't know a fucking thing."

She starts off, the coal apron pressing her down.

"Molly…"

"My mum run off, my da run off and now you've run off."

"I haven't."

Molly Reilly turns and looks me up and down like she's trying to remember something.

"Oh, Shoe," she says in a whisper, and goes back into the hotel.

After a bit of thinking but getting nowhere with it, I pick up my box and walk down to the Taylor's, where the old girl sits wringing hands at her kitchen table. The laundry tub is plugged, water laps at the sides and over them. I've got a reamer down but it ain't doing it. Mr. Taylor is standing over me, the fingers of each hand tucked into his vest's pockets.

"…and, of course, as I was recently disclosing to my dear wife that not only did the Wood Pulp Company's heavy off-white writing paper demand a firm, fine hand, it also required an excellence of manual folding, so that the edges possessed an order, a uniformity if you will, when one removed the correspondence, displaying a certain harmonious camaraderie with the elements. How did I put it my dear? If I may quote myself: 'A fine fold is as necessary as the communication that lies within the paper.' But the days are behind us young man, when men like me strode the world declaiming an excellence not easily found in today's layabout products. Hugh Stillwickle, chief cutter at the firm, often recalls one particular admonition I hurled at an upstart from the newsprint division on the far corner of the Wood Pulp floor. Seems the scalawag believed paper was paper and let it be known to his admiring cronies. Well, young man, I…"

"Something's down here that ain't got give to it, Mr. Taylor. I'm going to have to cut and pull."

The Mrs. has come behind me as I put away the reamer and lay out my saw and cutter.

"Is it bad?"

I look up at her and there's the sad smile they all get. Mummy had it too. Is it only in the Barrow, I wonder?

"Something's stuck. I've got to cut and pull."

"Oh dear."

"And so I crossed the Wood Pulp Company floor, samples in my hand. Drew this close to the young Mr. Know-It-All, held out my samples and exclaimed…"

"It's a chicken down there, is what it is," she says.

"A chicken?"

"Yes, it was a scientific experiment. It's trial and error."

"Oh."

"I must be sure I can get rid of the parts when I eventually do Mr. Taylor in."

I look at her, but the smile has flattened into sorrow. Mr. Taylor packs and lights his pipe with great attention.

"...and so, as I said, I stand toe to toe with the infidel and exclaim: 'The Wood Pulp Company's paper *is* indeed a superior product and here is the proof of the pudding!' My samples told the rest. Many a young man in the newsprint division learned a thing or two that day I can assure you."

And there *was* a chicken down there. The old girl will need a cutter and saw for sure if she wants him in small pieces. I'd like to help her. When I've got it back on, I take a banger on the steps of Victoria Hall. It's a bright day and Mrs. Bulmers gets them outside. I wave when I see her and she comes and sits and both of us watch them go.

"Young Mr. Horn," she announces in her deep voice as she sits.

She's getting fatter I think, but still that beauty you can't describe. She must be about what Mummy would be. Older maybe.

"How are you? I mean, without Bobby? Is it hard?"

"Yes."

"It's the right thing to do," she says.

"It's the only thing to do."

We watch them. The wee blind one and the wee mongoloid stand still. They don't jump or run like the others. I can almost hear them wondering where Bobby is, where the black hairy thing that barks and kisses is. They were one of Bobby's jobs, lunch pail or no, and one he did perfect.

"The day after tomorrow," she says without taking her eyes off them, "That's when you have your match."

"Maybe."

"Maybe? The announcements are everywhere."

"I never said I would."

I light one and smoke a bit.

"He's very good with them," she says.

I look at her.

"The giant. The one in the skins in the announcement. Sometimes he comes by and helps me. He understands."

"The McAvy knows things, it's true."

"Once he pointed to the sky and the children looked up. It was filled with gulls. I'd never seen them over Victoria Hall."

"They follow him."

"He said that. He's the biggest thing I've ever seen."

"He's still growing."

"And you're going to fight him?"

It's hot when I get to the fire station. They're out in front telling lies about burning shops and flaming houses. Half of the buggers smell like beer and move like they're full of it. They couldn't put out my cigarette. Arthur sees me and pretends he doesn't. The announcement is nailed to the door. The monster and the boy. I go up to the first mick I see.

"I'm the plumber."

"Captain's water closet. Upstairs."

The door's closed. When I knock nobody answers, so I go in, find the water closet and give it a flush. The tank above the toilet leaks like a faucet until it quickly empties all over the floor. I call Lowden.

"I need a new reservoir at the fire station."

"I believe we have that in stock. Listen now, the Blackpool gang's coming down too. They're big betters. The winner's pot will be well over a hundred."

My mind sees The McAvy dancing and punching as Rogers told me. My brain aches front and back.

"Are you listening, Horn? The giant will be in for quite the surprise, won't he?"

"I'll wait for the reservoir in front."

Phil's sitting next to his cousin Arthur when I come out. I light one and Phil's the only one not smoking. Arthur'd shit himself if he could see he wasn't alone on his bench. Addy Augarde walks by with her nose in the air until she sees me. One of the mutt firemen meows like a cat. The others laugh dirtily.

"Hello, Shoe."

"Hello, Addy."

She looks at the station behind me.

"I'm here to fix a water closet," I say, then "Irish," to explain what went wrong with the plumbing.

"Molly's a nice one. And kind."

"Don't get too friendly with him, Missy," I hear Arthur laugh out behind me. "He's going to be killed by a bloody giant in two days."

He lets go a louder laugh and his cronies join him. I turn to see their laughter coming out of sneering lips.

"It's true, Arthur. Looks like I'm dead already."

They laugh harder.

"But look, to show that there's no hard feelings, I must tell you that a certain bloody giant has heard a rumor that you called him a coward. He came to my house and asked me if it's true. He's growing, you know. He's much bigger. He punched at the brick wall in my alley while he spoke. Some of the damn bricks broke and fell."

The McAvy would as soon bother a flea than this fat little man. But their laughter has stopped.

"I told him I didn't think Arthur would say such a thing, but he said he heard about it from his uncle, who heard it from one of your cousins."

Arthur's listening but his eyes are searching the street.

"He's coming for you, Arthur, and I wouldn't want to be near you when he finds you."

Now the others look up and down the street. Two of them walk into the station.

"I…I…never…"

The other two go inside and poor Arthur's alone. Now I look up and down the street.

"Did you feel that Arthur," I say in a serious whisper.

"Feel what?" he says standing.

"There. That. The ground starting to shake."

"Dear Christ, I can feel it…Horn, help me."

"I'll do what I can Arthur. But I never seen him crush bricks before. I never saw his fingernails as long as bear claws."

"Sweet Jesus," he says and runs into the station.

If Addy has questions, she don't ask them. She knows what all the girls know. How to stir me with a look. Or a word. Christ but she's a full one whose hair tumbles crazy over that creamy face. If I know Lowden, he'll take another hour.

"Want to…want to see the water closet I'm fixing in the Captain's place?"

"It's not a toilet?"

"No Addy. It's a water closet."

She follows me up the stairs and into the place. The firemen are all loafing by their pumpers and if they notice her, they notice quietly. I don't know why but I actually point to the water closet.

"It's the reservoir, Addy. It's cracked the way the micks crack everything."

She looks at the thing as if she cares. She even runs a finger over it before turning around. Now that actress is in her. I see it pretty clear, or at least think I do.

"Do you love me, Shoe?"

Love you? Christ Addy, love you? I don't feel nothing since I gave Bobby away. I been too busy hating myself. Love you? No, for the love of Christ.

"Sure," I say putting my hands onto her hips. "Sure."

21

I let my pile fall and
line things up instead

"Listen!"

No one speaks above a whisper, even the little micks, even the boys from Blackpool with their whiskey bottles and fists. They turn to the corner as one, and though I promised myself I would look away, I could not help but swing with the others. Only the shadow gives him away. He never rumbles or clops and the long strides drop each foot in a calmness that seems impossible. When the shadow has compressed, it stops. A matches' glow sneaks out from around the corner and cigarette smoke follows. We wait. Even the whispering has fallen away. He steps out and faces the crowd, watching us as we watch him.

"Good Christ," one of the Blackpool crowd says, low and slow.

Could he truly have grown this much since I saw him last? Doesn't God have rules about such things? His head has become too huge for his cap and black hair hangs long and straight onto his shoulders. The jacket sleeves can't reach his wrists and the cuffs of his pants ride high over each ankle. The McAvy doesn't speak or look at me. He doesn't look at any of them. He walks to where the spot under the light is marked off with heavy rope, steps over it and enters the square. For a moment no one says a thing.

Mummy squeezed my arm once, when we walked to her elm and Bobby chased pigeons ahead. She said we are but a drop of water in God's great ocean, no more or better than any other drop. And Bobby was a drop too, she said. But The McAvy is a *wave*, Mummy. Or an ocean himself. His gulls fill the sky over him. Small birds, too, all looking down and wondering, if birds wonder, why this great thing is stuck to the earth. Surely it can soar and twist and sail like them.

It's as if everyone is trying to understand what it is they're seeing. Mr. Rogers comes over to where I'm standing.

"Let me tell them it's off."

"We can't"

"You bloody well have to tell them it's off, laddie."

Rogers motions to The McAvy's back.

"That's not a man. No one would blame you."

Over his shoulder I see my father, his face buried in his pail of stout. He is what he is. Lowden steps behind Mr. Rogers. There was no work for me today. I was to rest because the bastard said he had wagered a bit on me. I would wager my life he wagered nothing on me. What kind of odds could the dog give? I heard this morning that he had them going on how long I lasted. When I would die, if I did. Even if I'd show.

The McAvy still hasn't moved and my head clears enough to see he's in the throw of moonlight. Stars twinkle down too, so he's framed by them or is one of them. I start to walk to the square.

"For the love of Christ," Rogers says.

"Keep the money away from my father."

Rogers looks and sighs.

"That I will."

I slide under the ropes and hear Mr. Horn's reedy, ugly squeal.

"Here's the end of the beast now! Here's my boy! Cut him down, son! Make your father proud!"

246

Some of the beggars clap their hands. The McAvy still hasn't turned. Is he praying? He begins to roll his sleeves now and he's never done that. By the corner of the rope nearest to the light, Liz stands with Tom. Phil is between them. Tom has a sneer up. Liz has something else. She smiles at me and gives a wave no one else can see. I think of her under the sink and then in the chair. What's wrong with me? The McAvy turns suddenly, so quick I don't catch his spin. One step in and the buckle of his pants is at my nose. His look is fierce and that wide hard face is curled into a snarl. He bends as if in a threat.

"Take me down, Shoe," he whispers. "Take me down and keep the pot."

"I'm Shoe Horn."

"You are."

"I can't."

"You have to."

I say it again. What is wrong with me? I come up and shove him hard, only my push drives *me* back. The McAvy has not shook a bit, a piece of the cobblestone and sky. Push him? Move him?

"I can't," I yell from where I've stumbled.

"Remember all I've taught you!" Mr. Horn squeaks. "Around the Horn."

I circle to my left. The McAvy doesn't move or even follow with his great blue eyes. He's told me I was his only friend and I know he's the only one I had the time for in living Bobby Horn's sweet life. So, only friends. Is he as sad and afraid as I am? Could he be afraid?

"C'mon," Mr. Horn squeaks, "Take the filthy thing down!"

I don't see him even flinch but the back of his hand has slapped my cheek. My feet leave the ground and I sprawl in front of Liz and Tom. When I'm up I can see The McAvy's back is still to me, head hanging. His great shoulders seem to quake. The slap has given the crowd its voice again and they tell us what they want and how they want it. Mr. Horn's squeal cuts through.

"Take the monster down, for the love of Christ."

I hear the Gogartys snicker and see Lowden's happy face next to them. Petey Evans and Taber, point and scream at me. Are they laughing? I feel something now, moving out of my heart, up and down my body. Veins in my forearms flash out from the hot flow of blood. Fists seem to swell, shoulders hunch as I move in front of him, but it's all the others I want. I want to take them all with bleeders and kicks, want to end the life around me and bring my dirty lying pile down around my ears. The McAvy raises his eyes and sees me through the long wet hair. It's as if he's looking out from a forest and I'm looking in. I can't see him, though, only the others snarling at me like dogs. I throw one at The McAvy but really at Tom. Then Evans. Taber. The coward Arthur. Lowden. Mr. Horn, over and over and over. I know the crowd is screaming although I can't hear them for my own hurried breaths and shouts as I leap up to reach his eyes, his chin, his mouth. The McAvy's head doesn't move. The arms, as long and thick as rail ties, hang limp by his side.

"You've got the beast. You've got the beast now," Mr. Horn squeals.

Blood is falling hard from The McAvy's wide face and has matted clumps of hair onto his cheeks and forehead. He hasn't blinked. His eyes watch me and through me. My hands bleed from what I've thrown and, dear Christ, I've thrown them at my only friend. The crowd has stopped its roar. I step back and see what I've done.

"I was," I gasp, pointing, "I was punching at them."

"I know, Shoe."

"I was…I was…"

I was punching at the lying thing I've become too, punching at myself. I wobble to my knees as if I've whacked myself in the back of my head.

"Bobby!" I shout through my tears. I feel his great hand stroking the top of my head.

"It's alright, Shoe."

"Bobby Horn," I scream to the crowd.

My head bobs onto my knees. I have brought myself down. The liar's pile has fallen onto him. I cannot breathe or stand.

"Mr. Rogers," I hear The McAvy whisper.

Rogers comes out of the crowd. The McAvy holds his palm out and Rogers put the pot into it.

"It's well over a hundred."

"Thank you, Mr. Rogers."

He picks me up with his free arm, nestles me like a baby against him, and walks away from the silent mob.

"The monster and the boy," I mumble to the moon and the stars.

I hear her in the kitchen when I wake. Hear a small silvery voice singing something. To come back to the world in a song is a mysterious thing. Perhaps it *was* a dream after all, and I am the same old Shoe. Perhaps I've been cleaned again and nothing that has happened, happened, and that's why she's singing and Bobby may be smiling and holding Blacky on his thin lap. I swing my legs down and walk naked into the kitchen. She turns away from the stove when she hears me pull a chair and sit at the table.

"You're up," she says.

"I'm up," I say.

I don't remember falling into my bed but I do remember her coming in and sliding under the cool sheet, surprising me with a tender touch I didn't think went with her.

"Are you feeling better?"

"How did I feel last night?" I say and light one.

"You felt good, you bastard," Liz says with a laugh.

And what was I to do? Because I may not have wanted it to happen, or I might have wanted it. I just don't know. I feel the pile swaying side-to-side, flinging things off as I watch. She taps something on the table and it rolls over to me. I see that it's money wrapped tight with a bit of string.

"This was here on the table," she says, "Tea?"

We have a cuppa while I count it. Christ. One hundred thirty-two pounds. Liz watches me between sips. Watches the money close. She knows so much more because she's twenty-five or says she is. I don't have to think about looking at her in a visit because she grabs my hair and makes me. She's a Gogarty and her black eyes will always give her away. I am Shoe Horn and I'm known, only not to myself. She reaches over and counts out twenty, folds the bills and puts them in her skirt pocket.

"What's that for?" I ask her.

"What do you think?" she says, and crawls under the table.

Mr. Horn sits against the alley wall, waiting for me to leave. He pushes himself up when he sees Liz and me coming out the door. I walk by without a look.

"How did…how did we do?" he squeaks after me.

How did we do? The McAvy broke me with his face. He broke me with his hands down to his sides, then he carried me home and left the pot on the table. That's how *we* did. I turn and look at the thing my father has become. All at once I'm aware of changes inside myself. And even though the morning is damp and cloudy my poor brain isn't. Is this why the pile has crumbled so that some parts of it can be lined up in order and the rest tossed?

"I don't need much," I say.

"But how…how did we do?"

I reach into my pocket, count ten pounds and hand it to him. I have no idea who this man held up by the alley wall is.

"Bobby's your son. Do you know that?"

He looks at me and struggles for pride. It's gone.

"Yes."

"He's at a special school on Quince Island."

"Special?" he says slowly.

I look at Liz and think of Molly. I'm Mr. Horn's boy alright. I walk on and she follows. I shift the plumber's box from hand to hand. Liz lights one of my cigarettes and we share a few puffs.

"Well, Liz. I'm turning up to Lipper Lane at the corner."

"Alright."

At the corner she gives me a kiss. A small one that doesn't say much. I watch her walk a bit, finish the smoke, and think of what must be done and how I must do it. It carries me all the way to Lowden's shop. He's red faced and pacing when I walk in. I lay down the plumber's box and notice, for the first time, how swollen my hands are. How scraped and raw from the great bones of The McAvy's face.

"Where have you been, Horn? It's past seven for the love of Christ. The morning's mostly gone."

He stops at a desk, cluttered with parts new and old, picks up a piece of paper and waves it at me.

"It's like all of the bloody Barrow sprung a leak or got clogged. Toomey Jewelers has a basement leak, that's the first one. Then Craymores Shoes' water closet seems to have exploded during the night. Then…are you listening Horn?"

"Well, you'd better get at it."

"I'll drop you at the Jewelers, but then I've got the club so you'll have to…what did you say?"

"I said you'd better get at it because I'm not going to be slaving for you no more."

Lowden's face gets red. He gets his hands onto his hips. He can look as annoyed as he pleases, but I know what he's thinking. Lowden on his hands and knees trying to remember how to plumb his way out of all the shit.

"Now…now lad, let's not get…I completely understand how you feel after…after last evening. But no one could move the giant, he's…"

"McAvy. His name is McAvy."

"Of course it is. I was just…"

I turn and leave him to the pipes. I've learned more than he could ever teach. The card won't help where I'm going. What's inside my noggin ought to be enough and if it's not, well, the laughs on Shoe Horn. I walk to his lane and knock on the door. His mum answers with that sad Barrow smile. She's as tiny and spare as he is vast.

"Good morning, Mrs. McAvy."

"Good morning, Shoe. Come in."

She turns and closes the door.

"I'll make us all some tea. He told me you won the match."

"I didn't."

"I know. He's in his room," she says pointing at the hall.

I push the door and walk in. I have always wondered, what are his things? How does he sleep? A long, wide bed rests on heavy beams. His mum has sewn four mattresses together and they lay on a flat platform without springs. The McAvy is on it wearing a circus tent of a sleeping gown. He lay on his side toward me, his face completely hidden under the wild black hair. The room itself seems two rooms and a beam is floor to ceiling where a wall must have been removed. An enormous wooden chair with arm rests and cushions is turned toward a small coal stove. Behind that, posts are stretched across the ceiling and his clothing hangs, nearly to the great shoes below them. A high table is pushed against the far wall and there are papers piled on it. I pick one up and read what's written in a delicate, rolling hand.

"They're just stories," he whispers.

I put it down and look at him.

"I didn't know if you were awake."

"I'm always awake, Shoe."

The McAvy sits up and his hair clears from his face. The bruises and cuts and lumps jump off him.

"I like to write little stories. I put myself inside them and I'm the way I am only smaller. I'm much smaller in the stories. I'm a rabbit in one."

I take the money out of my pocket.

"I've brought the money."

"You won it."

"I didn't."

"I don't need it, Shoe. I'm not going to America. I can't leave my mum. She needs me, I think, and I don't scare her. Donald wrote that America would be scared too. He said that they're only human. 'Stay away' is what he said."

The McAvy crosses the room, pours a pitcher of water into his bowl and cleans his face.

"I'll need work. Anything. Maybe I can work somewhere. Maybe if I make myself seem smaller…I don't know."

Smaller? Can a mountain fold itself up? I look at his face and majesty rides across it, like Bobby knew. Yes, my pile is down and I see the world in a straight line. Maybe it's the only way I can think. Things one after the other and not balanced in a heap, stacked too high to know what's on top.

"I'm thinking," I say.

"You are?" he whispers seriously.

"I'm thinking I know what I know as long as I line it up and not pile it up."

The McAvy looks at me as if he gets it. I take the money and count out half.

"That's half."

"I won't…"

"I know what I know. Get dressed. We got to be somewhere."

"Where?"

"The jewelers."

* * *

253

One of the shop girls leads us to the basement door. The McAvy walks delicately between the cases of pearls and stones, keeping his head bowed so he can move under the ceiling. When she opens the door, the girl looks up at him.

"You're large."

The McAvy smiles.

"You're pretty."

The girl beams and walks back to the displays.

"What's in the basement?" he whispers.

Lowden's facing a swirling tide of brown water. His chalky, skinny legs look like they're painted on, standing ankle deep and pants rolled. He's got a big two hander wrench in his hands, but he's most likely forgotten how to use it.

"It's the outtake. You think, Mr. Lowden? Outtakes clogged good."

He's so relieved to see me he only starts a little at the sight of The McAvy.

"You're back. I knew you wouldn't let me down."

I don't move. He gestures to the flood.

"It looks like the outtake alright. A ream? You think?"

"Well, I don't know. Where would we get in?"

He looks around. Jesus Christ, he doesn't even have an idea where to begin. He points to the far wall.

"In…in that vicinity."

"No," I say.

"It's not there?" he whines.

"See McAvy," I say to him looming over my shoulder, "There's two big pipes. One that brings clean water into the house, that's the *intake* and one carries the dirty water out, that's the *outtake*. They always go in and out at the same place."

"Makes sense," The McAvy whispers.

"So…where?" Lowden asks.

"There," I say and point to the corner next to the coal chute.

"See McAvy, there's great order to plumbing. There's only one way to work. Not two or three. First the intake must be shut off, then the outtake must be reamed."

The McAvy nods.

"Did you know the word plumbing comes from *plumbum*? That's Latin for lead."

"Really?" Lowden blurts.

"There's true history behind this, you know," I say to The McAvy.

Lowden stands still. The water's cold and he shivers a bit.

"So…okay lad, let's get the intake off and we're in business."

"Look, Mr. Lowden, I hate to see you up to your knees in this filthy water, I do. Only, I gave you notice or don't you remember."

"But that was this morning."

"And this is this morning, too."

Lowden's got desperate eyes to go with the shiver.

"I'm sure you can find another apprentice and train him. Should only take some months."

"But there's too much work."

I'd love to see the white pig weep. I'd pay to see it, but that's not why I've come.

"Would you excuse us, McAvy," I say. "There's some business Mr. Lowden and I have to talk about."

When he's gone back up to the shop, I lift the plumber's box out of the water where the dirty phony has put it.

"These tools are wet now, they'll all need oil or grease before you finish up, late tonight, or they'll rust."

Oh, but Jesus this man wants to be at his club and not floating around a dark smelly basement, or he wants to be at his inventory, among the pipes and stems he knows how to count but not fix.

"Look Horn, the Plumbers Guild card is a very…"

"I don't care about no card."

I wait. He wants to fall in the water and have it float him away.

"Look, Mr. Lowden, maybe there's something I can do."

I see the club back in his eyes.

"I can give the week until Saturday. I'll work like a fool and clean your lists. And while I'm at it, I'll train another guy to take my place. Teach him all of it or most. What I miss, he's so smart and hard working, he'll learn on his own."

He's thinking hard. The bugger looks like a sack of flour in red suspenders.

"Another apprentice?" He says fighting a smile.

I know him. He's thinking another slave. Another dog. Another seven years. I nod.

"Yes, Mr. Lowden. Another apprentice, only this one you don't deserve. Not how hard he'll work or how bloody easy he'll make your life. But you can have him for two years only. Two years. And you'll pay him half again what you give to me. Then you give him his card and his trade."

"Two years? Nobody'd agree to that."

I turn to the stairs.

"Well, I suppose you can call the mick plumbers or Andersons. They'd be glad for the work."

"Wait."

I look down on a dog. He laughed at Bobby once, I remember. I tell myself that I am not here for that.

"Who?"

I point toward the shop without taking my eyes off the bastard. "The McAvy."

He steps back and the rising water sloshes up to his crotch.

"The giant, for the love of Christ?"

I shake my head and smile. I don't know much. But what I *do* know I know like Bobby does, inside my bones.

"He's not a giant Mr. Lowden, he's much bigger than a giant."

His wheels are turning in that puffy little head.

"People will be…My God, Horn, he frightens everyone. *Everyone.*"

The bugger's not fit to look on The McAvy, much less employ him but I tell myself again, I'm here for other things.

"Look, Mr. Lowden. The McAvy is the hardest working guy you could ever have. You know he's strong, but he's *smarter* than anybody else. I know people are afraid. Sure. But the first time he comes to plumb in their shops or their houses, they'll see how fine and kind he is. They'll brag about how The McAvy came to their place and they chatted with him, and when they see him on the street they'll wave and he'll wave back, and they'll say, 'There goes a friend of mine.' "

I take another step down.

"Don't you see, Mr. Lowden? Everyone who's afraid today, will be calling for him tomorrow. He'll be money in your pocket."

His small mean mind suits the body God has thrown him.

"Well…I always knew he was a fine lad and…and…kind you say?"

"It's true."

"Now, of course, the two years is…"

I start back up the stairs.

"Alright! Alright…You'll train him this week and then two years apprenticeship."

"Two years from today and half-again what you gave me."

"Agreed."

"In writing."

"Christ Horn, after all this time you don't trust me?"

"No, Mr. Lowden, I don't."

He borrows paper and pen from the jeweler, Mr. Toomey, and writes it out. The McAvy is talking to the shop girl by the china plates. It's two years, it's half-again, it's the card and, in all Lowden's desperation, it's a job at the end of it. Mr. Toomey signs it too as a witness. After Lowden has sloshed out to his truck, The McAvy walks over.

"What's it?" he asks in his whisper.

I hold the paper up. He reads it. He reads it again.

His mouth forms each silent word. When he looks up a river is flowing from his eyes.

"A...trade," he whispers.

"A trade, McAvy, and a week to learn it."

The McAvy gives one great sob. Mr. Toomey and the shop girl look over.

"Then teach me, Shoe," he whispers. "Teach me."

So I'm right about my wee brain and its way of thinking. Don't pile things, Shoe, line them up. Then you can walk around them and touch them and know them a little. Worry about the lies later. The shop girl and Mr. Toomey stand in the doorway of the shop and wave at the two apprentices who have drained the basement. We walk to the shoe store, our toolbox tiny in The McAvy's hands. Can he stand taller? The gulls follow us in widening circles, sailing above like crazy kites.

Yes, it's true. At first the startled looks and then the confidence his whispers show. A friend now. An enormous boulder of a friend. At day's end, after the mick school for more concrete in more of the dirty little buggers' shitters, he hands me the plumber's box.

"You take it McAvy."

"Me?"

"It's the only way to learn the tools. That, and how I lay them out in a proper order."

"I won't forget how you do that."

"And there's history behind us."

"I'll be proud of that, I promise."

"Be at Lowden's at four-thirty."

"I will."

The McAvy has made sure he's buttoned before picking up the box and walking to his mums'. He whistles something. Maybe he'll sleep this night. Phil steps up to me. We stare at each other, then walk to the Channel Lane Hotel. I light one and sit on the porch steps. The lies are somewhere away for a bit and Bobby Horn will be in a warm bed. If I didn't believe in his being warm I would wash away. I must believe that and tonight I begin knowing I must. The ocean laps its shore, coming and going, filling the Barrow with wavy music. I close my eyes and pretend it's Mummy singing Bobby to sleep in his small bed. Yes. Her voice *was* like the sea and deep as it too.

"I have her voice in my head," I say to my cigarette.

"Whose voice?" she says above me.

"Mummy's voice. It's here," I say and tap my noggin.

"My mum's in London."

"I know."

"She run off with Da's brother."

We go quiet. Phil stands off the step and walks to Bobby's lookout.

"Do you love me, Shoe?"

I stand and turn to her. Inside my head she's much bigger than this little girl. She's got a long grey coat on and her hair is wet and curled tight around her head. I don't have to think at all.

"Yes, Molly, I do."

She's careful, standing there in all she is. She closes her eyes and balls her fists.

"But it's got to be just you and me. You and me forever. Nobody else. Can you say that, Shoe? Can you say you will love me and nobody else?"

I step up to her.

"Yes, Molly. I can say it. I'll love only you."

And I believe it, too, like Bobby believed in Mummy's fat face and her sweet, sad song.

22

The Dropper tells it to me
and I get the fuck out

There's rope around the small trunk. Everything's in it but still it weighs half what the plumber's box did. In the mirror by Mummy's door the Sunday suit and cap seem out of place. I stare at someone I only guessed I knew. That bully boy looking back at me is half-made at best. Out of place in all that he is or thought he was.

My hand is on the door when I stop and put the trunk on the floor. There's something I've forgotten, I'm sure of it. I feel the money in my pocket, to know it's there. Now the trunk gets open, the rope pulled off. Yes. There is the picture of Mummy. There's Bobby. What's missing? The kitchen seems smaller than it did a minute ago, but whatever I've forgotten ain't here. Or in the other rooms. I sit for a bit in Mummy's parlor looking at the things she used to make a place in this dirty world for us.

"I'm forgetting something, Mummy. I know it."

The room is more than silent. It's empty. It's as if we drained her out of it.

"I don't think you're here anymore."

Phil is waiting outside in the alley where Mr. Horn is sitting against the wall. He's too drunk to push himself up. He just stares at me, stupidly.

"Do you…have money?"

"Yes."

"Can I…?"

"No."

I see him for the last time. Him and all his "disappointments."

"I won't be coming back."

"If you…could spare…"

"Bobby Horn is your son. He's on Quince Island."

He looks at me as if he has drunk his own child out of himself.

"Bobby Horn," I say again and point at his terrible face.

"Bobby…Horn," he whispers.

There's almost nothing left to say but what there is I say without anger. It's in my heart and I know it like my plumber's box.

"I hate you."

I turn away and Phil turns with me toward the narrow strip of rocks and sand that lead to Quince Island.

Last night, The McAvy and me finished up at the Taylor's. The Mrs. had dug a great hole behind her roses and, like the Vicar, cut into an intake. Muddy water roiled up and lapped at its side. We got it shut on the second try and she sat with her sad smile, under a small grape arbor, wringing her hands. Mr. Taylor had wonderfully lost his voice at the sight of The McAvy but found it again when we walked through the back door.

"What a lovely garden," The McAvy whispered to him with a smile. "My mum would love the way the roses climb the fence."

Now, Mr. Taylor's standing over us, thumbs inside his vest.

"…of course, *opponent* might very well be an understandable misnomer, given the lad's proclivity of evoking various phrases in French with, as I said, that distinct Welsh emphasis. Nonetheless I proceeded to accommodate him as best I could being, after all was said and done, his superior at the Wood Pulp Company. And yet there remained in him an intrepid, one might even go so far as to say devil-may-care attitude toward the aforementioned astonishingly superior Wood Pulp stationary that often forced me to feel a jumbling in my jejunums, which, by the by, is the middle portion of the small intestine between the duodenum and the ileum. And so one dreary, sunless afternoon I had…"

"There McAvy, when it's up like this it can often be wrapped and clamped," I say holding the length of pipe a few inches from the earth.

Mrs. Taylor has walked over and stands next to her husband looking down at the muddy plumbers.

"So it's better than a cut and re-threading?" he asks.

"Nothing's better than that but sometimes, if the leaks not coming from a large gash, a wrap and clamp will do nicely, and I've always got them in the box."

"And I will too."

Mr. Taylor looks up at the thick flock of circling gulls, takes his pipe from his pocket and begins to stuff tobacco into it.

"…and so I pointed sternly at the young miscreant whose task, by the by, whose occupation, whose very responsibility it was to promulgate a universal craving for the finest quality stationary. 'Where is your pride of product,' I boomed in a crisp, clear baritone I seldom used and yet kept in my vest pocket, reserved and at the ready. And at that, his cronies sidled away leaving him alone to confront a capacious truth, illuminated as it was, not by fancy, but rather incontrovertible certainty. And so I filled my lungs with oxygen and roared, 'Nothing compares with this, the finest poundage of stationary in the British protectorate.' A remarkable epiphany spread throughout the Wood Pulp Company and its paper cutting associates that afternoon, I can assure you."

"Do you think it's deep enough?" Mrs. Taylor asks us.

"Deep enough for what?" The McAvy whispers with his smile.

"Yes, Mrs. Taylor," I say. "This will do nicely."

"And it's a pretty spot too," she says, fondly looking at the flowers and ivy on either side of the hole.

"I think he'll like it," I say with a smile.

We left the box at his mum's and walked to the dock where the *Madagascar* was being loaded with moulds and machinery in the largest hatch on the waterfront. A guy operating a loading crane stopped and left the freight hanging at the sight of The McAvy. Some of the seamen working the deck called to others and they lined the ship's railing, watching him below and his gulls above. At the bottom of the gang plank, The McAvy whispered up to the man who seemed in charge.

"Is Mr. Haywood about?"

At first he couldn't answer. We waited. We understood.

"Uh…yes, yes he is."

He backed out of sight and a few minutes later, a tight, short man about sixty, with silver hair, strutted down the gang plank. He wasn't surprised by The McAvy.

"Mr. Haywood, I've decided I won't be coaling you to Boston. This is Shoe Horn. He'll be the coaler I was to be. He'll work hard. And, Mr. Haywood, Shoe is a great plumber."

Haywood jerked his head my way and narrowed his eyes.

"Plumber? Honest?"

"Yes sir."

"What do you know about a ship's boiler?"

"If there's water going into it and water coming out, I know everything."

"You look like you could load the coal good. Water closets?"

"I'd do everything you need, only I'm bringing somebody with me."

A half hour later, after showing me where I'd work and letting me get the boiler into my head, he walked us back to the deck and gangplank.

"Tomorrow evening, we leave at six-forty. You be here no later than four o'clock. This is a ship, lad, and I will be your foreman. Never be late and we'll get along good."

"Yes sir."

"She carries cargo and passengers. They'll be sixty, so they'll need cleaning and serving and the rest."

"We don't know much but we know work. I won't be late. She won't neither."

We have a pint and sit on the curb in front of the pub.

"...every fortnight?"

"Yes," I nod to The McAvy.

"I'll go each time. I won't miss one."

"I know you won't."

"He's a great lad."

"He is," I say.

I look at my only friend. He knows I'm looking but keeps his gaze out toward the Irish Sea and Boston. I'm thinking I'll walk out of Boston into America and I'm thinking I'll walk out for him too. His hair is beginning to curl back and the long strands flap a bit in the breeze. Phil watches us on the far corner in front of the flower shop.

"Are you real, McAvy?"

He laughs, I don't.

"Are you?"

The McAvy stands and takes some folded papers out of his pocket. He holds them out to me.

"It's a story."

I start to open them but he lays a big mitt on my hand.

"Read it on the ship."

He keeps his hand out and we shake.

"But McAvy. Are you? Real?"

His brow furrows like a field. The sun has gone. The half moon is behind him.

"No."

Phil and me stop in the middle of the bridge. I lean against the rail. From here I can see both the Barrow and Walney Island, cut by the Channel, rushing in, its tide making a whooshing echo under my feet. After an hour or so, stars twinkle down on this last Barrow night. Phil sees her first and I look where he does. She's walking slowly toward the bridge from the Walney side, skirting the throw of lamps to stay in shadow. I know things now but still my heart pounds and sweat oils the palms of my hands. As if by her command, clouds, heavy and wet, overtake the moon and many of the stars until what just a moment before was an almost sparkly night, now is weighty and confusing. Mummy said she'd seen her swoop over houses, a giant black bird, waiting. Waiting for what, Mummy? I know she's behind me now. I feel a peculiar heaviness in my legs. I hear her dry skirt crinkling, smell things mothy and sunless.

"That Dr. James is a delightful one, isn't he?" she says, slowly, in a bruised and scratchy voice that is tired and sad at the same time.

I turn and face her. She's moved close to the edge of the bridge where light stops at her feet.

"He…he told me you'd…he said you told him about…"

"Bobby," we say together.

"Bobby Horn," she says again.

I can't see her face but hear the smile in that weary voice.

"Virginia had been concerned, of course, and when she became ill that day, I watched him closely. Bobby Horn."

"I'm so…"

"Bobby Horn," she says again, only this time to the channel and its roaring flow. "He knew that I was…afraid to be with them…

in the morning…in the sunny afternoon. He understood when I pushed myself back into shade and held my hand and squeezed me for the joy of his life."

She steps closer to me. Her age and sorrow in eyes set deep in shadows of their own.

"I know where dusk falls, Mr. Horn. I know the lanes and alleys without lamps and can move through them with eyes closed, which I've done and will again. My reflection, even on wet cobblestones, vitiates me as surely as boiling water would scald my eyes. I prefer the echo of my life to the image."

She steps closer. There's lemon on her breath. Her sunken cheeks soppy with tears.

"There's still so much to do. So many of them. Those that can be in the life, like Bobby. Those that can't. But there's scope for them. There must be."

She stands tall and straight. She doesn't bury her face in her long white fingers or close her eyes but looks into mine and weeps. I reach for her hand and she steps back. Is The Dropper afraid of *me*?

"I know that lies and rumors were told about Mary Corony," I say, as softly as a hard plumber can.

She watches me and waits, her breathing stuttering and hard.

"I know that we were afraid and I was afraid and the crazy stupid words made something that wasn't there."

"The Dropper," she sobs and now her hands do fly to her face.

I reach again. This time she don't back away or flinch.

"I'm seventeen," I say, surprising myself.

"I know. I remember every single one. Thousands of you."

She looks beyond me, out to sea and smiles like a girl.

"I wore a skirt the color of brown but my blouse was always a powdery blue. I wanted mother and child to see the lovely sky over them. 'Push' I would say or to some I would whisper 'that's only an *urge* to push, resist it, my dear.' And the tools were mostly these hands."

Mary Corony held her hands out. We both looked at them as the moon showed a piece of itself. Phil paced on the other side, every now and then looking up toward the Barrow.

"I was young. Mother would bring me and teach me. The *hows* and *whys* of it all. How to hold the head in soft towels. How to rest an elbow onto their bellies and push down and out. How to know when a life is ready to turn and squiggle and writhe and take its opportunity. Because who else is firmly there between the warmth of the womb and this cruel uncertainty? And don't forget prayer. Mother taught the prayers for our arduous labors.

> Oh lord, Thou who created the
> Miracle, guide our poor hands,
> Take away the chains of pride
> so that we may be replenished
> by your holy spirit, every new day.

And I would say it each day and before each miracle like she told me to, until it was such a portion of this head, this body, that it needn't be said at all. It simply hung there, over my head like a blessed reminder. On the afternoon she died, I left her bedside to take Raleigh Pepper from his mother. Yes. I did."

Phil has stopped pacing and has crossed the street watching us. She rests her hands on the bridge railing and speaks to the channel.

"Sometimes though, sometimes she would tell me to leave the room…and I would linger just outside with the husband, waiting as he waited, wondering what he wondered."

A baby's cry flies over us. I can't tell if it's from Walney or the Barrow. It's screeching for something and it ain't asking.

"On those occasions my mother would take on a severeness that was outside of her character. She would assume a hard and critical role in the theatre of parturition. She would come to the door with a certain detachment, even aloofness and bring the husband in, leaving me alone in the parlor, or the den, or the kitchen.

When she finished and the man was weeping in other rooms, she... she carried the sealed bundle to the mortuary her friend, Carlton Roebuck, operated and which his son continues today. Nothing was ever frivolous with the devout elder Roebuck and when she would pass the bundle to him, he accepted it as tenderly as if it were a bird fallen from its mother's nest."

A couple strolled by, talking nothing and laughing. Mary turned away, almost folding into the night. When they were by, she spoke to their backs.

"I was young, I was young and wanted what other girls want. Romance and music and secrets."

She turned back to me.

"Good secrets. Sweet secrets. Secrets to pass through the air like gossamer and disappear with the first fragile breeze. Those are the secrets a girl should have and not the unshareable breed, crawling back no matter how many times you drive them away."

She began to walk back to the Walney side. I followed. Phil too.

"One afternoon, I remember it was a cottage on Shakespeare Lane, Jane Gorty was ready. My mother was quiet on the walk over, removed really. She always placed some flowers onto the tools in her bag, but this day she did not. I don't remember her speaking except once and that was to herself. She said, 'Jane is forty-three' and shook her head. Byron Gorty met us at the door, polished and suited. 'This is how I greeted the others,' he said to Mother. She had brought six out of Jane, but that was a long time ago and they were all grown or gone or dead. Mr. Gorty took back to his big chair, sitting straight and smoking English ovals and we went to her. She was moving her limbs, all of them, at the same time."

At the big lamp, where street meets bridge, she circled the throw of light quickly and slowed only at the darkest sidewalks. The nearer to the light she squeezed into herself. Now in the murky night she grew tall. Her feet moved under the long black skirt in such a silent slide she seemed to sail along.

"Mother played her hands over Mrs. Gorty's hard belly, put her ear close to it and looked at her tunnel. When Mrs. Gorty cried out, my mother told me to leave the room. 'There's tea on the table,' Mr. Gorty said without so much as a glance. I…poured a cuppa. I remember a chill in the air, or in me. I remember the smells of tea and Mr. Gorty's cigarettes. I carried my cup to just outside the door. I don't understand why, I have asked myself always, why I put my ear to it."

Mary's legs wobbled as if she'd fall. I steadied her and we sat on the curb. Clouds had sunk into fog. Phil went wavy in the small smoky breeze and blew away.

"I could only make out the tone behind the door. Voices low and stony blended into a single lamentation. Then the voices stopped. The only sound was the draw of Mr. Gorty's cigarette. Mother had sent me out as she had before. But now, this day, I became curious at the quiet. It was not serene or placid, rather it seemed an obtrusive silence, active and…potent."

Mary put her hand out and grasped at air.

"I opened the door and stepped into the room."

I followed her memory as if it were my own. Mrs. Gorty in her high bed. Mary's mother behind, not surprised to see her. Waiting perhaps.

"I see them both. Mother stares at me in stillness. Mrs. Gorty, an arm over her eyes. 'Mother…' I start to say. And then I…I…see it there. Oh dear God, at her feet. I stumble across the rug and fall to my knees. I reach for it but Mother stops me. 'Mother,' I cry. She goes to her knees too. There's some wee drops of blood under it, where it lay on its side as though sleeping. Mother rolls it over and points. 'Look,' she says, 'Look, Mary. Look.' and begins to weep as I have never dreamed she could. A girl yes…long limbs and neck… fine black hair. But where…where…bumps and skin…bumps and skin…instead of eyes. I pull Mother's work bag over to my side and lay out a tiny linen blanket. Mother cannot help me. I reach for the girl and place her on the blanket. At the first wrap of her feet, a stringy arm flops and fingers open and close. I…I…"

"Mary…" I say, to say something.

"I ball my shawl and press it over her mouth."

A ship's horn sounds and holds its tone until its own echo falls back onto the blast. We both turn our heads to the steady moan as if there's an answer out there in the fog. Her mouth is parted a little and her lips are cracked and dry even on this damp night.

"Mother remained in the shadows of the street, while I carried the bundle up to Mr. Roebuck Carlton, who met me in suit and tie. After he took it he said: 'Mary.' Nothing more."

A good blow comes and a whoosh with it, then stops.

"That night I was a girl no more. My bright skirts and shawls were no more. I married melancholy. From time to time, inside the wee rooms cut by lanes and streets, I would take the vows again to the cries of the half born and the muffled sobs of their mother."

Mary began to stand and I helped her.

"I never believed myself to be a tool of our Lord, Mr. Horn. I only thought of the cruelty of this world to the un-made. I have never understood the darkness He has left me in…but I accept it."

She looks at me and considers something.

"One evening I was called by a boy to come to where his mother was ready. There was no husband and the boy who fetched me ran back outside to play. The small place was very clean and flowers were on the table in the kitchen. Something white I remember.

She was a lovely small thing, lying there on the bed in a corner of her room. The lamp gave a yellow glow and I found two or three candles to help its light. She was a cheerful thing and, except for the size of her belly, quite ordinary. I felt relief in what I saw were no signs of a severe parturition. But where I touched her egg, the kick or punch was unlike anything I had ever experienced. And it came quicker than any, came along and red, thick black hair, fingers splayed to the light. A boy, he did not cry, but shouted into the room and the world beyond that."

Mary thinks for a moment. She lays her head sideways onto my shoulder, both of us in shadow now.

"I placed him onto his mother's breast and reached into my work bag for the small, soft blanket I always wrapped them in. When I turned back, he'd turned *himself* so that he faced me. Could a babe turn? He seemed longer still and the fingers opened and closed with purpose. And then…"

I felt her breathing come heavy.

"Then what Mary?"

She stepped away from me and looked hard into my eyes.

"And then he was *watching* me. Seeing me with eyes that truly saw he had come into an impossible, unthinkable circumstance. Something had happened, I knew. There was *something* in the room, I knew, that shouldn't be…She asked for water…when I returned from the pitcher in the kitchen, he'd grown longer still and this time I was sure of it. I stood in the door, by precious God, waiting for him to speak. When he didn't, I went to them and…lifted him off his weary mother. I felt him expand again in my arms."

"The McAvy," I whispered to myself.

"That evening was cool and starry. Where my steps had been crisp as I made my way from Walney to the Barrow, on my return, they slid as if they were not mine. At the bridge, I dropped my work bag and tools into the channel. I could not be an arbiter again of what is right and good. Who is fit and who this world will rebuke. 'Let the others drop them,' I said to the black water."

She backed further away and nearly blended into the fog and night. We looked at each other's silhouette.

"I'm glad," I said, "I'm so glad you didn't drop The McAvy."

A fine rain began.

"But, I did, Mr. Horn. I did."

* * *

I've got the trunk in one hand and a smoke in the other as me and Phil cross the rocky strip to Quince Island.

"It's one cheerio after another, Phil. I've said goodbye to the whole fucking world."

Phil don't talk, of course, but I wish he would. Trying to convince myself off this bloody Barrow ain't as easy as I'd imagined. There's a place here for me to sleep. There's plumbing too, even if Lowden could ruin a steak and kidney pie.

The school seems smaller than it did the last time. There was something heavy to it, solid like a two-hander. Now it rattles a bit and is maybe held to the earth by the weight of my hopes. I put my trunk down at the bottom of the stairs and finish the smoke.

"Look Phil, you don't have to go no further, but I'd like you to come in with me, if you would."

I stub it out and walk in. Phil, God bless him, is waiting inside the hall and is with me as I move to the stairs and Dr. James' room above us.

"It's a nice place, isn't it Phil?"

I stop at the gymnasium. The double doors are open wide and their games roar over me. Bobby is not among them and I move up the stairs.

"They play good. They have fun, don't they Phil?"

Dr. James isn't there either. From the corridor window I see the playing field near the sea cliffs. Mixed teams of girls and boys are chasing a soccer ball. One club in black and white, one in brown and red.

"Look Phil, it's Bobby. Look at him. Look at him go."

We cross the rail track and climb a worn path to the field. Dr. James in his white coat is calling it, with another young woman in white as well. Bobby's hair has been cut like a bowl and close above his ears so that his head seems larger and fatter, floating on his bony neck and shoulders. He looks wonderful in his brown and red uniform. A girl passes to him and he stops it and dribbles in his sweet halt.

"C'mon Bobby," I say under my breath. "Score."

Phil looks at me and smiles. Yes, he does.

Janey, the first one I met at the school, is in goal and she's standing in the middle jumping up and down as Bobby stumbles toward her trying to keep the ball ahead of him. When he gets in front of the box, he stops, steps back and kicks a soft wee roller right to Janey that she can easily cradle in her arms. Bobby runs over and congratulates her.

"Bobby Horn," I say with satisfaction.

Dr. James has seen me, standing on the far side of the field with my roped trunk. He calls Bobby over and points at me. He runs so well and fast he knocks me to the ground.

"Shoe . .. Shoe…Shoe…Shoe…"

"Bobby," I grunt with him still on top of me.

"I…I…I…"

"I know Bobby. I love you too."

"And…and…"

He pushes up from me and looks down at my face.

"I score goals."

"Goals?"

"Goals!" he shouts.

"Goals!" I shout.

He stands up and rocks side to side.

"…and…and…I have a place for…I read the Cowboy and Indian book…and I read it to Charlie and…and Janey too."

"Well this is a nice school, isn't it?"

"This is a nice school, isn't it. And we can have hot potatoes anytime we want…when it's not too late…I…I…I love hot potatoes."

We're quiet. He comes in and gives another grab. Hard. His bony arms squeezing for all their might. He pulls away and I brush what little hair he's got as if they hadn't cut it. I want to tell him how beautiful he is and promise I'll dream and think of him every day. But there are other things to say and I say them.

"I'm going to America."

"You're going to…to…America."

"America," I say again.

"America."

"Right…Boston."

His face goes even, as it does when he's lining up his words and ordering them out of his guts.

"Can…can…can The McAvy fly?"

I smile at his serious mouth and how it circles and forms all that he says and thinks. He puts wonder and amazement into every word he utters.

"No Bobby, The McAvy can't fly."

He thinks about this and points up, here and there, at a gull or black bird. I light one and we sit on my trunk. Phil has crossed behind Janey's goal and watches the game.

"I…I…"

"What lad?"

He points up to the clouds and doesn't speak for a bit. I look where he's pointing.

"What lad?" I say again.

He don't pull his arm away from the sky but looks at me.

"I…I saw him up there…I did…I saw him with the big gulls… I did…I miss Blacky, Shoe. I want him to kiss Janey."

Yes. I should have killed Mr. Horn. I feel the regret of it to the bottom of my feet.

"Well, Blacky misses you too, lad, and you know there's nobody in God's world he'd rather be with, but he had some business up…up at Windemere."

"Win…Windemere?"

"Right…uh…see, there's some poor wee blind girls there…"

"Like…like…like birdy?"

"Just like birdy and…they needed Blacky to…kind of…explain things."

His eyes go wide.

"*Explain* things," he says with awe.

"Yes."

"I…I…I love him."

"I know lad. And I know that he loves you."

He walks in a circle. When he's back to me, his eyes are full of tears.

"I want…I want Mummy," he says loudly, banging his fists onto his thigh.

"Bobby…stop that…Bobby, I want Mummy too."

"I want Mummy."

I pull him back to the trunk. I know exactly what he feels.

"She…she…her face was fat."

"Like yours, Bobby Horn."

"This fat," he says with joy. Happiness and sadness and anger rolling through him as he puffs his cheeks out and holds his palms away from his face.

"And her pies and cakes," I say.

"Pies…pies and…and cakes."

"And songs…"

"Songs…" he says, as if a great mystery came out of Mummy's mouth when she sang "Molly Malone" or "The Chick and the Hen."

"Will you show me where you sleep, Bobby?"

"I…I…I will."

He runs across the field and tells Dr. James who nods and waves. Bobby picks up a ball they're not using in the game, squeezes it to his belly with both hands and runs back to me.

It's a long wide room with twenty beds. Each bed is made neatly and each has a different blanket. Bobby has Indians praying on his. There's a box under each bed for treasures and a chair in between. The room smells like pine sap and sun comes in the windows that open on either side. Bobby proudly shows me where the water closets are and the sinks and three large bath tubs. It sparkles. After I inspect the fixtures we walk back to his bed where he lies on it and I sit on my trunk.

"What a lovely spot you have, Bobby."

"It's…it's…it's a…lovely spot."

I reach over and pet his forehead, for me more than for him. For the comfort of it. To feel part of it. He closes his eyes and smiles, then bolts up, gets off his bed, and pulls out his box. He hands the Cowboy and Indians book to me.

"Why look at this Bobby. I wonder what it's about."

"Oh…oh…oh Shoe…stop," he giggles and slaps the bed.

"Read…read."

I lie down with him, our heads on his pillow, and lasso the moon and stars once more.

He's got the soccer ball clutched when we stand outside the school. Phil is behind Bobby, but watching the sky. I look at my trunk, think about what I have and it ain't much.

"I got the plumbing, though," I say to Phil. "I got the skill."

Bobby's not listening and bounces the ball. The sky above is clear with warm afternoon sun, but there's a blackness coming over the sea. It'll be raining when the *Madagascar* sails.

"So it's a goodbye now, Bobby."

He keeps bouncing, watching the ball hard.

"It's…it's…it's a…goodbye now, Shoe."

"America," I say softly.

He throws the ball up and forgets it, his arms wide.

"America!" he shouts.

"America!" I shout.

We laugh and he comes in with his head under my chin. Dear Christ, my brother feels like my life. What more do I need? Where am I going? He pulls back.

"America. There's Indians in America. Are you…are you scared?"

I am Bobby. I am scared of America and scared of Shoe Horn. All of me is scared.

"No," I say.

We go quiet. He's thinking and I'm watching him think. He's taller or maybe it's his uniform.

"It's a goodbye now, Bobby."

"It's…it's…a goodbye now, Shoe."

I pick up my trunk.

"America!" he shouts.

"America!" I shout.

He bounces the ball once and catches it.

"So…so…so I'll see you tonight."

"What?"

"After…after you go to America…I'll…I'll see you tonight."

My brother bounces it again, concentrates hard and catches it.

"Goodbye Bobby, learn what they teach you."

"I…I will and…and I'll score goals."

"You will."

"I will."

"You're a great good guy, Bobby Horn."

"And…and…and you're a…a great good guy…Shoe Horn."

I move fast over the strip of ground that connects Quince to Walney, looking at the ground as if trying to put each pebble into my memory. Phil looks where I do, and neither of us look back.

She's sitting on a case smaller than mine, held together by rope, too. We don't have much. Maybe that's the way it's supposed to be. People pass her carrying leather luggage and walk up the gangplank where the smartly dressed Ship's Captain welcomes his guests aboard.

"Shoe," she says.

"Molly," I say.

She looks at my trunk and hers. I said it before. It ain't much.

"Do you love me, Shoe?"

"I do."

"Only me?"

"Only you."

And it's true. I do. Only this little mick, who I think about and wonder about. The lies get squeezed out and I'm cleaned up and down and inside out. She kisses me and squeezes as hard as Bobby. She steps back and picks up her case. I pick up mine and we walk to the gangplank. Phil stays on the dock. I stop and look back at him.

"What," Molly asks.

Phil gives a little wave and walks back up towards the house of the Gogartys.

"What?" she asks again.

"Nothing."

I find Mr. Haywood below and he shows us where we'll be. It's a dent in the wall with two small beds stacked on top of each other and some cloth hanging that separates us from the corridor.

"It ain't much," I say to Molly.

"It's perfect," she says.

We put our stuff onto the beds and walk back through the oily belly of the ship to Mr. Haywood who tells us where Molly is to go. She kisses me and climbs up to the maid's assembly. The other coaler, an old wog, has got the boiler stoked good, throwing in a shovelful every minute or so.

"This here is Charlie. He don't speak English but he's a good old lad. Mr. Horn, I've got some plumbing if you're up to it."

"I am."

"Plumber's box is over there behind the bin. Nobody knows what's what about plumbing here, so you might need more pieces. Look it over and I'll send a runner if you need more. Captain's shitter is plugged, boiler showing some pressure loss and the bilge pump is working but not pumping water out."

I pull the box and look it over. The tools are rusted but quality ones. I'll need a two hander, extra hammer, wraps and clamps, three or four guts of the water closets, a reaming snake, and a good plumber oil to soak the old tools in. I hand my list to Mr. Haywood and then climb up to the Captain's water closet, which turns out to

279

be a toilet with newspaper jammed up it. What? Has Mrs. Taylor had a go at the Captain's pipes?

When I walk out to the tiny walkway circling the Captain's room, the dark clouds have floated over the Barrow. Rain is right behind and starts heavy by the time I reach the deck below and the stairs to the boiler. A girl in a blue maid's uniform with a bright yellow scarf, her hair in a net, is waiting just inside for the rain to stop. I run in but not quick enough. I'm soaked through.

"I think it's raining," I say.

She looks at me solemnly.

"You're wet," she says in a Scots' roll.

"Am I?"

"You'll catch cold."

I smile at her and she does too. A little one anyway. She's almost as tall as me.

"I'm Shoe Horn. I'm a coaler and plumber."

"I'm Anne McClaren. I'm a maid."

The rain increases to little drums all over the ship.

"That's a pretty name."

"Thank you."

She bows her head a bit and her cheeks get red just like Addy Augarde's used to. Like Dorothy Wickford's did when she knew it was me.

"Have you worked here long?"

"I'm on at Saltcoats. That was four days ago. I'm getting off in Boston."

"Why, me too Miss."

"My fiancée is going to meet me."

She can't be older than me. We all get onto boats and run.

"He's mending the railway or something. He's going to meet me."

I watch the black sky and rain. Is it all sunshine and dollars in Boston?

"He hasn't written in awhile but he's busy I'm sure. Can you imagine how large the railway must be? America and all?"

Yes, I can but I'll *walk* out into it like I promised myself and The McAvy. She speaks so softly it might be to herself.

"Hasn't written in…in a year or so."

I watch the rain and maybe hear her small whimpers between the drops. I catch the smell of Worcestershire but understand it's just my small brain playing me for the fool. I know for sure to keep things lined up and not piled up. I don't think in a pile. I think one thing after another, a straight row that I can circle and look at and be sure won't come toppling down leaving me flattened under my fucking lies. I know this and am sure of this. But then what's a *little* pile? A wee heap. It's one thing to be a dolt and another to know it. Christ. I reach out and brush my fingers over her hand.

"There, Annie, don't cry."

She looks at my fingers, then at my face. I wonder what it shows.

"He must…he must be busy."

"He must be."

The rain is down to a drizzle.

"Well," she says in the soft roll, "I'd better be at my linen station."

I watch her walk away. She knows I'm watching. There's a line of sun now coming down in the distance. It looks as if it might push the rain away.

"Annie McClaren," I say to myself so I can remember that it will be a wee pile, if one at all, and what happened may not really have happened even if it happens.

Charlie is throwing coal with a stupid grin on his face. I put the plumber's box behind the bin. There's nothing to be done for the boiler or the bilge outtake until Mr. Haywood's runner gets back with the rest of the tools. I pick up a coal shovel and gesture to Charlie to rest. He smiles, puts his shovel down, and kneels and bows on a small rug facing the hull. In a half hour we'll be away from the Barrow, swallowed by the Irish Sea, then the North Channel, around Ireland and into the Atlantic. Boston's out there and I'm feeling the blood flowing through my fucking veins. I get the bully boy face, flat and hard, and go at the coal like it's a brother plumber, under the light.

23

The third night out and she's sleeping. She says she's having bad dreams because I'm looking. I might be, but how would she know? Every night we turn in our wee beds, me above her. This night I squeezed into hers and she turned to the wall.

"You're looking. I know it," is all she said.

After a bit I climb to the small deck above the stairs and light one. It's clear and the sea is flat as a pond. Stars and moon reflect off it. I wonder about Boston but I don't know the use of it. Whatever will happen, will happen. I won't lie my way out of America. Or hope I won't. I feel the papers in my pocket and remember them now. I move closer to the small light at the back of the stairs and unfold them. Some of the ink has run against my sweat but I can read through.

For a long, long time the boy was just the same as every one. He wasn't tall and he wasn't short. He wasn't fat and he wasn't thin. His face was nicely round and his hands and his feet were very nicely the same as everyone else. One morning he woke to find that his sleeping gown was much too big. And when he put his feet into his shoes, he found the shoes much too wide.

"Mum," he asked his mother. "Am I getting smaller?"

"Why, yes you are."

When he went out to do errands for his mum, he felt people staring at him and some of his friends stared too. One of his friends said:

"You are getting smaller. I am afraid of you."

"Why?" the boy asked.

"Because you are not the same as we are."

The next morning he was smaller still. Only his mum did not mind. She fed him and buttoned him up.

Every morning he became smaller and smaller. He had to shout to be heard and his mum had to pin back his clothes so they would not drag on the ground. His friends did not want to be his friends and people stared at him and pointed at him.

Soon the boy was as tall as his mum's knee with a voice like a whistle. No one would give him work. No one liked having him around because he was not the same as them. He wanted to run away and live like a mouse in a field. And then he wanted to go to sleep and never wake up.

He still had one friend. A friend who did not stare and who was not afraid. One morning they flew a kite.

"There is no place for me," the boy said, trying not to be stepped on by the people in the park.

"Yes there is a place for you," his friend said.

And that was enough for the small boy. He would not be afraid any more to be what he had become.

"Thank you," the boy said, "for being my friend."

* * *

Phil is patient. I smoke three under the cemetery arch, lighting each at the end of the other. When the last one's on the ground, I hitch my pants and button all three buttons on the suit coat. Four of me could fit inside my clothes. I pat my thin hair down but the breeze throws it back up in a point. My legs have been given the commands but stay still as if they want to be asked, rather than be told, what to do. They're my legs alright and I'm hinged to them, still they've got a mind of their own and it ain't on my shoulders. Maybe if I think of something else than this place and its stones and mounds. But what? I tap my head.

"There's nothing else up here, Phil. Not a fucking idea. I can feel chowder sloshing where my bloody brain ought to be."

He smiles and my legs get moving on their own.

"That's it boyo," he says quietly.

The last time I was here, I remember better than twenty minutes ago. Bobby danced ahead with Blacky in his arms. Mummy was between two small berry bushes. Robert Nelson too. My legs want to go faster but can't. What comes is a march of some sort. A high step on the slate path.

"For the love of Christ, Phil, I'm bloody marching."

But Phil has stopped and looks down on seven small stones.

"What's it?" I say.

"Me," he says with a point to a stone.

"Tom?"

He points to another.

"Liz, too?"

He points.

"She was a good one. She was a beauty."

He looks at me.

"Well, she was, you fucking ghost."

He doesn't say anything.

"I didn't...I was joking Phil. I'm glad you're with me."

He gives a little smile and my parade begins again. We cross a small bridge over a pond. Mummy is across the flat, past the soldiers' crosses lined like a regiment and up a small hill. I stop at the bottom of the hill and I don't know why. It's not to catch a breath. There's not enough air in the world for me. I have the lungs of a fly. When I look up, I see them all around her newly dug grave. Her friends, Mrs. Bolton and Mrs. Wallace, who washed her and prepared our house for her wake, the Reverend Cryer and his young wife, Mummy's sister and brother down from Blackpool. Mr. Horn himself, swaying like a dry black branch, moaning words he bloody well should have said at the time to say them. Myself and The McAvy, holding Bobby between us. I point for Phil.

"Do you see? That long night before the grave, Bobby danced and twisted and screamed in his bed. I sang her songs to him, I said her prayers she taught us, but I could not bring him down."

I see how sleeplessness has softened his shrieks down to the long hollow coos of a morning dove. I look at Phil and look back. They are gone. The grave is old again and so am I. I see the tip of her stone. I don't know a thing. I've learned nothing in eighty seven years.

"Boyo," he says softly.

"I...don't want to Phil."

"Shoe Horn," he says.

"I'm afraid."

"It's alright."

"It's not. It's not alright."

I look up to the stone. The hill has become a mountain but I begin marching in place. When the legs are ready, they go, and I ride them. At the top, I circle the slate to the front of her stone. I step around to all I know.

"Mummy," I whisper.

In the coolness of the clouds, I reach for the knot in my red tie, to be sure it's true, and blink my eyes free to read.

GETRUDE KIND HORN

1885-1919

ROBERT NELSON HORN
1904-1904

ROBERT WILLIAM HORN
1908-1951

*I kneel at the stone. The birds and trees watch me go to my hands,
then spread myself onto the cool and mossy grass, so I can hold him
and feel him once again inside my tired old bones.*

"Bobby," I puff to the moss and pebbles. "My Bobby Horn."